PRAISE FOR ALL TH[...]

KW-153-749

'An expertly crafted sequel. Amie Jordan is a master at storytelling.'
@billreadslol

'. . . the perfect blend of fantasy, mystery and slow burn.'
@ascorpioreads

'What an absolutely incredible, warm hug of a book!
I will be shouting about this from the rooftops!'
@evavstheworld

'A brilliant sequel – witches, werewolves, romance and found family,
whilst still keeping me desperate to see the mystery solved – what more
could you want from a supernatural novel?! An emotional rollercoaster,
and I cannot wait to see what Amie has in store for book three!'
@_rebeccareads

'I was gripped from the very start and was completely consumed
by this book . . . an absolute joy to read and I am willing to sell
my soul for book three because there's no way I can wait over
a year to find out what happens next after THAT ending.'
@takealookinsideabook

'Mind-blowing and a true heart-warmer,
it will have you utterly captured from the first page.'
@stuck_in_the_book_loop

'A wonderful mix of mystery, folklore and the complexity
of love in the face of mortality. This book was heartfelt,
fun and had me guessing right up until the end!'
@sophi3saur

'Vivid and electrifying – your new favourite escapism!'
@andonshereads

RACE THE LOST SOULS

A MESSAGE FROM CHICKEN HOUSE

This violent supernatural mystery/love story is one of my favourite series of all time. It's funny, arresting, cool and deeply charismatic. This time, our detective duo leave Downside to investigate trouble in the French mountains where tensions between witches and werewolves are running high (not to mention the tension between Sage and Oren . . .). Brilliant twisty crime and cracking romance.

BARRY CUNNINGHAM
Publisher
Chicken House

ALL THE LOST SOULS

AMIE JORDAN

2 Palmer Street, Frome, Somerset BA11 1DS
www.chickenhousebooks.com

First published in Great Britain in 2025
Chicken House
2 Palmer Street
Frome, Somerset BA11 1DS
United Kingdom
www.chickenhousebooks.com

Chicken House/Scholastic Ireland, 89E Lagan Road, Dublin Industrial Estate,
Glasnevin, Dublin D11 HP5F, Republic of Ireland

Text © Amie Jordan 2025
Cover illustration © Micaela Alcaino 2025

The moral rights of the author and illustrator have been asserted.

All rights reserved.
No part of this publication may be reproduced, transmitted, downloaded,
decompiled, reverse engineered, used to train any artificial intelligence
technologies, or stored in or introduced into any information storage and
retrieval system, in any form or by any means, whether electronic or mechanical,
now known or hereafter invented, without the express written permission
of the publisher. Subject to EU law the publisher expressly reserves this
work from the text and data mining exception.

This book is a work of fiction. Names, characters, businesses, organizations,
places, events and incidents are either the product of the author's
imagination or used in a fictitious manner. Any resemblance to actual
persons, living or dead, events or locales is purely coincidental.

For safety or quality concerns:
UK: www.chickenhousebooks.com/productinformation
EU: www.scholastic.ie/productinformation

Cover design by Micaela Alcaino
Typeset by Dorchester Typesetting Group Ltd
Printed in Great Britain by Clays, Elcograf S.p.A

FSC
www.fsc.org
MIX
Paper | Supporting
responsible forestry
FSC® C018072

1 3 5 7 9 10 8 6 4 2

British Library Cataloguing in Publication data available.

PB ISBN 978-1-915947-48-2
eISBN 978-1-917171-03-8

For Major –
the most loyal wolf I know.

Now this is the Law of the Jungle —
as old and as true as the sky;
And the Wolf that shall keep it may prosper,
but the Wolf that shall break it must die.
As the creeper that girdles the tree-trunk
the Law runneth forward and back —
For the strength of the Pack is the Wolf,
and the strength of the Wolf is the Pack.

Rudyard Kipling, 'The Law of the Jungle' (1894)

I

OREN

Oren stared up at the dark bedroom ceiling.

Every night he relived the same memories in his nightmares: Sage covered in blood, gasping for air, and he couldn't save her.

Even now, the thought still made him feel physically sick. The . . . *helplessness* he'd felt. The realization that his magic, so integral to his very being, which had never failed him, had simply gone like someone had flicked a switch.

She could've died. And that made his chest feel so heavy he could hardly breathe.

The way her hand had grappled with his collar, pulling him close, telling him to let her die, let her become a ghost, let her stay young with him forever? The fact that for even the briefest of moments he'd considered it made him feel equally as sick.

He'd never been perturbed by death his whole killing career, he had no right to be afraid of it that night. But he just couldn't face the finality of it at that moment. The abrupt end to . . . *what if*?

Anyway, he'd saved her. Against all the odds, he'd managed to keep her alive. And wondered every day since whether he'd made a mistake. Had he made the right decision by saving her life? Or should he have let her freeze herself in her youthful, ghostly body forever? He still didn't know.

I don't regret getting to watch her live, he'd told P when they'd sat up quietly talking that night, and he'd meant it. But both of them knew that decision came with a cost. Werewolves aged like humans, so Sage was the only one of them who would grow old and frail. It was an impossible decision, and every side lost.

Oren sighed and glanced at the clock on his bedside table. Barely four. The sky was still dark outside his window, but he wouldn't get back to sleep now. He kicked off the covers and grabbed a T-shirt from his drawer. He pulled his bedroom door shut behind him with a soft click and crossed the hallway to the door that was never fully closed. He nudged it gently with his shoulder to ease it silently open.

Of course, she was in there. He could scent she was from across the hall, and hear the slow, rhythmic breathing of her sleep. But he just needed to see her without the gouge in her chest and the lingering scent of blood that haunted his dreams. Her back was to the door, hair tied in a knot on the top of her head. She wore some silky designer pyjamas Berion had gifted her in a Yuletide box.

'She's still here,' a quiet voice said from behind.

'I know.' He pulled the door shut and turned to face the silvery ghost.

Only the top half of P's body was visible through the carpeted floor of the landing, her legs dangling underneath. She was watching him with a suppressed smile.

'She'll still be there tomorrow, and the day after.' Her eyes filled again with that look that understood him all too well. 'So will I. We're not going anywhere, Oren.'

The lump in his throat was back. He swallowed. He hated it when she made him feel so human.

She gave him a small, encouraging smile, like she knew speech was impossible. 'Toast?'

He nodded, and she disappeared through the floor into her kitchen.

A couple of weeks into Sage's recovery, they'd squeezed on to the sofa in their old apartment, Berion and Hozier too, for pizza and Netflix.

'There just isn't enough room, is there?' P had sighed.

'Maybe we should get a bigger one,' Oren had said.

He'd meant a sofa, but the next day P had thrown colour-coded printouts from a Downside estate agent on to the coffee table. And that was that.

Now he lived in a four-bedroom, three-storey townhouse with a large kitchen for P and garden for the BBQ parties she was planning.

He lived with his friends.

His friends.

People he cared about, who cared about him.

It horrified him.

Every day when he woke from that nightmare, he realized that he'd allowed himself to become so attached that when he'd thought Sage was about to die, he'd known he'd rather die too than allow her to leave him alone again. Bereft of the acceptance and understanding she represented. A feeling he'd thought for so many years he'd neither wanted nor deserved.

He hated himself for it. Hated the vulnerability of it.

How many would target her if they knew she was his weakness, in revenge for death sentences he'd passed on their loved ones? What bounty had he placed on her head?

He heard the tinkling of cutlery in P's pristine kitchen, and thanked whatever gods might be listening that only one of his two beloved housemates still had a life force to be taken. If he had to face the possibility of losing both of them—

He shook his head. He was Oren Rinallis. He feared nothing.

But as he set off down the stairs in hunt of his breakfast, he couldn't shake the feeling that it might not be so true after all.

2

SAGE

The warlocks didn't do themselves any favours.

Those who did work for the Arcānum were more cliquey than a particularly bitchy group of teenagers, and those who didn't still kept themselves to themselves, socializing only within their own circles. They didn't integrate like everyone else in Downside.

Basically, they were stuck-up.

So, as their Friday team meeting was held in the function room of a pub, and their captain, Roderick, covered the first round of drinks after from the staff budget, it was a surprise to all of them that the courtesy extended to Sage. The only werewolf in the team. The sore thumb.

Though she still didn't rule out her drink being laced with poison. Or at least a mild laxative. In fact, she was quite sure that was probably the end goal.

Oren would rather die than socialize, and she had it on good authority – aka Hozier – that in what they now termed the 'Pre-Sage Era', he'd shift right out of the room as soon as meetings ended. But she'd slowly cajoled him into taking advantage of his free drink, at least. So these days he knocked back one stiff whisky before promptly striding out as Berion ordered wine for the rest of them.

So . . . he hung around perhaps an extra forty-five seconds.

The Warlock's Cloak was one of the oldest pubs in Downside. It reminded her of the smoky olden-days pubs Upside where men would down a pint after a hard day's work in the mines. The benches lining the walls were covered in the kind of fabric she associated with grandma carpets. Not the modern spot you'd expect for such a gentrified, twenty-first-century, supernatural city. But she supposed this pub was as old as some of the warlocks that frequented it, so maybe that had something to do with it.

'I love that jacket, Sage.' Berion's white eyes looked over the leather appreciatively as they filed out of the function room after a particularly boring meeting. 'Where'd you find it?'

She twirled, grinning at his raised brow. 'Your wardrobe.'

'You think I didn't realize it was missing?'

'I'll lend you one of mine?' she offered.

A warlock with bright green hair laughed, throwing Sage an appreciative smile. Nothing any of them owned would satisfy Berion's luxurious taste.

'It wouldn't kill you to be more social,' Sage muttered to Oren under her breath as they reached the bar. P spent her

Friday nights in Vampire Slayer, at a knitting group led by a local gargoyle artist, and she wouldn't be finished for another half an hour yet, so what was he gonna do? Sit in silence and sulk?

Probably.

Despite the run-down nature of the pub, it was still popular: one side of the room a thriving hubbub of chatter, darts tournaments and card games. Three satyrs pushed each other around, arguing over who was keeping score of their game, settling down as they noticed the whole of the Arcānum spilling out towards them. Only an old mothman, his tall wings withered and red eyes dulled from what smelt like a lifetime of too-heavy drinking, didn't seem to notice or care that Oren Rinallis was standing beside him with a face like thunder.

She watched Oren gulp his whisky that the wraith behind the bar always had ready, as two bottles of red and three wine glasses were pushed towards the rest of them.

'I'll see you at home.'

'Not so fast.' Another voice cut across the chatter.

Sage's least favourite warlock appeared, clicking off whatever call he'd just taken and slipping his phone back into his pocket.

'What do you want, Roderick?' Oren growled. 'Team meeting is over.' Translation: *I have absolutely no obligation to acknowledge your existence.*

'Last-minute request for a case transfer.' Roderick's

smile turned cruel as he looked right at Sage. 'There's trouble brewing in the Jura mountains in eastern France. Witches. And werewolves.'

She wasn't sure why her cheeks flushed. Something about the way Roderick directed the statement was accusatory. Like she was somehow personally responsible for the misdeed of every werewolf that existed.

She refused to think about their last case.

No.

Shut it down.

But it was too late. Her heart was hammering in her chest, and she felt faint. The whole left side of the room, the Arcānum side, quietened just enough to pretend they weren't listening in. She glanced around. Saw averted eyes. But she could practically feel the burn scorching her skin as she noticed someone who wasn't even bothering to hide their interest.

Bitch.

She'd made Flora's acquaintance a few weeks into the new year. The female warlock had been away in the weeks leading up to the Yuletide Sage had spent with Oren. But, man, was she back now.

Hozier had delighted in telling them of the time she and Berion had caught Flora sniffing one of Oren's jackets. Oren had scowled as he'd admitted to taking her for a drink nearly five decades earlier in another country entirely, and five minutes into that encounter she'd smashed the end of a bottle against the bar and thrust the sharp end towards the barmaid, threatening to rip out her throat for smiling at him. He'd shifted right out without even a goodbye. 'I prefer one-night stands who are not batshit crazy,' he'd shrugged, and he'd thought that was that. Until she'd turned up in Downside and joined the Arcānum.

Sage and P had found the idea of Oren having a stalker hilarious.

Until that stalker, unhinged and slightly wild-eyed, had cornered Sage in a coffee shop with Berion and warned her to keep away from Oren. *Or else.* Berion had had to intervene when Sage laughed and Flora's hands had glowed red.

She felt a brush of Oren's magic, warm and comforting, bringing her back to the room.

It's done. It doesn't matter. I don't care.

It'd become their mantra, their gift to each other to forget their pasts, their sins, their self-loathing.

When she looked back at Roderick he was watching for her reaction.

She gave him nothing.

'Peace is tenuous at best,' he went on. 'Neither witch nor wolf is willing to resolve whatever petty grievance is going on and they have requested Arcānum assistance.' His brow rose; the insinuation that he didn't think she'd be of much assistance was clear. 'Word has spread of the werewolf in our ranks. The French have put in a request to borrow you, Sage, in the hope you'll be able to communicate with the alphas better than them.'

'Well, as long as she doesn't know any of them personally, right?' Flora's girly voice floated across the bar, unable to resist the opportunity. 'Or the perpetrators might get away with it for longer than necessary.'

The room stopped pretending they weren't listening. Even the side full of patrons who had absolutely nothing to do with the Arcānum. The repetitive thud of darts on the dartboard faded out and the chinks of pool balls knocking into each other halted.

Everyone had heard the truth about the Silver Serial Killer, Sage's first case with Oren. About how he'd been her friend. Harland. How he'd nearly killed her with a silver dagger, before Oren had saved her and killed him instead. It'd been on the cover of every Downside newspaper for over a week.

There were a few awkward looks. A few outright smirks.

Hozier told Flora to do something that would've usually had Sage laughing out loud. But it didn't matter. Her face was on fire again. Roderick could've called them to his office, given them this case in private. Instead he'd chosen to do it in front of everyone. He was grinning like a feral cat.

But it was Berion's voice that spoke loudest.

'Well, I also knew Harland,' he said. 'Or should I say, Liam MacAllister. Spoke with him enough times that perhaps *I* should've noticed he was a murderer. I, after all, am a century into this business. Sage hasn't yet racked up six months.' Berion stared at Roderick, his boyfriend – that was a long story. The smile slipped off their captain's face. Then Berion looked at Flora. 'What do you think?'

'Think about what?' she snapped, but the wicked enjoyment had faded now she had an opponent she could not beat.

'Should I not shoulder some of the blame for not noticing that Liam MacAllister was a murderer?' Berion went on. 'Shouldn't Hozier? She met him too.' His smile turned indulgent. 'What about Oren? Go on, Flora, tell Oren how he should've spotted what Liam MacAllister was.'

Flora's face went puce. She said nothing.

'I didn't think so.' He smiled.

Hozier snorted into her wine glass.

Oren had actually been the only one who'd taken an instant disliking to Harland. 'Sage, you're expected in the Alps tomorrow at noon,' Roderick snapped with a tone of finality. 'Don't come back until it's sorted . . . and try to avoid any more silver daggers.'

Another punch to the gut. The scar on her chest throbbed, a reminder of what that silver dagger had done to her. A constant dull ache lingered there.

How long would she be in France? What about P? The thought of a new case, and a big one, by the sounds of it, did stir something a little like excitement inside her, but she hadn't spent more than a week away from her best friend since before her parents had died. Even after she'd been turned, she still saw P Upside on weekends. She didn't like leaving her behind.

'Don't worry.' Oren slammed down his empty whisky glass. 'I have no plans to let her die on me yet.'

'You're not going,' Roderick sneered.

'Excuse me?'

'I'm not wasting two of you on a bunch of werewolves that can't play nice. You used to insist on working alone, Oren, you'll manage for a few weeks without her.'

She saw his back stiffen. And felt the whole room hold a breath.

'You wouldn't separate any other team, Roderick,' Oren said calmly. 'You're trying to put her in an impossible situation to prove a point. You're being an arsehole.'

A few stifled gasps.

A single giggle, and she could guess who that belonged to.

Roderick drew himself up, lifting his chin. 'I am your captain and I'm telling you you're not going.'

Oren didn't flinch. 'And how do you suggest you'll stop me?'

Roderick stared at him.

Sage stared at him.

The charade that Roderick was his superior had always been a game Oren had tolerated for more than a century, because the alternative was becoming a Cariva assassin again. But now Oren was deciding to challenge that authority: nobody had true control over him. Nobody other than eight ancient warlocks – the Elders – on the other side of the world. And he was doing it for her.

She could see the internal dilemma playing out behind Roderick's eyes. He hadn't truly realized until now that Sage was a battle he would not win. But how could he let this challenge pass in front of everyone?

Maybe he should've called them into his office after all, huh?

'Oren.' She put her hand on his elbow before it could descend into anything worse.

A heartbeat pause . . . but he nodded. 'We'll have to be packed tonight to get there by noon tomorrow,' he told her. 'Shall we go?'

'She can finish her drink,' Berion said, handing Sage the large glass of wine he'd already poured. He eyed Oren pointedly. Oren's reputation had been curated over decades, but Sage was still building hers. If she left with him now she'd look like she was fleeing, embarrassed and upset. 'I'll walk her home shortly.'

Oren nodded again and shifted out of the bar, his golden magic fading in his wake. And the chatter picked up. Now it appeared her humiliation was over, the room came back to life.

Berion turned his back on Roderick, calling Flora something uncharacteristically graceless at the same time. Roderick stormed off. Hozier returned Sage's awkward grimace.

Turns out, Berion's on-off-on-off affair with his boss had

been going on under all their noses for over five decades. Apparently, Roderick had wanted something more serious, but Berion had always resisted, because if they couldn't make it work, well, they'd still have to sit awkwardly in team meetings. But he had agreed to go official, as long as Sage got her job. When Berion had told her what he'd done, Sage hadn't been comfortable with the bargain, not at all, and was shocked by the whole relationship . . . but she also got the feeling that it was the excuse Berion needed to take the plunge without feeling like he'd lost any pride too. So she let it go.

She hated Roderick, and he hated her. But as aghast as she was that someone as kind and funny and confident as Berion was with someone like Roderick, she also understood just as well – *too* well – that sometimes the heart wanted what it wanted, even if it didn't necessarily seem . . . right. She might not like Roderick, but she wouldn't be the one to make Berion choose between them.

'Promise me you'll check in on P every single day,' she said, sighing as she leant against the bar.

'I'll move in, just until you get back?' Hozier offered. 'So it won't be so lonely in the evenings.'

'Are you sure?'

She knew it was probably Hozier's idea of a nightmare. They loved her and she loved them, loved coming round in the evenings to gorge on P's food, but Sage also knew she appreciated having her own space. So did Berion. The pair of them, so fiercely independent that even after decades of loyal partnership, owned adjoining apartments rather than live with each other, like most Arcānum partners.

Hozier winked back. 'Of course. And, Sage, she'll be fine. It's just a few weeks.'

Sage could feel the temper still radiating off Berion in red-hot waves. So she waved at the wraith to pour a round of tequila. 'It doesn't matter, Berion.'

'Yes, it does,' he muttered as he turned from the bar, the three of them forming a little circle as they chinked their shot glasses, knocking them back as one, each pulling disgusted faces as they swallowed.

Blerghhhhh. She shuddered. 'I don't care.'

'You do.' He rolled his eyes.

'I'm more bothered by Flora being the world's biggest cow,' she admitted quietly.

Hozier waved her concerns away with a hand. 'Oh, ignore her. You've already won that battle—'

'And what battle is that, exactly?' said Flora from behind them.

3

SAGE

When she turned round there was genuine, feral fury in Flora's eyes. They'd embarrassed her in front of Oren. In front of the whole room. And apparently she wasn't ready to let it go.

'Oh, Flora, *piss off.*' Hozier's eyes nearly rolled out of her head. 'The excitement's over. Let us have our drink in peace.'

But Flora's eyes were fixed on Sage. So she held her gaze, and slowly took a sip of her wine.

'Drinking with warlocks,' Flora seethed under her breath. 'Not enough to simply work with us?'

Sage almost laughed. The tequila had gone straight to her head. 'Drinking with my friends, actually.' She let the rest of it hang in the air.

Friends. Of which you aren't one. So get out of my face.

'Ignore her, Sage,' Hozier said loudly, turning her back on Flora and blocking her entry into their little group.

'Friends?' The faux-girly voice rang through the bar. 'So they know, then?'

'Know what?' Sage yawned.

'Well, I heard that pet poltergeist you have is only Downside because *you killed her*.'

She froze.

The world around her froze.

The entire room went utterly silent.

The ground disappeared beneath her as her heart all but stopped in her chest. Of all the things she ever could've imagined coming out of Flora's mouth, it wasn't this. Never this. This secret that was so painful, so horrendous, and not Flora's, not even hers, not anyone else's to tell.

How did she even know? Where had she heard it? The blood drained from her face as her heart started to thunder, blood rushing to her ears. And Flora knew at once. Saw she'd hit jackpot. Her smirk turned into a wide, feline grin.

Berion recovered first, his usually impassive expression furious. 'I swear to the gods, Flora.' He pointed a bejewelled warning finger in her face, and it started to glow purple. 'That's a low one, even for you.'

'Well, Sage, is it not true?'

She couldn't speak. She knew she needed to. Knew she needed to refute it before it was too late. But the lump that rose in her throat was so strong she could barely even breathe. She couldn't even open her mouth.

'She was your friend, wasn't she?' Flora covered her heart with a hand in pretend horror, but she was giggling. 'Before, I mean. Before you mauled her to death. Brutal stuff.'

'Do one, Flora,' Hozier hissed. 'Of course she didn't—'

But her friend's voice trailed off as she looked back at her. Sage's eyes already stinging with tears as she watched the moment Hozier realized it was true. Hozier's eyes went wide, her own mouth dropping open.

Sage's heart was pounding in her chest under all the endless stares of horror. She couldn't breathe. Her ears were still ringing. Her face was burning.

Shame.

Shame and embarrassment and guilt came flooding back as the room full of warlocks watched. She wasn't sure if it was the room that was starting to spin, or maybe she was about to collapse. Flora's laughter sounded far away. Her own breaths were shallow, tight, and she could feel the dizziness building behind her eyes.

She had to get out. She couldn't pass out here.

She wanted to drop to the floor and die all over again. Every horrific, awful, terrible memory flashing in her mind's eye. Blood. Torn skin. Her parents. Her brother. Even that wolf she'd killed to protect Oren.

'Well, now the secret's out,' Flora sighed dramatically. 'They deserved to know what kind of friend you really are. I'm doing them a favour, if you think about it.' She gasped dramatically. 'Wait until Oren hears.'

As tears began to overflow, Sage put down her wine glass, and turned for the door.

'Sage, wait!' Hozier called.

But she couldn't. She fled to the sounds of Flora's gleeful cackles.

'Werewolves. Couldn't even control herself enough not to kill her best friend. Pathetic, really.'

Pathetic.

Couldn't even control herself enough not to kill her best friend.

The words rang through her ears, Flora's high, tinkling voice shivering down her spine.

Her whole body jerked as it tried to flee and freeze all at the same time.

And *it* woke inside her.

Couldn't even control herself enough not to kill her best friend.

Pathetic.

Pathetic.

She didn't realize what was happening until it was done. Didn't really think about it. Not until the pain of transforming was shattering through her body. She howled in agony. Scraps of clothes fell from her in ribbons as what started as a scream of pain ended in a snarl of fury. Gigantic white paws landed on the sticky wooden floor of the bar.

Flora's smile slipped from her lips.

Berion already had an arm around Hozier, dragging her away from whatever was about to come next. But Sage was too fast. She barely touched the ground as she crossed the length of the room in one giant leap, teeth bared and ready to rip out Flora's throat. Like that wolf she'd killed for Oren. She'd sworn she would never do that again . . .

She didn't care.

She'd *kill* this bitch.

Blood thrummed through her veins.

Shouts went up. Screams. She heard dropped glasses shatter. She saw flashes of light as hands ignited in magic. But no one was quick enough for her. Not now she was powerful and *whole*. Her sights were locked on her target, and nothing would stop her. She landed on top of Flora, smashing her head into the floor and pinning her shoulders under her paws.

'Sage!'

The voice didn't tremble, not like the ragged breaths of the rest watching on in horror, or the whimpering, incoherent sobs of the body trapped beneath her. That voice feared no one. Certainly not her.

It brought her back to life.

The jaw that'd been ready to crush Flora's bones paused a hair's breadth from her face. Flora's yellow eyes were squeezed tightly shut.

Good. She wanted Flora to know she was millimetres from death. Wanted her to feel razor-sharp fangs centimetres from her face. Wanted her to beg for her life.

The rest of the bar was still frozen, but she sensed magic being quickly extinguished. The monster's keeper had arrived to deal with her, and none of them would get in his way.

'Let her go, Sage.' Oren's voice was closer now. She was still panting, her chest heaving with anger and shame and everything in between. 'She's not worth it. Let her go.'

She ignored him. She was still ready to do it. She wanted to. She didn't care. She had killed for Oren. She'd kill Flora for herself.

She'd killed P.

The pain in her heart felt like it could kill her.

She felt a hand on the fur at the back of her neck. Reminding her to keep control. And that he was there with her. That when he was, she didn't ever have to be afraid.

It's done. It doesn't matter. I don't care.

Shame welled inside her again.

She let him pull her away and back to his side, only feeling his fingers loosen as her head came level with his shoulder.

He looked around the room. 'What the *hell* is going on?'

'She attacked me!' Flora shrieked, leaping up and pointing an accusatory finger, taking full advantage of the fact Sage couldn't answer first. 'The bitch attacked me!'

'You started on her first!' Hozier's voice was shrill and shook with fear. Fear Sage had caused. It pierced another shard of shame through her heart. But Hozier was staring at Flora in disgust, and it was her only salvation: that she was more disgusted by Flora that she was scared of Sage.

'I only told the truth!' Flora screamed back, her make-up smudged down her face as she panted, the shoulder of her

T-shirt hanging off. 'She's a murderous dog!'

Sage lunged again. Or at least she tried – something wrapped around her neck. Strong, but gentle.

Oren didn't even look at her. His face remained a mask of calm as he gazed at Flora. 'What did you just say?'

'The truth,' Flora snapped, emboldened as she realized Oren's magic held her attacker back. 'She killed that poltergeist you live with, you know? Nearly three years ago.' Her eyes were wide, daring him to call her a liar. 'Look it up if you don't believe me, Oren. It's all true!'

'Who told you that?' He stepped towards Flora.

'Heard it on the grapevine.' She shrugged, pulling the shoulder of her T-shirt back up. Then her demeanour shifted as she realized. 'You . . . you already knew?'

'Of course I fucking knew!' he roared.

Flora jumped. Everyone in the room flinched. Then something erupted from his hand. Long and steel. Not silver. The whole pub recoiled as he pointed the tip of his dagger in Flora's face. 'So I won't ask you again. Who told you? Because it hasn't come from me, and I'm certain P hasn't confided in you. So who . . . the hell . . . was it?'

Her mouth opened and closed as she stared at the dagger. She swallowed, but before she could answer, another movement. Only slight. A hand scratching a nose.

Oren must've sensed it too. He turned his gaze, just as Berion did the same.

'It was you.' Berion's voice was quiet with shock. He

stared at his boyfriend.

Roderick's face was stony. 'No.'

Oren's dagger turned on his boss. 'Bullshit.'

'How would I know any of that?' Roderick demanded.

'Because you have unrestricted access to every record in the archives. Even staff members,' Berion said, stepping towards Oren's side. It was an act that said enough. 'You can pull Sage's file from the restricted section. We can't. Not even Hozier.'

Hozier, still at the bar, nodded gently. Confirmation that Roderick had only recently gone into the restricted section – which she meticulously logged. 'Last Wednesday,' she mouthed to her partner.

'She's only a werewolf.' Roderick shrugged, giving in. 'She'll die within decades. It's not a big deal.'

So Roderick had found the dirt on her and waited for the opportune moment to reveal it. P had died on a full moon: the one night wolves weren't held fully accountable for their actions, so it wasn't illegal. But he'd wanted to cause her the most hurt and embarrassment. Tonight, he'd seen the perfect opportunity in an angry Flora.

When Berion turned to look at her, a single tear rolled down his porcelain-white cheek. 'I'm sorry,' he whispered.

But there was no way to answer him. Not like this. All she could do was stare into his white eyes full of pity and guilt. She didn't know if Oren let his magic release her or if Berion had used his own to override the restraints, but suddenly she could move again. She padded close to her friend and pressed her muzzle into his cheek, the only act of kindness she could offer.

'Look at you,' he murmured approvingly into her ear. 'You're monstrous.' He smiled as he pulled her back, but it was forced bravado. 'Come on. Let's get you home.'

She knew he needed to get out of there as quickly as she did, so she bowed her head and let him turn her towards the door, past the staring red eyes of the old mothman, who had at least been brave enough to stay and watch. Most of the rest of the bar had made a swift exit at some point.

Berion paused only once, to bend down and pick up her necklace from between the scraps of her shredded clothes, the moonstone Oren had given her and which she never took off. Her heart jolted as she realized she'd nearly lost it. He put it in his pocket for safekeeping.

'You won't be able to save her forever, Oren,' Flora spat from somewhere behind them.

As Berion pulled open the door for Sage to pass through they heard Oren's voice, shaking with suppressed rage.

'There's nothing she can do that will ever be worse than some of the things I've done. I will never be interested in you, Flora, not ever, and that's got nothing to do with her. It's because you're *insane*. Do anything like this again and I'll kill you myself.'

4

OREN

Although he lived with Sage and P now, he hadn't sold his old apartment. He didn't really know why. Maybe because some days he woke to the smell of food and the sound of laughter and still thought it was all too good to be true. That it'd come to an end soon enough. And when it did he could skulk back here to this lonely place.

After Berion had taken Sage away he hadn't followed. He needed time to calm down. And to think. Now an hour had slipped by.

He could've killed Flora. He should have. He had the unrestricted assassin's licence of a Cariva to kill whomever he wanted, and nobody, not even Roderick, could do a single thing about it. But it would've made the whole sorry mess even worse. He already knew he'd have to let what Roderick had done slide, in return for making sure Sage faced no consequences for tonight. Flora deserved every part of it . . . but an arcānas attacking anyone like that in a public space was still grounds for dismissal.

He'd bide his time.

One day he'd flay Roderick alive.

He'd done it enough times to perfect the skill. He'd make sure it was a long and slow end for that warlock.

For now, he needed this to pass. Maybe their punishment trip to the Jura mountains would be a blessing in disguise. Get her away. Out of sight, out of mind.

'So . . .' came a voice from the doorway.

'So, what?' He didn't move from his seat at the dining table. He hadn't magically locked the door. He'd expected someone to come looking soon enough.

'So, she's a white wolf.' Berion's expensive shoes clicked as he crossed the darkened apartment. 'Which is . . . rare.'

'I know.' He took a swig from the glass he was staring into. The liquid burnt the back of his throat. 'I wasn't planning on letting anyone else see. She doesn't change other than the full moon. It wasn't supposed to be too hard.'

'This is the real reason she won't change of free will, then?' Berion asked. 'Guilt.'

He gave a curt nod.

'Well.' Berion slid into the chair opposite, a glass appearing in front of him too. 'It was probably the one thing that might lead her to murder someone in a bar full of Arcānum . . .' He sighed. 'Sage has locked herself in her bedroom "to pack" and P's worried you haven't come home. I said I'd find you.'

Finally he looked up at Berion; the white-eyed warlock looked haggard. 'I knew Roderick didn't like her but I didn't think he'd—'

Oren shook his head. He didn't want to hear it. He knew Berion choosing to leave the pub with Sage was a decision about his relationship with Roderick. And that was enough.

They sat in silence for a while.

'Does she know?' Berion asked at last. 'How she . . . came to be *that* kind of wolf?'

He shook his head. Memories of Liam MacAllister's father – the pack alpha – echoed in his ears.

True white wolves are rare. They say they're touched by moon magic.

'She knows the story of Amhuinn, obviously. And the MacAllister family. She knows that Amhuinn tried to create illegal magic werewolf hybrids, and Liam MacAllister's father gave permission to experiment on his children. That Liam – Harland, as he became – was the only surviving hybrid, as far as we know. She knows what I did to the rest of them too.'

'And she hasn't made any connection? Oren, if Sage is . . . If she is one of Amhuinn's original creations—'

A bang echoed through the room as his fist slammed into the table. 'If she is and the Elders ever found out, they'd demand she be executed. Demand *I* execute her. Amhuinn's method of making hybrids is illegal. *She* would be illegal. They would not let her live.'

It made him feel sick. More blood. More final words and execution rights.

Sage.

Red flashed. The blood pooling under Hozier's shaking hands, and streaming in rivulets down Sage's body.

He shuddered.

'That wasn't what I was going to say,' Berion said gently.

'What, then?' he demanded, and it came out louder than he'd intended. The fury bubbling inside him felt uncontrollable.

'If she was turned by a warlock – Amhuinn – if she has our magic as well as moon blood, well, she is partly one of us.'

'They'll never accept—'

'No. Oren. I mean, she's nearly the right age. She . . . Oren . . . she could settle.'

It shattered his chest.

Settling was the warlock slang for the process that slowed ageing into millennia. Warlocks were not truly immortal, but it was close enough. He hadn't dared even think about it.

In spite of the danger and the lifetime of hiding what she was, it would be the answer to their prayers. A stop to all the nights he'd lain awake wondering whether he should've let her die, turn herself into a ghost rather than be the only one of them all to wither and age. Even just a few hundred years would be enough. Time to spend together and . . .

It terrified him. The thought of hoping and being wrong.

He shook his head, unable to speak.

'Isn't that what you wanted?'

Oren shook his head again.

Berion hissed. 'Don't lie!' His worn expression turned angry, rallying in her defence.

And he realized he was grateful for it. He'd watched Sage and Berion together, knew their friendship was real. He knew he'd scared most of her other friends away and that allowing Berion in was the only thing he could offer to make up for it.

'I heard her,' Berion went on, 'begging you to let her die, so that you didn't have to watch her get old. I heard you say you didn't want that either.'

'So what?' he snapped back. 'She lived. I saved her – we all did. That night is history—'

'And how many times have you regretted it since?'

'I don't regret it.'

'Bullshit.'

'What do you want me to say?' He felt like exploding again. 'That I wish she was dead?'

'I want you to admit that you're in love with her.' Berion lifted his chin, daring him to deny it. 'And that it's clouding your judgement.'

Oren froze.

Berion chuckled bitterly. 'Oren Rinallis, the warlock with a heart of ice, thawing at last. And you thought it'd gone unnoticed?'

He didn't know why the truth made him feel so angry.

'I came here one morning, remember? To give you some results for an older case.' Berion refilled his glass wearily with a flick. 'And you told me that the night before, she'd *killed a werewolf* to save your life, and you were trying to pretend you weren't freaking out. And I couldn't figure it out at first. She'd killed that wolf but you've done worse. Her wolf was no threat to you: you could have killed her in a heartbeat. So what were you so scared of?'

'I'm not scared of anything.'

Berion shook his head sadly. 'Her feelings for you were abundantly clear with that act alone, but I realized you'd started to wonder if you might actually care for her too.' He smiled. 'I made sure she looked beautiful that night of the moon ball. I wanted to give you a little . . . *push* in the right direction.'

And hadn't she? He'd seen it written all over her face, that for once she actually *felt* beautiful, and it'd given her a radiance he'd never seen before. A confidence he hadn't realized she'd been so lacking until then. He hadn't thought of the hair constellations of his people for decades, but that night he was able to see clearly exactly how her hair should've been braided.

Berion shrugged. 'You're not scared of anything, you say. But the sound you made when you saw her dying and had no magic to save her? *That* was fear. I knew then that you'd accepted you love her too.'

The lump in his throat was painful. 'She wouldn't even

entertain the idea.'

'You've not given her the chance. She thinks she's going to die while you stay young forever.'

'That might happen,' he argued back. 'Even if she is a hybrid, that's no guarantee of settling. She could still age a human lifespan.'

'But if she doesn't?'

He shook his head. 'I can't risk giving her false—'

'She has a right to know, Oren.' Berion sounded annoyed again. 'Has she shown any other signs? Any physical magic?'

'Not how we'd use it. I've seen no colour.'

'Well, her size is another pretty big indicator, by the way. Excuse the pun.' Berion pulled a face. 'But she's huge. Especially for such a small human form.'

He also knew that. It wasn't definitive proof but . . . wolf size did tend to follow human size.

'She can partially transform at will,' he admitted. 'I've seen it. She can stay human but change just her fingers to claws, or take on fangs and wolf eyes while her face stays human.'

Berion choked on his wine. '*That's* not just a sign, Oren, that's impossible!'

'She doesn't realize that.'

'Oh,' Berion snapped. 'Something else you haven't told her?'

And the other thing.

For weeks he'd been confused, wondering why the hell he was feeling a whole range of emotions that not only had

~31~

he schooled himself not to feel over many decades, but that didn't remotely fit the situation he was in. It'd taken him a while to realize that they weren't his feelings at all . . . they were hers.

Empathic skills were not a trait of warlock magic at all, not even a rare one – like his shifting. He hadn't dared ask P or Hozier to research it. So why in the name of the gods was he feeling what she was feeling? Whatever was going on felt ominous. He wasn't going to tell anyone about it, not even Berion, until he had figured it out.

'Anything else?' Berion asked.

'She's volatile,' he said slowly. 'She's not been easy to talk to recently. Mood swings. I can see the anger on her face, and she grows claws without realizing. Then she flips one-eighty and hides away, thinking we can't hear her crying.'

'Irrational anger, mood swings, behaving out of character – it's all the start of settling, you know that.'

'They're also signs of a human not coping with all the bad things that've happened to them,' Oren pointed out. 'Post-traumatic stress. That's what P is convinced it is.'

'She still has the right to know that she might be a hybrid.'

He shook his head. 'I can't tell her what I suspect and then walk into the *Jura mountains*, of all places – surrounded by wolf packs and witch clans – and expect her to keep it together.'

'Well, I disagree, and I seriously advise you to reconsider.'

Berion sighed deeply through his nose. 'Let me be clear, Oren. If you wait until you return, I'll tell her myself before letting you keep her in the dark any longer. She has to know. And then we have to plan. Because we won't be able to hide it forever. Not if she develops proper magic, with a colour. It'll be impossible to hide until she learns to control it and that takes years of practice.'

He knew, despite all this rage he felt inside, that Berion was right. And they'd need his help. This wasn't something he could risk burning bridges over.

'Fine.'

They sat in silence for a little while.

'I need to go home.' Oren drained his glass.

Berion nodded. 'I'll have to stay there too. I can't go back to mine tonight. Roderick will be staging an ambush. He'll try Hozier's but he won't dare knock on your door. Not after tonight.'

'Sage won't expect you to leave him.' He pulled on his coat. He still couldn't meet Berion's eye.

Berion looked disgusted. 'I have more self-respect than you give me credit for, Oren. Besides, I believe the humans call it "bros before hoes".'

Oren snorted. He knew the term.

'Hozier's waiting at your place with P too. She came back home with her after P found out what happened – P went to the pub herself and threw a drink in Flora's face.'

5

SAGE

Her body was on fire.

She'd refused to change on the walk home. Berion had offered to magic some clothes, or at least a dressing gown, but she'd opted to keep walking in silence. And once they'd got home she'd gone straight upstairs and left Berion to deal P the double blow that she and Oren were about to leave with no return date, and that the whole Arcānum now knew how she died.

She'd transformed back only once she was inside the sanctity of her bedroom, and had slammed her door firmly shut. When P had knocked a few minutes later she'd barely managed to control her hyperventilating, silent sobs to call through that she was packing, and would come down for something to eat later.

Thankfully P had left her to it.

So she sank to her knees, let her head fall against the side of her bed, and cried.

An hour or so later, she still hadn't moved. The tears had subsided but the aching in her limbs after the process of her bones shattering and re-fusing themselves into different shapes had hit her full force.

She closed her eyes, the events of what'd happened in the bar replaying over and over in her mind. Every moment was awful. But she couldn't stop herself. Couldn't stop replaying it. Torturing herself with it.

A tap at the door, and as the handle turned without waiting for permission, she knew it wasn't P.

Light flooded from the hallway into the dark room lit only by the small fairy lights dangling over her bedhead. Oren's outline stood there, looking down on her. She felt the warmth of his magic ripple over her body, and the aches and pains vanished.

He held out his hand without a word. She put hers in his calloused palm and let him lift her to her feet.

'Are you angry with me?' she whispered.

He was centimetres from her, his chest close enough that she could lean forward and rest her head there if she dared, which was preferable to looking up at him. She couldn't stand to see the disappointment. He'd fought so hard for her. He'd gone to bat against Roderick, against threats to terminate his contract. He'd agreed to a partner after all those years of a solitary life, knowing the only way to guarantee her a position was to take her on as his responsibility.

And she'd shown him up. Lost her temper in front of them all. Not even a year into the job.

A finger came to her chin and lifted it, forcing her to look up.

But she found none of the anger she'd expected. None of the disappointment.

'Are you OK?'

She nodded. 'I'm sorry.'

He shook his head. 'If Flora had done that to anyone else in that room, there would have still been a fight, Sage. Just less fur and more magic. Nobody will actually be surprised you tried to kill her.'

'Just surprised that I killed my best friend?'

He sighed. 'I've still done worse. And that was what we agreed. That you will witness unconscionable things at my side before we're through. But we go to hell together.'

And so nobody else's opinion mattered.

It's done. It doesn't matter. I don't care.

She wanted to cry all over again.

She couldn't bear to go downstairs and look P in the eye.

'Roderick—'

'I'll deal with Roderick.' Oren practically growled his name. 'I'll be paying him a visit before we leave tomorrow. There will be no repercussions, not when he was the one who gave Flora the information.'

She knew Oren would kill Roderick if he could. He'd hated the bastard for decades. But he would have to let it go to keep her in the Arcānum.

She wasn't sure she deserved it.

The hand that'd lifted her chin brushed her cheek. His gentleness always surprised her. Ever since she'd learnt the truth of his past. She'd never quite been able to reconcile the man she knew with the terrible things those hands had done.

She wanted to lean into his touch. How embarrassing, that she, a nineteen-year-old werewolf who could barely contain her temper, who couldn't even transform without almost killing someone, could dream to stand before the infamous Oren Rinallis and be described as anything other than inadequate.

She didn't know what must've flickered across her face, but he sighed. Then he wrapped his arms around her and let her fold herself into his chest.

She thought often of that night they'd danced together at the moon ball, and how being in his arms had felt. That for the first time in a long time she had felt safe, and that was because of him. How sad she still was for the girl she'd been before him. How alone, and unhappy, and afraid, and she hadn't even realized it until all those things had started to melt away. How different things were now. That dance felt like a lifetime ago.

His voice hummed quietly against her cheek. 'Why are you crying?'

'I don't know,' she whispered.

That was a lie. He knew it was too. So he simply waited.

'I wish we could've stayed on that dance floor forever,'

she admitted. The pain in her heart was so strong.

'Does it really matter to you?' he asked softly, still holding her close. 'If we don't have forever?'

They hardly ever acknowledged it. The possibility of an alternative future. One where they could be more to each other than they were now. Neither of them ever discussed that night not long after he'd saved her life. The night he'd strode into her room and told her that if she ever tried to die on him again, he would fight his way into the afterworld and drag her back kicking and screaming, as he did not want to face a future where they were parted. And then he'd collapsed into the chair beside her bed and wept into his hands.

'Yes. It does matter to me.' She pulled back just enough to look up at him. 'I'm sorry.'

The one truth she'd been certain of from the start. She could not, would not, allow herself to love someone who she would eventually feel obliged to let go of, to watch him find someone else who was not the old woman she'd become. Someone who could still match him. Someone still his equal.

'Sage.' He looked pained. 'Sage, what if—'

'No, Oren. I don't want it.' She almost choked on the words. She didn't even mean them. She hated the lie. But she couldn't stand to hear him try and convince her otherwise. She just couldn't put herself through it.

He looked deep into her eyes, and all that pain he

usually hid away was so clearly there in his. He looked like he maybe wanted to say something more, but whatever it was . . . it got the better of him. 'There's nothing to be sorry for.'

She knew that wasn't true either. And it broke her heart that he was willing to lie for her anyway. So just this once, a single memory to keep forever until she aged and withered and died without him, she lifted her hand to his face, and brought him closer.

She could feel his breath tickling her lips, slow and steady, sure and confident, just like him. A stark contrast to her quick shallow breaths that gave away her nervousness. But if he knew it, he didn't laugh at her. Instead, he nudged her nose with his, an offer: he was so close, he was right there, and he wasn't pulling away, but it was her choice to close that final gap between them.

And she did want to. Despite every instinct roaring at her that it was a terrible idea.

She closed those last few millimetres, until she felt his lips soft on hers, and she couldn't stop her eyelids fluttering closed as she leant into him completely.

But then it was over. Fleeting. Like this rare moment of painful honesty.

When he pulled back, his eyes were still closed tight. And when they opened again, he shuddered, shaking off the vulnerability he rarely showed. He cleared his throat, and any emotion lodged there. And she saw that wall descending between them again. The one that locked all feelings away.

'You're still my best friend.'

'Always,' he said gently.

'This conversation never happened,' she whispered. 'Neither of us cried. Reputations remain intact.'

'No.' He smiled sadly. 'None of this happened.'

He understood. She understood. They hadn't admitted anything to each other at all. Because it was the only way that either of them could live with it.

Oren stepped back and let go of her.

'Be ready for ten,' he told her as he backed out of the room and shut the door behind him.

6

SAGE

She woke early, after a bad night's sleep.

Late in the evening, once Berion had settled upstairs and Hozier had returned with her packed bags to move in, and Oren had stopped pacing his room, P had floated up through the floor.

They'd talked late into the night, and P had taken her still mostly empty rucksack and told her she'd deal with it. She'd check in with the fairies who glamoured the Downside sky to look real and who somehow knew the weather forecast in any given city at any given time, and sort what needed to be packed while Sage slept. Because of course she would.

Because she was P, and none of them deserved her.

But though Sage felt at peace by the time she'd closed her eyes, her dreams were haunted by the old nightmares filled with her brother's rasping breaths. She hadn't had them in a long time – not since she'd met Oren, who had refused to allow her to feel guilty for surviving. Last night, though, they'd made a guest appearance.

Her head throbbed from tiredness as she made her way down the stairs. She had no idea when she'd sleep in her own bed again, but she could smell the bacon P already had waiting for her. At least she'd share one good, final meal with her friends before they left.

'Oh.' She jolted to a stop as she opened the living room door and found a stranger on their sofa.

A handsome stranger.

Surprise turned to confusion. He looked . . . exactly like Oren. Like they could've been twins? Except for the hair. His was entirely black, and he had a short beard. Oren was never anything but clean-shaven.

But other than that, uncanny.

Oh, he was a delight. And he was sitting on their sofa?

He looked up and smiled politely. Her headache paled into insignificance and her legs went a bit jelly.

'Um,' was just about all that she could manage. 'Hello?'

'I apologize.' He got to his feet and held out a hand. He was tall too. 'Kane Attaia.'

His accent was a lot stronger than Oren's. That slither which sometimes reminded her he was from somewhere far, far away, but lost in the time he'd spent Downside. She'd very much have liked Oren to have kept this accent.

And the tan.

She took his hand. The skin was soft and warm. No weapon callouses.

Stop drooling!

'Sage,' she just about managed to get out. 'Sorry, who are you?' She blinked. 'I mean, you're Kane Attaia, you just said that, I mean—' She was fluffing all her words.

He grinned. 'Why am I in your house?'

'Well.' She sighed with relief that they'd got there at last. 'Yeah.'

'I'm waiting for Oren.' He looked around the room, faintly bemused. 'I was told by the ghost at the entrance to the city that he lives here now. I met P, so you must be his other housemate.'

'Yes.' In her momentary brain fuzz, she hadn't realized P wasn't there. Neither were Berion and Hozier. They must still be upstairs.

'P has gone to find him. I'm only in the city for an hour before I leave for Paris, so . . .'

Her stomach lurched again. Had Oren gone to see, *to threaten*, Roderick?

She took the narrow but comfortable armchair opposite the sofa – P's usual perch away from anyone that could pass through her by accident – and Kane sat too.

'I don't know whether I'm surprised or not to find he's living with two lovely women.' Oh, a charmer too? 'He doesn't—'

'Like people very much?' she offered.

Kane gave her a knowing smile.

'Yeah. It took a long time to break him.'

'Break him?'

'Let me be his friend.' She refused to acknowledge the heat rising in her cheeks even as she said *friend*. She guessed that was what they still were this morning. She'd refused to hear him suggest anything else . . . before she'd kissed him anyway. She was such an idiot. She was so embarrassed at how quickly she'd caved.

'Ah.' She was sure Kane had noticed her pinking cheeks. Was he wondering why?

'So,' she said after a slightly awkward pause. 'You look . . .'

'Similar?' he finished her sentence. 'Cousin. My father and his mother were siblings. Oren is less than a year older, so we grew up together. Everybody thought we were twins.'

'You knew *child* Oren?' Her eyes lit up.

Kane nodded, smiling. 'We got up to a lot of mischief.' Then his smile faded. 'We were as close as brothers. But he changed after his parents were executed. Shut himself off. My parents wanted to take him in, but he chose to board at school all year round. Otherwise I don't think he would have . . . well, things might have been different. He died with them. The Oren I remember, anyway.'

The smile slipped from her lips too. His parents' deaths was a subject she thought he should only talk about when he was ready, and he hadn't touched on it since the first and only night he'd ever brought it up: the same night she'd told him about P.

'You do know about that?' Kane looked mortified as he

misread her expression. 'I assumed—'

She shook her head hastily. 'No, don't worry. I know they're dead. Mine are too, so . . . it came up.'

'I'm sorry to hear that.' He was polite enough not to say what he could clearly scent; that she was a werewolf, and it was therefore likely her parents died in an attack she survived.

'Kane?' She turned to see Oren in the doorway, his face slack with shock. 'What are you doing here?'

'Passing through.' Kane got to his feet again, with a slightly determined air, arms wide in embrace. Oren stood stiffly, as Kane dragged him to his chest and said something in Arabic, the language of their homeland. When Oren answered, it took her breath away. Out of all the differences that separated them, it was funny that *this* made him feel so far away. Another reminder he'd lived so much life before she'd existed.

'Well, you never return my letters. What am I supposed to do?' said Kane, smiling. 'And what has it been? Twenty-five years?'

Twenty-five years. They hadn't seen each other in longer than she'd lived. And yet neither looked older than that. It made her shiver.

'You look just as I remember. Except . . . more muscle,' Kane conceded, stepping back and observing his cousin.

She snorted. Kane threw her an appreciative glance, and Oren an annoyed one.

'Tea?' P chimed over Oren's shoulder. 'I'll get some more tea!'

'I've not finished my first—' Kane started as she disappeared through the wall, but Oren shook his head.

'It's not worth it,' he said. 'Accept whatever she gives you.'

Sage was about to follow P when Oren looked at her.

'We need to go,' he said pointedly. Any kindness he'd shown as he'd wiped her tears and kissed her in the privacy of her bedroom last night was gone.

'Uh, what about breakfast?'

'P can wrap something up.'

'I haven't said goodbye to Berion or Hozier yet.'

Oren turned and shouted Berion's name through the open doorway. And when he looked back at her his expression said: *problem solved.*

'Oren. Please.' She eyed him wearily. *You're being rude.*

'No, Sage.' His tone was final. 'We're leaving. Now.' Oh, he was annoyed, all right. He was not willing to be strong-armed into any family reunion.

She flared at once, irritated he was turning on her the attitude he usually reserved for people like Roderick. 'Don't speak to me like—'

But as her speech slurred, and his brow betrayed him with a little twitch, she felt a moment too late that fangs had started to elongate in her mouth.

It was happening more and more recently, every time her temper flared. But the fangs must've made him realize they were about to descend into a fight because he sighed, his jaw locked and expression tight. She felt the brush of his warm magic down the back of her neck that said the apology he would refuse to voice in front of his cousin. The fangs retracted at once.

'You get used to the bickering,' P said brightly as she floated back into the room with a fresh teapot. 'They fight *constantly*. Exhausting. It's a good job I don't need to sleep.'

'I was only two floors up,' Berion called as he descended the stairs. 'No need to be so—' He froze in the doorway, his white eyes wide. 'Hello.'

Sage looked at P. P looked at her. All traces of her temper with Oren evaporated as the three of them suddenly tried desperately not to grin at each other.

'This is Kane.' P recovered quickest, gesturing in an over-the-top manner at their visitor. 'Oren's cousin – just . . . passing through.'

'On his way to Paris,' Sage said, eyeing P again. 'We've never been to the city of love, have we, P?'

P managed to cover her giggle with a little cough. 'We haven't, no. It's on our to-do list.'

Berion's canary-yellow velvet suit and chiffon white shirt clearly startled Kane, who took a moment to recover before smiling, and taking the extended hand Berion offered.

'But you can stay for breakfast, surely?' he asked Kane.

Berion was holding Sage's moon necklace, and swiftly swooped it over her head and fastened it, all without taking his eyes from their handsome visitor. Kane watched his nimble fingers on the clasp with mild interest.

'Hozier, my work partner, is just dressing. She'll be . . . devastated to miss you.'

P made for the kitchen at breakneck speed, and Sage knew it was to hide the snort she couldn't contain any longer.

Oren looked outraged at their fussing. Kane's eyes turned on his cousin. 'Do you mind?'

'You think I get a say?' He gestured furiously at Sage and Berion.

'The Oren I know wouldn't let that stop him,' Kane said quietly.

Oren said something in a language she didn't understand. Kane didn't reply, but he swallowed.

'Rubbish,' Berion said smoothly, seeing the need to break some more tension and pouncing. 'Sage is just big enough to put up a fair fight if she transforms.'

'Your control is excellent.' Kane gestured to his mouth, referring to her retracted fangs. 'I've never seen a werewolf only partially transform. Didn't realize it was possible. How long did that take to master?'

She blinked. She hadn't taken any time to master anything. She looked at Oren, confused. He didn't look surprised at all.

'She just has good natural control, it seems.' He said something again in Arabic. Short. The tone said *end of conversation*.

She stared at Oren. He looked right past her and at P.

'We'll take ours wrapped. Your bags are still upstairs, Sage?' And without waiting for an answer, he shifted out of the room.

Their farewells were pretty swift after that. Oren appeared again and ignored Kane entirely as Sage wished him a safe journey and kissed Berion on both cheeks, and Hozier crashed into the room demanding to know if she was going to leave without saying goodbye.

Her face lit up. 'Who have you been hiding here, Patricia?' She rounded on the ghost. 'He was not here when we all went to bed last night! Did you sneak him in?'

P's silvery cheeks blotched opaque and Berion smirked. Oren strode across the room, and Sage knew the moment he touched her they'd shift and be gone. She looked at P, the one friend she couldn't hug goodbye. P nodded encouragingly, wishing her well on this new adventure. She'd be fine at home with Berion and Hozier.

Sage wasn't sure if she herself would be.

But as Oren's hand reached her elbow, and she saw Kane's handsome face surrounded by three grinning cats, she couldn't help feeling sure that if anyone wasn't going to be fine, it was him . . .

7

SAGE

'No more,' she gasped, letting go of his arm a dozen shifts later. 'Is this it?' she panted, looking around and forcing bile down her throat. 'Please tell me this is it.'

Trees.

And mountains.

That really was all there was to look at as they stood in a steep valley. Terracotta rooftops of a town in the distance were as small as doll houses.

A couple of shifts into their journey they'd landed atop white, sprawling cliffs. Dover. Barely a few kilometres from the ferry port. The fields behind were far-reaching, and ahead, with no barrier to stop them plunging to the sandy shores below, was the sea. The calm water had glittered where the morning sunlight reflected off the surface. She'd let go of Oren's hand for a moment as she gazed at it.

She'd never been afraid of water, but for the moments she stood there looking out on so much empty space, there was such an overwhelming pressure in her chest. The thought of being stranded out there, adrift, floating, just . . . alone.

So tiny and insignificant in a vast, never-ending ocean. Lost forever.

And now, as she stared at this endless landscape, so remote and isolated, she felt the same.

'Yep,' Oren said grimly. 'This is the Jura mountains. And that's Poligny.' He gestured to the toy town with his chin. 'We head for the limestone cliffs to the east. A warlock will meet us.'

She looked back towards the town as they walked. She'd learnt about it in school. It was infamous, for her, at least. When the humans in England and beyond held witch trials, this place had held werewolf trials too.

She didn't know how many of those trialled really were werewolves. Most of those condemned for witchcraft were simply misjudged human women. But it was that relentless persecution which had pushed both the witch and werewolf communities here up into the mountains to escape. In the deepest parts of the Jura, where four wolf legs or a broom-stick could travel where humans could not.

Over time it'd simply become a safe haven, and witches and werewolves alike crossed the country to make the Jura their home. So she could see how it might be getting a little overcrowded. How tensions would start running high.

They soon reached the trees that stretched up into the mountains. A warlock stood in the shadows there. Sage had scented her already.

Unsurprisingly, Oren didn't bother to introduce himself,

hanging back like an oppressive spectre while she conducted the formalities.

'Hello.' The woman looked just a little older than Oren, and held out her hand.

'*Salut. Enchantée.*' Sage took the hand politely.

'Ah!' The woman's expression brightened. '*Vous parlez français?*'

'No,' she admitted with a sheepish smile. 'I didn't get much further than that, in my human school before I was turned. Our supernatural schools don't teach languages. I can tell you my name and favourite colour, but that's it.'

The woman laughed. 'Don't worry. I didn't learn to speak English until I was nearly two hundred years old. You have plenty of time yet. I'm Annette.' She placed a hand on her chest. 'I work for the Arcānum team based here in the Jura – we cover the whole mountain range, as well as the towns in and around it.'

'I'm Sage, and this is my partner, Oren.'

To give her credit, Annette tried to hide how her smile strained. But it was there. The gut reaction of fear that always came with the name. Oren ignored her completely. His disinterest in most people was genuine, but it was also a part of the persona he kept firmly maintained.

'So.' Sage forced past the awkwardness. 'Can you give us a little more information? What's been going on?'

'Come, I'll explain on the way.' Annette nodded towards the steep incline behind her. 'It flattens out in a kilometre or so. There are six wolf packs,' she went on as they set off under the thick canopy. 'There used to be seven witch covens but over the last century they've merged, and there's just one witch mother now who oversees the whole host. Wolves and witches reside on opposite sides of the mountain. They use the River Ain as the official boundary. Both sides generally keep themselves to themselves, but when paths do cross, it's traditionally . . . aggressive.'

'And it's got worse recently?'

Annette nodded. 'I don't know how much experience you have with true packs, but they can be less civilized.' Sage didn't think it was the time to recount how the last pack they'd strode into unannounced had tried to kill them. 'It's the same with the witches. Worse, even. We make . . . exceptions in these mountains. What would usually fall to the Arcānum to deal with in terms of punishment, we often let the alphas or witch mother sort it out, if it keeps it contained within the Jura and away from the human towns. It's . . .'

'A lot to deal with?' Sage offered with a reassuring smile.

Annette nodded, relieved. Sage knew she was probably worried about what she said within earshot of Oren. Although she knew that he didn't really care about Arcānum protocol.

'The separate wolf packs are usually rivals, but now they've joined forces and turned, as one, on the other side of the Ain. So they're about an even match for the witches.

And the two sides have been at each other's throats for months. A few of the alphas are reasonable. But frankly,' Annette gave her an apologetic smile, 'I don't envy you.'

'Oh, my captain in England is definitely hoping they're unreasonable.' Sage rolled her eyes. 'I think he's hoping they decide to try and kill me instead. He's furious he had to give me a job in the first place. But I won it fair and square. Solved a case he didn't think I could.'

'We heard.'

'You did?'

'Everyone did. There's never been a non-warlock in the Arcānum before. It was big news.'

Oren tutted. 'Please. This partnership is only big enough for one of us to be so arrogant. Don't let it go to your head.' Sage called him something that turned Annette pale. Oren ignored her, and turned back to Annette. 'Why are they fighting?'

Annette pulled a face as if to say, *who knows*. 'Some of the werewolves say things have been happening – like livestock going missing, or a bad crop – but a lot of it just sounds like bad luck.'

'And what do the witches say?' Oren asked.

'Nothing. They've ignored all attempts at communication.'

'Great,' Sage grumbled.

'Quite,' Annette said. 'But both sides look for excuses to take a swipe at the other. I suspect that's all this is. Neither side believes the other should even be in the mountains. It's an excuse to fight.'

'Why?'

'Politics older than any of us here.' She shrugged. 'Both argue they were the first ones to take refuge in the mountains, thus the land is rightfully theirs. And since populations are growing, both sides would undoubtedly seize the opportunity to expel the other and spread out, if they got the chance.'

'So this whole thing could just be an excuse for a land grab?'

'I think it's possible,' Annette agreed. 'You're staying with the Meute de Dubois. The Dubois pack. Celeste Dubois is the youngest alpha here and by far the most reasonable. It was Celeste who contacted us, once she'd collected support from other alphas. She will be your biggest ally – if you maintain her trust. She's sent an envoy from her pack to meet us. He will take you further into the mountain.' Annette frowned, moving her head from side to side to peer around the endless trees. 'You'll like him,' she winked just as a figure moved in the distance, and a young man stepped into view. 'He's handsome.'

Sage snorted. 'At this distance, he can totally hear you.'

'I hope so,' Annette muttered. 'He has to get bored of werewolves some time, right?'

He wasn't *Oren*-handsome. Nobody was. But that didn't mean Sage couldn't appreciate the thick, light-brown hair cropped short, and pretty green eyes. He was tall and slender, his physique more like Berion, though as he stepped forward and held out a hand to Annette with a slight lip-curling smile, he didn't quite achieve the same level of grace.

Annette muttered greetings in French as they shook hands. It reminded her of Kane and Oren conversing in Arabic, the language of their childhood, and she pushed away that weird feeling it kept giving her.

He turned to her with a smile. 'I'm Gabriel, we're grateful you've—' He froze, his eyes locking on to hers. 'You're a werewolf.'

'You . . . didn't know?' She glanced at Annette who looked vaguely surprised at his reaction.

'*Je suis désolée*,' she told Gabriel, looking between them. 'I . . . didn't even think to mention it.'

Sage thought it was a pretty big thing not to think to mention, if she was honest. But even some of the nicer warlocks she'd met still possessed some level of ignorance towards other races, and it didn't particularly surprise Sage that Annette had not considered how this information might impact the pack hosting them.

'Well.' She forced a *who-cares* smile to cover a surprise sudden onset of nerves. 'Here I am.'

She could tell from his expression that this wasn't a *who-cares* situation. She knew what MacAllister's pack had thought of her working with the Arcānum, and she didn't expect this pack to think much different. But she needed this greeting to go well if there was any hope for it working out here. Sure, Oren would technically keep them safe . . . but she wanted to be able to do it on her own, gain her own respect, without his presence always scaring everyone into submission.

But Gabriel seemed to decide it wasn't the time to push it either. And so he smiled again, straightened, and held out the hand he'd momentarily retracted in shock. 'And here you are,' he echoed. 'Welcome. Thank you for making the journey.'

And *ooh la la*.

Yep. Accents.

Ooh la la indeed.

'Sage.' She took his hand, hoping her face wasn't going puce. 'My partner.' She cleared her throat and turned to him, realizing with mild horror that he was staring at her with a wide-eyed, slightly accusatory look. 'Oren.'

Gabriel's expression had changed again, just as Annette's had. 'Rinallis?' he asked, as if clarifying. But she could see that he already knew. His features held the kind of contempt that werewolves especially held for Oren.

'Well,' Annette said, louder than was necessary. 'This is where I leave you.'

'Thank you, for bringing us this far,' Sage said earnestly. She still couldn't shake the immense gratitude she felt when any warlock was kind to her. 'Hopefully we'll meet again.'

'Hopefully . . .' Annette's eyes flashed to Gabriel, then back at her with a smirk. But she was already backing away into the trees.

8

SAGE

She knew she was unfit compared to the warlocks who worked out in the training rooms every day, but bloody hell. Her lungs were on fire by the time they'd practically climbed halfway up a cliff edge, and she was trying her hardest not to show her exhaustion.

The trek would be easier on four legs, Gabriel told her when they'd set off, but the jolt in her stomach at the idea was quickly remedied by the resentful glance he'd thrown at Oren. They would remain on human feet out of forced politeness for the warlock who couldn't change. And she hadn't bothered to tell Gabriel that Oren probably would've preferred shifting along beside them anyway.

Clambering over the top of the steep slope she jolted to a stop, still on her hands and knees, staring up at, well . . . a small village? She couldn't see clearly past the first row of tidy little cabins, but she could see a long, wide earthen street, grass worn into hard dirt by endless footsteps, with smaller streets branching off to either side, leading to more bundles of cabins.

She didn't know exactly what she'd expected, but it wasn't this. Solid dwellings, with garden walls made of piled-up stones, gates with welcome signs, windows decorated with flower boxes . . . there were even street names screwed on to the corners of every end cabin.

Oren refused to show any surprise at all, but she knew he was taken aback, if only by his lack of sarcastic comment.

'We were told this is the largest pack?' she asked.

Gabriel nodded. 'We have just over eighty members. Some are married, and most of the younger ones live with friends. There are nearly fifty buildings on our land. Most are dwellings. The rest are used for things like storage, or medical attention. And enclosures for our livestock.'

'That's a lot of land.' She puffed out her cheeks.

He smiled. 'The Jura is around three hundred and sixty-two kilometres long.'

'The Arcānum implied there was an overcrowding issue,' Oren said. 'That both sides of the river would prefer to drive the other out.'

Gabriel's back stiffened almost imperceptibly at being addressed directly by Oren, but he answered politely. 'There are limits to how far we can spread. There are other . . . things that live in these mountains. Things it would be wise to keep at least some distance from.'

Oren didn't comment further, and Sage didn't ask. She wasn't sure she wanted to know just yet.

Gabriel led them through the little cabin village.

'Where is everyone?' she asked.

It was suspiciously quiet. She'd noticed a face watching from a cabin window – an older woman with grey hair tied back – and a younger man ripping chunks from an apple as he watched them. She wondered if they could tell what she was on sight, or scent.

'Work,' he said simply.

Work? Where? But before she could ask, they were already at the largest wooden building – what she supposed might be a village hall in a small countryside community, tall and wide with double doors already flung open for them.

Her heart pounded in her chest as the reality of their situation fully settled over her. They were in the middle of another pack, a pack that might not want her there once they knew what she was, and she had no idea when they would be able to go home. But that familiar warm brush of Oren's magic against her side was comforting, and when she glanced at him he gave her a small nod.

Nothing is as horrifying as I am. And here I am with you.

They ascended three stone steps and entered a wide room.

A 'small village hall' made her think of the community hall where she grew up, where she was human, and she and P had attended Brownies every Tuesday night. A floor covered in cheap linoleum and stacks of plastic chairs. The walls of this hall were decorated with incredible drapes, rich colours embroidering scenes of varying stages of transformation, and wolves in full hunt or battle. This floor was a deeply varnished wood covered in thick Persian rugs and long tables she could imagine piled high with food for a banquet. In the centre was what looked like a throne, and sitting on it was a woman dressed in black jeans and a cream knitted jumper.

'This is our alpha, Celeste Dubois,' Gabriel said. 'And her main advisor,' he added, nodding to the man beside her. 'Benoît.'

Celeste Dubois stood and Sage could see now that the throne was a seat carved into the trunk of a felled tree and that the whole hall had been built around it. The varnished floorboards paused just before the gnarled roots burrowed into the ground below.

The woman was tall, with high cheekbones and blonde hair scraped back into a bun. She looked to be around forty, the faintest of crow's feet starting to grace the skin around her piercing brown eyes.

Gabriel hurried ahead, speaking in French. Celeste looked surprised, her eyes flitting between her and Oren, and Sage could guess what the envoy was revealing. Benoît's head snapped up, his nostrils flaring as he breathed in deeply, scenting her.

'A werewolf?' Celeste repeated, in English now.

They'd stopped at a respectful distance, but close

enough to be heard. Oren's hands were loose in his pockets, and he made no effort to reply for her. Good. She needed to deal with this herself, even as her heart still thundered with anxiety in her chest.

'I am. My employment in the Arcānum is new, and a first, I believe.' She stepped towards the alpha in a gesture she hoped was symbolic. A step away from Oren's side, an offer to bridge the gap between both sides.

In one swift movement Benoît was before her, his palm raised. Whatever he was shouting she didn't understand, but she understood the tone. She flinched. She couldn't help it, but furiously wished she hadn't. It was a weakness she was trying to overcome.

'Benoît—' Gabriel gasped, shocked.

But it was drowned out by a cry of pain, followed by the sound of Benoît's clipboard clattering to the floor. Gold mist had grabbed Benoît's wrist and twisted it behind his back.

Gabriel yelped, and Celeste shot forward, shouting Benoît's name.

Sage whirled on Oren. His face was impassive, his hands still slack in his pockets as he stared at Benoît writhing against his magical restraints.

'Unhand my wolf at once!' Celeste ordered loudly, and though Sage was not a member of this pack she heard the authority in the alpha's voice, and the wolf inside her began to move. It was hard, even for her, to defy such command.

'If he raises that hand again, I will snap it off,' Oren said smoothly, looking at Celeste at last. 'Am I clear?'

Celeste lifted her chin.

'Am I clear?' Oren repeated.

Sage swallowed. 'He won't raise a hand again,' she said, her eyes fixed on the furious alpha, urging her to let Sage be their intermediary and defuse the situation. 'And Oren will have no need to interfere again. I will swear that to you.'

The alpha's brown eyes met hers at last, and Sage nodded slowly. Another offer. The bridge between them was still open, if Celeste was willing to help her build it. Another beat passed, and then Celeste nodded too.

'Oren,' Sage said firmly. 'Let him go.'

And thank God he did.

Benoît's hand fell to his side. He muttered furiously in quick French. But whatever order Celeste gave had him falling silent. Rubbing his wrist, he returned to his place beside her tree throne.

When she glanced at Gabriel, who she now realized had reacted rather calmly to discovering what she was, he seemed to take pity.

'It's illegal here for any wolf to cross boundaries into a pack that's not their own,' he explained. 'A wolf uninvited and approaching an alpha without permission is seen as a threat.'

'But I was invited,' she countered. 'By the alpha.'

'The Arcānum was invited,' Benoît growled. 'We were

not aware there were any wolves in their employ.'

She didn't really know what to say to that. She could see their points entirely. But she knew she couldn't back down and she definitely wasn't going to apologize. It wasn't her fault they hadn't been adequately warned.

'Fair enough.' She shrugged. 'But I am here now. Will it be a problem?'

'Now we've had a moment to take it in,' Gabriel glanced at the alpha, 'it could be a bonus, *non*?'

'We're here to do a job,' Oren said. 'What Sage is will not make her biased.'

'Oren is right,' she admitted. 'We've been sent with a job to do.'

Something registered in Celeste's face. 'Oren Rinallis.' She looked at him again, as Gabriel and Annette had.

He said nothing.

Celeste took another moment, perhaps wondering whether this had all been a mistake. Then she turned back towards her throne, as if it and all it represented was a comfort. Benoît still flanked it, and Gabriel stood between them, watching everything unfold.

Still, Oren said nothing. But as Sage glanced at him again, she knew that face. A derisive smirk for the alpha's small display of power.

'Thank you for coming all this way,' Celeste said at last, but her smile was tight. 'Shall we begin?'

9

SAGE

They followed Celeste to the back of the hall, where there was a large wooden table and chairs topped with thick cushions.

'Sit,' she gestured. 'We hold most meetings here, we won't be disturbed.'

Sage noticed that Celeste didn't bother to sit at the head of the rectangular table, instead taking a seat halfway down, Benoît still at her side. A dynamic she watched Oren observe quietly as they sat in seats directly opposite, Gabriel joining them. Interesting, she thought. He was not an advisor, or at least he hadn't been introduced as one. He'd been little more than their tour guide so far . . . But perhaps that would be his job for the duration of their stay. Their escort, the alpha's spy?

'Benoît is my most senior advisor,' Celeste began. 'He oversees the day-to-day living, finances, workload, etcetera, of the camp. Any issues, or queries, he will be able to help.'

Sage didn't think he *would* help, judging by the look on his face, but she said nothing.

'Tell us.' Benoît leant forward. 'How did you acquire a place in the Arcānum? This is impossible, *non*?'

'I solved a case my boss thought would be impossible,' Sage replied calmly, 'and he had no choice but to honour the job he'd promised when he believed I would fail.'

Celeste smothered a smile. 'How old are you?'

'Nineteen.'

'Young,' Benoît muttered.

She refused to let her cheeks burn.

'I'm one hundred and forty-nine,' Oren said, glaring at him. 'So we average out at eighty-four. Is that old enough for you?'

Benoît didn't reply. Gabriel cleared his throat awkwardly.

'These are for you,' Benoît said curtly instead, sliding two pieces of paper across the table towards them. She looked down the list of packs and the details of their alphas as he began to reel off the information. 'Meutes de Dubois, Monreau and Garnier voted to invite you here. Meutes de Duplantier and Egli did not. Meute de Bassett was un-decided. The *mère sorcière*, Sybil Crows-Caw, did not respond to our request for their input.'

Celeste gestured towards the list. 'The pack that abstained is wary of outsiders, but if they see you're not here simply to interfere with our way of life, I expect they can be won over.'

Sage nodded. 'We were told that there were some who

strongly opposed our presence.'

'To put it lightly,' Benoît said bluntly, glaring. 'You will be even less welcome there than here.'

She wasn't sure why he was treating her as if she'd intentionally tricked him. Someone not thinking to offer additional information was not the same as deceit. She could feel an irrational anger – becoming more and more familiar these days – start to flare inside her.

'You will not win over the Meute de Duplantier or Egli, no matter how hard you try,' Benoît continued. 'Their alphas are the oldest. Most stuck in old ways and traditions. They are not worth wasting your time on.'

'And the witches?' Oren asked.

Gabriel shook his head. 'Will be deliberately unhelpful. Our camp is only one of two that borders the river. I spend more than half of my time preventing all-out war at the crossing.'

'Gabriel is the head of security here, and he oversees the team of guards that patrols our borders day and night,' Celeste said, providing some clarity on their extra member at last. 'The witches never cross the river. And, not that we don't trust our wolves, but, well . . .' She grimaced. 'The younger ones are easily distracted by the pretty faces hovering on the other side to wash their clothes and hair, and the witchlings know what to say to cause trouble.'

'I have tried to make contact,' Gabriel admitted, rolling his eyes. 'The witch mother has not presented herself at the border despite many requests. Whether my messages are even being passed along to her, or if she is hearing but simply ignoring, I don't know. She is getting old, and her witches are very protective. Perhaps they have decided not to bother her with this at all.'

'But what exactly has happened?' Sage asked.

Celeste sighed. 'Strange things, more than usual. Enough to call it more than coincidence. Crops are dying with no explanation. Livestock have caught unknown diseases, with many having to be slaughtered. The animals of one pack have been so unsettled they've stopped producing milk altogether. Our own paddock is securely locked each night but the next morning it's open, no forced locks, animals gone. Last week there was a storm and two separate cabins caught fire—'

'Acts of nature?' Oren could barely control his derision. 'A witch's curse?'

A witch's curse. It sounded like something out of human fairy tales.

Celeste clenched her jaw, as if she knew how it sounded too. 'We don't know what started the fire. The storm was wind and hail, not lightning. And the wood was very wet.'

'Anything else?' he asked.

'We can't speak for all the packs, you'll have to go to them yourselves, but we do know others suffered the night of that storm, and there has been sickness among werewolves too, and not in the packs where the livestock were sick.' She sighed as she saw Oren open his mouth again. 'I know. All these things have plausible explanations. But all at once? After many decades of quiet? Well, that's what's causing unrest.' Celeste looked at her. 'Werewolves can be superstitious.'

She nodded. She knew that. 'We'll need to speak to some other packs first, I guess.' She looked down the list.

'Those that voted for your assistance will answer your questions.' Celeste nodded. 'But . . .'

'I can deal with the other two, if necessary,' Oren said quietly. Every head turned to look at him. He looked right back. Then he looked at Sage, and when he spoke again it was as if he were addressing her, but she knew it was for their benefit. 'We don't need permission to speak to anyone. If there's a problem, I'll make that clear.'

'Fine,' she said. '*If* they decline my requests first.'

His nostrils flared. But he nodded.

'Rest for today. You've travelled a long way to get here.' Celeste rose; the meeting was over. 'Gabriel will be your escort while you're with us, and he will see you across the borders. And to your cabin. There is running water, siphoned from the closest river. It's clean enough to wash with, but boil it first if you're going to drink it, just in case. Wildlife and all. You're welcome to eat in your cabin, though this hall is open every evening between seven and nine to bring your food and eat in company.'

'That's very social.' She eyed Oren, trying not to smirk as

they rose too, knowing he'd rather chop his own head off.

'While many live together, others live alone,' Gabriel said. 'Everybody has the opportunity for at least one meal a day where they are not lonely. My mother—'

Sage froze.

Oren froze beside her.

'What did you just say?' She felt instantly sick. The ultimate rule of werewolf turning: any change or death caused by a werewolf was only permissible on a full moon. By accident, not carried out when the wolf was in complete and total control. Werewolves still birthed human children, and it was highly illegal for any human child of a werewolf to be turned intentionally. That was one of MacAllister's sins, last year, in their last major case. He had *offered* his children to Amhuinn. He had let his alpha intentionally change his son Harland.

'Celeste is your mother?' she asked. 'By blood?'

Before anyone could answer, Oren added, 'I hope you all have a *good* explanation.'

'It was me.' Gabriel's eyes were wide as he looked between them, willing them to believe him. 'I was turned, when I was a small child. And then a month later, on my first turning, I bit my mother.'

Sage looked at Celeste, who in turn was gaping at the expression on Oren's face, perhaps realizing at last who held the real power in the room.

'It's true,' she said, lifting her wrist to display two faint white scars. Barely pinpricks. 'A much less brutal scar than many of my pack. Less brutal than yours, I imagine.'

Sage still avoided looking at the brutal gash across her own hip in the mirror, the lasting proof of what some were-wolf had once done to her. It was rare that parents and children both survived the brutal attacks that turned were-wolves. Sometimes siblings survived, because their parents had died protecting them. Most were like Sage. Sole survivors by luck or chance.

She looked back at Oren.

He looked at her, and nodded once.

He would accept it as truth.

'You should've reported the wolf that turned Gabriel,' she said quietly.

Celeste shook her head sadly. 'We were homeless. We lived on the streets of Normandy. I didn't know anything about the supernatural world. For such a long while I believed we were two of very few. By the time we discovered these mountains it was too late. We'd forgotten the finer details, and I felt no inclination to drag it all back up again.'

Sage nodded. She understood that. She'd never had any inclination at all to find out who had turned her. Drag all that back up again.

'Thank you,' she said. 'For telling us the truth. And letting us stay with you.'

She willed Oren not to say a word as they turned to leave.

'I apologize for Benoît's outburst,' Gabriel told her as they made their way to the exit. 'But I will be honest with you, Sage, you will face some mixed reactions here.'

'I know that.' She lifted her chin.

It bothered her all the same to face rejection from her own people. She knew wolves that lived in true packs were very different to the lifestyle she enjoyed in an integrated society like Downside. The longer pack wolves resided together, allowing the magic of wolf blood and pack loyalty to take hold, the harder it was for them to integrate outside pack life again. But she would not feel ashamed of associating with anyone outside her own race, and dared anyone ever to try and make her choose.

Gabriel led them back out of the hall and left, coming to a stop at the small path leading to the cabin that would be theirs, almost directly facing the doors of the hall they'd just left. She wondered if that was intentional. To keep an eye on them.

'This is you.' He looked between them as he started to back away, but now that he'd got over the initial shock of their meeting, the smile he offered her was genuine. It flooded her with relief. 'Ask where to find me, if you need anything, or have any questions. I might see you at dinner.'

'Maybe.' She smiled back.

Or maybe not, if the look on Oren's face had anything to do with it.

10

OREN

'This is nice, right?' Sage called from her bedroom.

The cabin was larger than it looked. There was a small but fully fitted kitchen, a living area with a sofa and a shelf filled with well-thumbed books. In the middle of the room was a round dining table and chairs. And two compact but cosy bedrooms.

'It definitely makes that hut MacAllister lived in look like a hovel,' he agreed, poking his head into her room to see if it was the same as his. Same single bed and wooden dresser.

'There's an en suite,' she gasped. 'Like, with running water! How have they got all this up here when MacAllister lives in a city and his commune is . . . a hellhole?'

He shrugged. 'Don't forget MacAllister spent a decade hiding his pack away. He forfeited comfort in his quest to evade anyone that might want to punish him for his sins.'

He wandered back into the main living area. He needed a cup of tea.

When had he become so British?

That was P's influence, the click and hiss of a kettle the soundtrack to his new life with them.

But as he looked around the kitchen he realized they didn't even have one. He flicked a finger and a small travel-size kettle appeared on the counter. At least they had electricity to boil it. But this glorified camping was not his ideal set-up. Not at all.

'So . . .'

He glanced at her. She'd followed him out into the main living area and was checking the time on her phone before tossing it on to the table. As she crossed her arms he knew what was coming. He turned his back on her and filled the kettle. The water pressure wasn't great. Something else to add to his list of complaints.

'Shall we talk about Kane now?'

He knew she'd see his back stiffen. Knew it'd happened before he could control himself to stop it. That annoyed him.

'There's nothing to say.'

He sat the kettle back on to its base and turned to face her while it boiled. He folded his arms stubbornly across his chest – two could play at that game – and leant back against the surface.

'He's very handsome,' she edged.

He knew what she was doing. Trying to break the tension with a cheeky joke. They did it to each other often but . . .

Every other time she'd made this kind of joke, she hadn't just kissed him the night before. He saw her remember that in real time as her cheeks started to heat.

He'd thought about that kiss a lot that morning. Every time he'd held his hand out to shift and she'd taken it. Every time he'd caught her glancing at him. Every time her cheeks turned pink. He knew she was thinking about it too.

He couldn't even begin to count the amount of people he'd kissed in his lifetime. He knew he wasn't her first either. And . . . he wished she hadn't done it. Because now it was harder to look at her and not feel all the things he'd been forcing himself not to think about. Because if he didn't acknowledge them then they couldn't be real – right?

He refused to admit the thought of her kissing anyone else made him want to summon one of his favourite daggers and point it at this imaginary perpetrator's chest. He understood that her choice for their relationship to only ever remain a working one meant that one day she would likely find someone she could grow old with. He'd accept that. He had no other choice.

But . . . what if she did settle? What if that meant she aged like him?

No. He wouldn't think about that either. And curse Berion for planting the seed of possibility that it might. He would not let it grow.

'Of course Kane's handsome,' he said finally. 'He looks like me.'

She was trying not to smile too. 'You don't reply to any of his letters?'

'I have nothing to say,' he repeated.

She nodded. Of course she did. That was their gift to one another. No judgement. No pressure. Nothing from the past would change their present. He'd been working on sharing more and he'd been getting better but there were still some things . . . some memories . . . His childhood was not a conversation he was ready to have yet.

'You know I don't care about any of it,' she said quietly.

'I know that,' he said, equally quietly.

The kettle clicked, but it was only as he turned back to pour two drinks he realized they had no milk. He had no choice but to give up on the tea. Infuriating. If P were here she'd flip out. He turned back to Sage.

'There is something else we need to talk about.'

Her cheeks instantly exploded again. 'Like what?'

'Like how are we going to eat without P?'

She practically deflated in relief, and he couldn't stop his laughter sounding just a little bit cruel. He'd got her thinking about that kiss again. 'I told you we should have stopped in Paris.' He pointed an accusatory finger before opening the fridge to show her the milk they did not have. 'If we're going to starve, we should've done it after a good final meal.'

She straightened a little faster than necessary, shaking her head to regain some composure as she shoved him out of the way. She opened one of the cupboard doors and found a half-empty packet of penne. 'There's pasta. I can make pasta.'

'You're telling me you can cook?'

'You're telling me you can't? You survived a century and a half without P.'

'She complains endlessly that I'm too thin.' He threw himself on to the sofa, stretching his arms over the back and resting one ankle on the opposite knee. 'I was actually talking about Flora — what she said to you in the pub,' he admitted. 'Should we talk about that?'

'Oh.' She dragged out a dining chair and sat down facing him, propping her chin on her hands. 'I'm kinda relieved the secret is out.' She sighed. 'Well, not to everyone. But with Berion and Hozier. You know like when you don't mention something for so long it then becomes a whole big, weird thing by the time you do actually tell them?'

He nodded and reached for that weird bond between them where he could feel what she was feeling, but . . . nothing. He knew she couldn't control it; she didn't even know it was happening, since he hadn't told her about it yet. But he'd come to realize that, similarly to the partial changes, he felt the flashes when she was most anxious — like when they were about to walk into that hallway to meet Celeste and he'd felt her overwhelming fear of rejection. He'd sent a wave of his magic to remind her he was there, and the feeling had calmed.

But right now, she wasn't stressed about Flora. She meant what she'd said.

That was a relief. He changed the subject.

'So, what do you think of the case?'

She straightened, as if it still surprised her that he actually *wanted* her opinion.

'I understand why the packs are getting twitchy. That's a lot of bad luck to happen at once, and, yes, it could be bad luck.' She pointed at him to stop him interrupting before she'd finished. '*But* it is odd after years of nothing.'

'Fine.' He couldn't stop his eyes rolling. 'You also can't deny there are logical explanations. Different packs or not, the sickness between livestock and werewolf could be linked. Sure, packs supposedly keep separate, but I'll be damned if some young werewolves don't sneak over the borders to have a bit of fun.'

'I do think it is all coincidence,' she admitted with a sigh. *Ha.* He knew it. 'But we're still going to have to convince the werewolves it isn't a curse, otherwise it'll blow up sooner or later. And Roderick won't let us go home until it's under control. I don't want to be here forever, Oren.'

'I know.' He sighed too. 'Me neither. With any luck, we'll get it under control in a couple of days and be back in Downside. Roderick will be furious.'

'That's true.' She smiled, but he knew that even talking about home made her miss it. It made him miss it. That was something he never thought he'd feel.

He smiled at her. He could hardly believe the person before him was the person he'd met at their first crime scene. The nervous ball of jittery fear, her heart fluttering like a panicked bird. And now he was sitting here, missing the home he'd built alongside her. A home full of laughter and promises and the smells of good food and—

That bloody seed. It was all he could think about now it'd been planted. Or maybe he just wanted to kiss her again. He hoped to the gods that urge calmed down as the passing days took them further and further away from last night.

'What?' she demanded, noticing his smile.

He shook his head and jumped up. 'Have a shower. Chill. Read a book.' He waved a hand at the bookshelf, the spines shimmering a soft gold as the letters started to shift and change into English. 'I'll shift into the town to get some supplies. You can wow me with your never-before-seen cooking skills.'

The sounds of her swearing at him faded as he shifted out of the cabin.

II

P

'How do you cook a carbonara?'

P laughed. Sage's panic was coming across Face-Time loud and clear.

'That's cheating.' She heard Oren's voice in the background.

P propped her phone up against the tiles in her kitchen. She'd promised a batch of home-made soup to the local soup kitchen run by volunteer fauns to feed struggling families, and she had lots of veg to prepare.

Hozier clambered on to the kitchen island behind her to chat and to dice carrots.

'Oren, I told you I'd cook pasta and I am.' Sage's tinny voice filled the room. 'There were no rules on how.'

Hozier snorted.

It took around twenty-five minutes, and P knew she would've done it better. But she didn't think that Oren would complain too much when the alternative was, well, nothing.

As they cooked simultaneously while hundreds of

kilometres apart, Sage filled them in on the case.

'Well, I mean,' said Hozier, the only one visible on the phone screen – the knives and vegetables P was using simply floated in mid-air – 'it's not exactly the plagues of Egypt, is it? Trust me, I'd know.' She rolled her eyes lined in black kohl, reminiscent of depictions of Nefertiti and a constant reminder of where she hailed from.

'Exactly my point.' Oren, who had been silent for most of their chat, butted in from where he was lounging on a small sofa behind Sage, leafing through a battered-looking book.

'Sure,' Sage agreed impatiently. 'But even if it is all coincidence the timing is—'

There was what sounded like a knock at the cabin door.

Sage looked over her shoulder at Oren.

He reluctantly got up, throwing the book down and muttering something about her already being on her feet. He moved out of sight of the camera, but P heard him pulling open a slightly creaking door, and . . . then a sexy French accent?

'I came to escort you to the hall,' the mysterious voice said as Sage's head turned to look at their visitor too. 'If you want to join us. I suppose the pack has to see you some time, eh?'

Sage had already told them about the scene some guy called Benoît had caused. P had felt a sinking feeling in her stomach. She knew it would be important to Sage to fit in, but she wasn't a pack wolf, and they'd never truly understand her lifestyle in Downside.

Oren reappeared on the screen, his expression an outright no.

'Who's that?' P hissed, pressing her face as close as possible to the phone. Hozier was trying to get a better look as well.

Sage ignored them, but P could see her cheeks going pink. Ha!

'Oren's got some paperwork,' Sage lied smoothly, giving him a look that dared him to openly contradict her. 'But I'll come. I've just finished making dinner. Give me a minute to dish it up.'

French Accent politely excused himself to wait outside as Sage started to open random cupboard doors for a container.

'What will you do?' she asked Oren.

He shrugged. 'Have fun.'

'Sage!' P hissed again. 'Who—'

But she'd hung up.

'Rude!' Hozier gasped. 'He was definitely a hotty, or she wouldn't have cut us off. Didn't want us to embarrass her in front of Oren.'

P snorted. Hotty. Hozier was nearly two hundred years old, which was quite easy to forget when she looked early twenties and barely came up to most people's shoulder, but easy to remember when she came out with phrases P's own grandmother might've used.

'Who's a hotty?' Berion appeared in the kitchen doorway, holding up a handful of brown folders. 'Kane isn't back already, is he?'

P snorted again. 'No. We just heard a sexy French accent before Sage cut us off. What are those?'

Berion threw the files down. 'Roderick's giving us the two case files he was going to give to Oren. I told him we don't work cases any more but . . .' He let it hang in the air between them.

Hozier rolled her eyes. 'Punishment for walking out of the pub with Sage?'

He pulled a face that said everything. 'They are gruesome ones,' he admitted. 'I had a flick through. I can see how nobody else would want them.'

Before Oren had stalked into Downside and faced off against the worst cases Roderick had to offer, Hozier and Berion had taken on most of those tasks with the least complaining.

'I'll help, if you want,' P offered, tossing a tasting spoon into the sink. 'I won't have much else to do.'

That was true. She'd told Sage she would be fine while she was gone and she'd meant it, for the most part. But she couldn't help worrying, anyway. Not just for Sage, but for Oren too. The pair of them in the middle of nowhere like that? With unknown wolf packs and a witch coven at war. Oren would keep Sage safe, sure, but . . . she'd been worried about Sage for a while now. After losing Harland – despite all that he was, well, there was only so much death one person could take, and Sage wasn't taking it as well as she believed she was.

Her emotions were all over the place, and her temper fragile at best. And that incident last night in the pub? P knew Sage was touchy over the way she'd died. So seeing that white wolf for the first time since it'd cleared a dark field in a handful of leaps and killing P on impact, slam its way into the hallway and take the staircase three at a time, a pale Berion not far behind, she'd known something had happened that was entirely out of proportion.

And Oren.

Oren could deal with her physically but the poor bloke still couldn't deal with emotion. How he was going to handle one of her bad days, P wasn't entirely sure.

Berion's thrilled gasp brought her back into the room. 'You're sure?' He sat down at the table. A little velvet cloth appeared in his hand and he started to slide off his rings one by one, ready to polish them. 'You don't mind looking over the files?'

She shrugged. 'Give me the paperwork, I can put it in order through the night.'

She did it for Sage and Oren, meticulously combing through and writing up everything while they slept, so they didn't have to do it through the day. It'd been Oren's dream come true when she'd admitted she actually quite enjoyed it, not to mention the thrill of sneaking into the archives in the dead of night.

Roderick would never allow it officially. After the contempt he'd shown for Sage, they hadn't even bothered to request official access into the archives for P. She knew, though, that the work she did was the reason Oren let her have full rein on his credit card, and didn't complain every time she opened a new delivery box to produce yet another piece of cookware. He hadn't been able to wrangle her a wage, but Oren made sure she was compensated in his own way.

'You are a star!' Berion gave her his most gracious smile. But then it fell a little. 'P. We need to talk. There's something I have to tell you – about Sage.'

If she could faint, she would.

If her body were still alive and able to shut down from shock and horror, it would.

Hozier was back on the kitchen island, frozen, her jaw hanging open.

'Oren doesn't know I've decided to tell you this,' Berion said, idly pushing around his rings with a finger. 'And we don't know for certain.'

'Bollocks,' she hissed.

Berion and Hozier looked at her, shocked. *Don't know for certain?* She knew the second the words came out of Berion's mouth, the second he admitted that Oren suspected Sage was an illegal hybrid, that it was true.

Oren was certain, whatever he said to Berion. Oren had kept it a secret from *her*. And he told P everything. Every little worry and fear. She'd lost count of the nights she'd been tidying her kitchenware or sorting her spice rack, and he'd shifted into the kitchen right behind her and spilt his guts like an anxious child who'd let the mundane worries of the day grow out of proportion in the dark hours of night. Sage helped Oren sift through his past, but P helped him sift through the present: the new things he felt because Sage had started to chip away at the barriers he'd built: his old coping mechanisms to get through everything that comes with being the supernatural world's most powerful and feared assassin.

For him to have kept this from her, that meant he knew it was true. He just hadn't come to terms with it yet. Didn't know how it made him feel. And he knew that in telling P it meant that he would have to face it. Because she'd make him. And then she'd make him tell Sage.

The worst part was that it all made complete sense to her. Sage's wild mood swings and irrational reactions, all of it getting increasingly worse in the last six months. She trusted Oren, knew if he believed it then it was right. But she'd done her research on hybrids too – in her own grief, she'd wanted to understand the man she'd thought was her friend, Harland, before Oren had executed him.

She couldn't believe she hadn't made the connection before.

She'd been so caught up in human diagnoses. Stress. Trauma. Depression. She hadn't considered there could be a supernatural answer.

'Well, then.' She breathed deeply through her nose. There was no point pussy-footing around it. 'We find out as much as we can now, and then we go from there.'

Berion nodded. 'My thoughts exactly. We need to figure out all our available options. We need a plan.'

'But where do we start?' Hozier asked. 'There isn't anything in the archives.' She paused, eyeing P. 'I take it you've been in the restricted bits even I can't look in?'

P nodded. 'It doesn't tell us anything Oren doesn't already know. Most of the information available in there is Oren's own reports of the Amhuinn investigation, and account of the night he went to the camp and killed them all.'

The words hung in the air between them.

He'd killed them all.

He'd torture himself over that – probably already was. He'd only been doing his job and he was very clear he had few regrets when justice was deserved; but by killing any witnesses, he had lost them all the opportunity to learn about Sage.

But even a warlock as powerful as Oren couldn't see the future. Even Oren couldn't have known the one girl that'd make him feel alive again might be one girl that he'd have to sentence to die.

'Then there's only one person left to ask, isn't there?'

Berion said.

'Looks like it.' She nodded.

Berion sighed and stood. One by one he slipped each ring back on to his fingers, holding his hand out to examine his work as he did so. 'I need to change first. Whatever Sage may or may not be, we're going to the moorlands and these shoes *are* Westwood.'

12

P

She paused on the outskirts of the trees and watched the movements beyond. A few bodies milling about, walking between cabins. One throwing a few logs on to a campfire in the centre of a dark clearing. A primitive existence. She knew she'd hate it.

Berion had refused to take a train full of rowdy and drunk humans up towards Winter Hill so late on a Saturday night, and she didn't ask how much the private car Upside actually cost.

Now her friends were waiting for her at the boundary into the camp. Best not to risk it, they'd decided, after the last time Sage and Oren turned up here unannounced. She swallowed, lifted her chin, and floated out into the clearing.

Nobody noticed.

She wasn't sure why she was nervous. She feared very little any more, not in the sense of danger for herself or her life. She couldn't die a second time, right? No, she supposed she was more scared of what she might learn. Her chest swelled with it. Their decision not to wait hadn't given her time to let the whole thing settle in. Hadn't given her time to properly think it all through.

She was so lost in those thoughts that she jumped when a disembodied voice spoke from behind her.

She whirled to find a face she hadn't missed.

'I wondered when I'd be seeing you again.' MacAllister's unblinking yellow eyes were hollow as he stared up at her. She lowered herself until her face was level with his. 'I've been expecting one of you to come, soon enough.'

She blinked. 'You have?'

He gave a curt nod. 'Come. We'll talk in my cabin.'

She followed as he led her deeper into his camp, past the few still outside their own dwellings. Hanging out clothes to dry. Sweeping twigs from the doorways. All of them paused to watch. All of them saw her now. She recognized some of them from the moon ball.

MacAllister pulled open the door of the largest cabin — still only a cramped wooden hut. She ignored it and floated in through the wall.

It was as claustrophobic as she expected it to be, and just how Sage had described it, when she'd finally got round to telling P exactly what'd happened that night. The night they'd tried to kill Oren. She'd tried not to let her voice shake as she attempted to justify why she'd killed that wolf. Tried to blame it on other things, but P understood that Sage just found the idea of another friend dying in the jaws of a wolf intolerable.

She straightened the folds of her own ravaged jumper and turned to face MacAllister.

'Can you take a seat?' MacAllister asked, gesturing to the two wooden chairs by his small table covered in dirty bowls.

She nodded as they sat. 'I wanted to ask a few questions. If that would be something you'll allow.' She swallowed. 'About . . . About your son. Harland.'

'That wasn't his name.' His back stiffened.

'It was his name to me,' she said quietly.

MacAllister's breath seemed to catch in his throat, and she realized she was surprised to see real sadness there. It almost made her pity him. Almost.

'Tell me about him,' he rasped. 'You . . . knew him better than me, in the end. What was he like?'

She shook her head again. 'I don't know what he was like. Not really. I didn't meet him, the real him, Liam MacAllister, until he confessed to his crimes.'

But he simply said again, 'What was he like?'

She didn't speak for a moment. She looked down at her fingers. 'Angry,' she settled on at last. 'And it had consumed him.' She didn't know how to say any more without sounding insensitive. 'It . . . seemed to have driven him into madness.'

'Did he . . .' He paused, as if he wasn't sure he could bring himself to pose the question. 'Was there anything but hatred for me?'

There was no point lying. MacAllister knew the truth, it

was written all over his face.

'If it's any consolation, his feelings for you were almost outmatched by his hatred for Oren.'

'He saw, then, what happened that day? When Oren Rinallis came to kill us?' MacAllister asked. She nodded. 'She killed one of my pack to protect him, you know. One of her own kind.'

'Oren is one of her own kind.' She lifted her chin defiantly. 'Far more than any wolf she's never met.'

'He knows what she is.' It wasn't a question.

'And what would that be?' she challenged. She refused to admit anything to this man. And perhaps his answer would be revealing.

But he was sharp. He knew the game she was playing. So he played it back, ignoring her question entirely. 'He hasn't killed her for it.'

'He'll kill you if you report her for anything,' she said. It wasn't a threat, it was simply the truth. A polite warning.

MacAllister's brows twitched. Then he shrugged. 'I have nothing to report.'

She didn't want to show him the relief this statement made her feel. But the rising panic she'd been refusing to acknowledge in her chest all evening was screaming to come out. 'I need your help,' she whispered. 'Please.'

He stared at her, those unblinking eyes boring into her with such intensity it made her shudder.

'We don't know where to start. First and foremost we

need to be sure, and then we can plan accordingly. But we don't even know what we're looking for. So how?' She felt breathless. 'How would we know, for certain, that she's a hybrid? What signs would there be?'

'You will try to hide this?'

'She transformed in a room full of Arcānum,' P admitted. 'People could ask questions. And the captain of the Arcānum is looking for an excuse to report her to the Elders for anything. This would be his dream—'

MacAllister hissed, his face suddenly contorting with rage. 'I knew that night I saw her transform here in this camp. She was so large . . . she thought my pack backed down because she'd killed that wolf, but the truth is, she's even bigger than me. And any wolf bigger than the alpha has the automatic right to challenge for leadership. If she had challenged me I would've had no choice but to engage in combat. If she'd won, she would be the alpha now. My pack paused because laws prevent them from interfering when a challenge has potential to take place. They could all see it too.'

She stared at him, taken aback. She hadn't known. Sage hadn't known. She betted that Oren had.

'But what if she's just . . . very big?' she pushed. That'd been one of Hozier's arguments in the car on the way there, one of her desperate attempts to argue that a report to the Elders would be silly on Roderick's part.

He snorted. 'There are wolves that are big, and wolves

that are the size of bears. No wolf is that large without being touched by magic. You'd better hope no one in that room has seen many werewolf transformations, and they didn't realize what she was.'

'Will she get bigger?'

He shrugged. 'None survived past the age she is now. Mr Rinallis saw to that.'

'Do you know if it's guaranteed that she will have magic? In the way that warlocks use theirs? Harland did – his colour was blue – will that happen to Sage?'

He looked up at her, his eyes wide. He hadn't known that about his son, then. Harland's magic must have developed in the years after Oren had shattered his way through their pack.

'She should,' he said at last. 'Though . . . we never quite figured out a pattern for it. Each hybrid was different. There was no consistency with age or maturity – just . . . whenever it was ready.'

'Is there anything else?' It was a fight to keep the desperation out of her voice. 'She has no tangible magic, other than her size. We still can't be sure?'

MacAllister frowned. 'She . . . wasn't a member of our own pack. She must have been turned on a full moon. That was the only time Amhuinn left the camp.' He paused, and swallowed. 'Sometimes he positioned himself close to humans. He . . . planned to turn them and then watch their progress from afar. See how the warlock magic presented itself in a werewolf that wasn't aware of what it was, in an environment that didn't know either. See if it made a difference to their development.'

P felt sick. And angry. And disgusted. Perhaps it showed on her face because he grimaced.

'He was our alpha. It was not our place to challenge him,' he said.

'It was not your place to alter the course of your own children's lives,' she shot back. 'You offered them to him.'

He closed his eyes. 'Werewolves only birth humans,' he said finally, not that it was much of an excuse. 'If we didn't allow them to be changed, Amhuinn insisted they be sent to live with humans. Care homes. Adoption. We didn't want to lose our children.'

And look how it'd turned out anyway.

'But Sage was turned a few weeks before Oren came for Amhuinn,' she pushed on. 'So I can only assume, if he did sire her, it would've had to have been the last full moon he lived through.'

MacAllister's face had gone slack.

'What?' she demanded.

'If that was the case, that would mean,' he swallowed, 'she was changed . . . here, then? In these moorlands.'

'How do you know that?'

'We travelled for a while. Trying to find a new place to call our home.' He shook his head. 'At last we ended up here. It was the last place we knew that Amhuinn had spent his full moon. Oren Rinallis made us denounce our alpha, but wolf loyalty is strong. It was our homage. To settle in this place where his last true wolf-self roamed.'

She was pretty sure that settled it.

Amhuinn was Sage's sire. She had to be hybrid.

That was the evidence they needed.

'She can partially transform,' she admitted. 'Change just her eyes, or her teeth, or her claws, but keep the rest human. Berion says this should be impossible. Is this a trait of the hybrids you knew?'

He nodded. 'Only the more powerful ones could do that. The ones who had practised control.' He frowned at her. 'She didn't know until recently?' P didn't dare answer him – just in case. Gut instinct told her she could trust him . . . but just in case. He sighed. 'I don't know what to tell you. She's going to be very hard to hide. Even for the most powerful warlock in the world.'

'Then he's the best hope she has.' She hadn't meant for the bite to be so sharp, but the panic in her chest was growing ever stronger. Then she quietened. And decided to ask a question that wasn't on the official list she, Berion and Hozier had compiled. This was supposed to be a proof-finding mission, nothing more. But . . . 'Do you know if she'll settle?'

MacAllister looked at her with eyes that had seen too much. 'If it was anyone but Oren Rinallis, I might pity them,' he said. 'But I don't know.'

She nodded, and rose. 'Thank you for your time.'

'She's . . . one of us. We would protect her, hide her away, if she needed it,' he said, standing too. 'If he . . . would allow it.'

Oren would never allow it. P nodded thanks again and floated from the cabin.

'Well?' Berion's pale face was stony as he stood in the darkness at the camp boundary, Hozier at his side wrapped in a thick coat.

P opened her mouth, and closed it. Any hope Berion had been clinging to that Oren might've been mistaken was gone.

But they both seemed to understand.

'We're fucked,' Hozier muttered.

She nodded.

'This will be the end of them both, you know?' Berion's white hair glowed like the moon through the shadows as he shook his head. 'If they want to execute her, he won't just let it happen. They'd have to kill him first.'

'More recently, I've been getting the feeling he won't let her die without him anyway.' She let the tears she'd been holding in all night roll down her cheeks at last. 'Whatever happens. Whether it's now or in sixty-five years.'

'So she won't settle?' Hozier asked, and her expression was strained too.

'He doesn't know.'

Berion looked like he wanted to cry too, for their friends,

for the love that was forbidden. For the love he had just lost that he'd so far refused to talk about.

'Well.' Hozier cleared her throat. 'It's the darkest retelling of *Romeo and Juliet* I've ever heard.'

13

SAGE

The hall had transformed. The tables were covered in the plates and dishes of pack members who'd come together to eat, and the room hummed with chatter. Old wolves. Young. Groups of friends, a pair here and there.

All of them looked up as she walked in at Gabriel's side. As one, the room seemed to collectively sniff. It felt like the first time she'd walked into an Arcānum staff meeting after she'd recovered from the silver dagger to her chest. Her stomach still squirmed at the memory of some of the expressions. Disbelief, a few smirks. *She won't last long, partnered with him.* And, honestly, this wasn't much different. Shock that she was one of them. Mild hostility as she intruded on their pack. Some . . . interest, she thought? Perhaps, like Gabriel, they assumed this would give them an advantage in the case.

'Over here.' Gabriel pointed to two seats opposite a werewolf with dark dreadlocks and bulging muscles under a tight T-shirt.

'Patrice is my housemate. This is Sage.'

He was eating from a plate piled high with vegetable stir-fry that had her stomach grumbling at the smell of it. It looked better than her botched carbonara, for sure.

'Your partner isn't joining you?' Patrice asked neutrally.

'He's not a fan of my cooking.' She offered a tentative smile, gesturing to her bowl. 'Paella is his favourite and this . . . is not that. I suspect he might sneak into the human town, see what restaurants are down there.'

Patrice ignored her attempts at making him smile, and pulled a face. 'That's a long way to go – the sun will set before he arrives, and he will not be able to get back here in the dark.'

'Oren can shift.'

'Shift?'

How did she explain it? 'He can . . . disappear from one place and reappear somewhere else.'

Gabriel paused from pulling the foil off his own plate, which she now realized was another batch of Patrice's stir-fry. Both of them stared at her.

She supposed that being isolated in the mountains, their interactions with the outside world at a minimum, she could understand why this thought seemed alarming to them. Hell, it still alarmed her.

'He can really do that?' A female who hadn't been part of their conversation, but who was obviously listening, leant in.

'This is Estelle.' Gabriel sounded exasperated. 'My sister.'

'Sister?'

'Adopted.' Estelle, a blonde girl who looked maybe a couple of years older than herself, gave Gabriel an affectionate smile. 'I was found wandering in the trees close to the town. I'd already been turned, my family must've abandoned me there. My . . . Celeste, she took me in and raised me with Gabriel. Is your partner single?'

Patrice rolled his eyes. Like he knew Estelle well and wasn't surprised by the question.

'Oh. Um.' She knew she had no right to feel the jealous pangs at the thought of him with this werewolf. Even if she was . . . very pretty. 'As far as I know.'

'Excellent news.' Estelle picked up her empty bowl, smiled again at her brother, and left the hall.

When she looked back at Gabriel, his expression was stony.

'Do you think he will be interested?' he asked evenly.

'In Estelle?' she asked. No, he would not. At least, *he'd better not*, something lupine inside her growled. But she did want to make friends so she tried not to sound too blunt. 'Not if she's looking for a long-term boyfriend.' That sounded diplomatic enough? 'Oren's never really done . . . attachment.'

'He attached to you.'

That made her stomach squirm again.

'We're work partners and housemates back home.' She shrugged. 'Not in a romantic relationship, if that's what you're figuring out how to ask.'

It was, clearly, as he and Patrice glanced at each other.

'What's it like living with Oren Rinallis?' Patrice asked. 'Don't you worry he'll kill you in your sleep?'

Gabriel's head whipped towards his friend. A question he clearly wouldn't have asked, not yet anyway. But perhaps something they'd wondered before Gabriel had collected her to eat with them? But she knew she'd face this kind of passive hostility, didn't she? And the only way she could gain anyone's trust was by facing it head on.

'I don't expect any of you to understand. You all know Oren has done . . . many things in his life.' Patrice pulled a pointed face as he turned back to his food. 'But I promise you, he won't harm anyone in these mountains unless there is a very good reason.'

'You can assure us of that, can you?'

'Yes,' she said bluntly, refusing to break eye contact.

None of them spoke for a few moments. Until Gabriel obviously felt he had to try and break the rising tension. 'So, you live . . . in a house?' he asked, as if the concept sounded alien.

'Where else would we live?' She laughed. 'We are just normal people. Kinda. We spend most of our time arguing over who ate the last biscuits, or whose socks are left on the bathroom floor.'

Patrice snorted derisively. 'Sounds like a happy little family. Do you have pets too?'

'We have a poltergeist. And she cooks, cleans all our clothes, and basically looks after us. We didn't realize until we got here how much of a problem her absence would be. I spent nearly an hour on FaceTime tonight trying to figure out how to cook this.' She gestured at her lame dinner. 'A dog is the last thing we need.'

Both looked like they weren't sure if she was being serious.

'How did you get yourself such a helpful poltergeist?' Gabriel asked. 'Don't they attach themselves to a person? She's your poltergeist?'

Her throat went instantly dry. Visions of Flora's face, smug and cruel, flashed before her eyes.

Couldn't even control herself enough not to kill her best friend.

Pathetic.

She'd meant it before when she'd told Oren that she was relieved the secret was out. But all of a sudden, her chest was filled with thick anxiety. Maybe because this time she was speaking to wolves and not warlocks. She realized she couldn't answer.

Oh, God.

What could she say?

A voice she hadn't expected spoke behind her. 'Sage and P had been friends for a very long time when P died. Sage was nearby when the accident that killed her happened. It tied them together.'

Gabriel and Patrice went instantly pale. She spun to see the last fading bits of golden dust disappear where Oren had shifted into the hall behind her. The lump in her chest instantly quelled at the sight of him. She both loved and hated that he could do that just by existing.

Everyone turned towards him. At least he'd backed up her shifting claims, she supposed.

When he looked down at her, he smiled. It was a smile that to anyone else would look cruel and cold. But it was his smile for her, that came with the warm, comforting brush of his magic down her side. It made another small lump rise in her throat, but for different reasons.

He held out a small, flat cardboard box. 'I went into the town.' Before she could say anything else, his eyes flashed. 'I won't wait up.'

And he disappeared back into nothing.

The hall was silent. Staring at the space where he'd just been.

She opened the box to find a cheese-topped garlic bread he'd picked up for her. He knew it was her takeaway favourite. When she offered a piece to Patrice and Gabriel they recoiled. She shrugged. More for her. It made her bland carbonara slightly more appealing, though she was quietly grateful to know that he'd save her some of whatever else he'd bought for himself.

But the conversation was well and truly dead after that. The room that had been willing to pretend there wasn't an intruder in their midst while they subtly listened in, deciding how to judge her, had shifted its mood. Now everyone was on edge. Chatter restarted, but it was strained, and Sage could feel the extra glances in her direction.

The second the last spoonful of carbonara touched her lips, Gabriel stood. 'I'll walk you back to your cabin.'

She didn't argue.

'Do you want me to come?' Patrice said pointedly, looking at his friend and roommate.

This time Gabriel's smile wasn't strained. 'I'll be fine.'

And that showed just how much of a threat Gabriel had assessed her to be. She didn't know whether to be offended as she followed him from the hall and out into the night.

'I'm sorry if that was awkward for you.' She eyed him as they headed for her cabin. 'Me sitting with you, I mean.'

He threw her a sidewards smile. 'I told you it wouldn't be easy.' He shrugged. 'It'll take a bit of time for some of them to come round. You weren't what we were expecting. And it's even less expected if you don't automatically side with us.'

'You seem to have come round quickly enough,' she said, ignoring the taking-sides comment. And when he laughed, she was surprised to find it made her laugh too. 'Or is your mother just commanding you to be nice to me?'

'I saw your partner nearly break Benoît's arm.' They stopped outside her cabin, but he was still smiling. 'I'm not stupid enough to wave my hand in your face and shout.'

'I see. So it's a fear of Oren more than a desire to get along with me?'

'Oh, well, I didn't say that.' He folded his arms across his chest, but his eyes sparkled. 'Now I know he isn't your boyfriend and won't behead me for even speaking to you, I'm a little more inclined to be friends.'

Her stomach twisted at the idea of Oren being her boyfriend. But she'd made that decision, and she had to get used to living with it.

And she could befriend werewolf boys too, right? There was nothing wrong with that . . . right?

'So,' she said quickly, hoping none of her inner thoughts had shown on her face, 'did you manage to get a message to any other packs?'

He nodded. 'The Monreaus, our neighbours, they're expecting you tomorrow. They border the river, like us, so have more interaction with the witches than anyone else. They'll be the most helpful.'

'Do you believe there's a curse?'

He was silent for a moment. 'I think there's no such thing as coincidence,' he admitted. 'Not on this scale. But . . .' He looked around him, as if the words he was trying to find might be printed on the leaves of the treetops. 'Who knows.'

'What do you think the chances are of the witches cooperating?'

'Oh. None at all.' He smiled at her again. 'But I'm excited to see you try.'

14

OREN

He woke to the sounds of urgent chatter and footsteps outside, and someone barking orders in French. Watery sunlight was seeping into the ink-black sky and he knew he hadn't slept anywhere near as many hours as he would've liked.

'Can you hear that?' he groaned.

He knew she hated when he did that. It didn't matter what room she was in, her wolf ears would pick up anything no matter how quietly he spoke. And unless he specifically tuned his hearing in he couldn't hear her reply, so she had to get up and come to him to chat. He did actually tune it in more than he let on. Like now. Just enough to hear her growl under her breath and the rustle of covers as she threw them off her legs. He chuckled under his breath.

She heard that too, and he heard what she called him.

He tuned his hearing back out and got up too, dragging on some fresh jeans and a hoodie – whatever this new washing powder was smelt great. He made a mental note to tell P.

He shook his head at himself.

He felt so . . . domesticated these days.

If only his enemies could see him now, huh?

She was leaving her bedroom at the same time.

'How was last night?' But he could tell that it was too early for her to be even slightly interested in taking on his derisive smirk.

'Tell you later.' She dismissed him with a wave. 'Let's see what's going on.'

They didn't have to go far to find out. Not even a foot out of the cabin. Because as soon as she pulled the door open a pair of goats merrily trotted by.

'What the—'

'They got out again, then?' he said dryly.

A werewolf came hurrying by, following the runaway goats. She was middle-aged, and dressed in overalls and thick wellies.

'Can we help?' Sage tried, hoping the woman would understand.

The woman paused, standing upright with her hands on her hips, and took a few deep breaths. Clearly she'd been running around for a while. 'Thank you.' She spoke in English, though her accent was thick and it was clear she was not fluent. 'That way.' She pointed towards the hall, the doors flung wide open even at this early hour. A llama was being led past it, back to wherever it'd come from.

Sage nodded and thanked the woman.

'This would be a disaster on a full moon,' Oren said darkly.

Sage *hmm*ed agreement as they set off for the hall. 'You could magic the paddock gates for now.'

'Depends on what we're up against.'

She tutted. 'Your magic locked me into our apartment overnight so a werewolf murderer couldn't get in.' She avoided his name. 'You can magic a paddock against a witch's curse.'

He didn't reply other than to snort. The *curse*. Of course.

As they reached the steps into the hall, he heard the ever-familiar, sinister caw of a raven. Sage glanced at him. He shrugged. They'd followed him for decades, he was hardly surprised they'd managed to find him there. Not with treetops full of watchful birds overhead chirping between themselves.

In the hall, a female wolf with her coat and wellies pulled on over pyjamas stood beside Celeste's empty throne, clipboard in hand, as a young man in overalls stood beside her jabbering away, listing things against his fingers.

'How can we assist?' Sage said in response to the woman's inquisitive look. 'I'm Sage.'

'I know.' The woman looked her up and down. It wasn't necessarily unkind, perhaps wary. But after a small pause, she nodded. 'My name is Elle. And we're still missing two goats, three alpaca, one llama and a cow.'

'We've just seen the goats running past our cabin,' Sage

offered, to a relieved sigh from the overalled man. He moved for the door as Elle called their street name after him. He gave a thumbs up as he hurried away.

'Can we see the bolts?' Oren asked. 'Or padlocks – whatever it is that's being opened to release the livestock.'

'Follow me.' Elle nodded. 'This is the second time this week,' she said over her shoulder as she led them back out of the hall. 'Two days before you arrived.' She sounded worried. And rightly so. He'd never give Sage the satisfaction of admitting it, but this was going to be a real problem if they couldn't get to the bottom of it quickly. 'It's becoming more frequent. Before that it was at least two weeks, and nearly four weeks before that.'

'How many have you lost entirely?' Sage asked.

'One cow, and a goat.' She led them down the path behind the hall and away from the cabins. The manure had him muting his sense of smell with his magic at once. And he sent a thin layer of gold to encase his trainers against the squelching – he didn't even want to consider what that was. 'Both on the same night. So we ruled out somebody trying to steal them for milk or meat, or we would assume that some would go missing every time.'

Sage nodded. He didn't say anything either. This was her rodeo as far as he was concerned. He'd get involved soon enough, but only when he had to. The ground was becoming softer and her trainers started to squelch too. He watched her look down and realize he was already using magic to protect his own footwear. Her scrunched-up face was cute, and he'd half done it only to see her turn it on him. But as he grinned he sent a faint gold glow over her trainers too.

'This is the first one.' Elle came to a stop in front of a high wooden gate leading into a paddock fenced off with thick, criss-crossing wire. 'You can follow the path and look at them all, though they're exactly the same.'

'This one will do,' he said, looking at her pointedly. *Get out of my way.*

She did. Quickly.

It was a standard sliding bolt lock. He ran his hand over it. Gold hummed at his fingertips. Somebody had already picked up the padlock that'd been discarded into the mud. It wasn't broken. It looked like it'd been opened with the key. His fingers still glowed as he clicked the lock shut, then opened it again with his magic.

'Nothing broken,' he confirmed. 'But nothing else.' Then he handed it to Sage. 'Like old times. What do you smell?'

'Like old times,' she replied. 'Nothing.'

'Exactly,' he said. 'Somebody unfamiliar would leave a scent. Unless it's purposely been disguised.'

She turned to Elle. 'Is it possible somebody in the pack is doing this?'

Both of them knew it was a long shot. Pack loyalty made this suggestion almost impossible – and the look of horror on Elle's face told her as much but . . . they still had to ask.

And he admired Sage's determination to do so, despite knowing the reaction it'd get.

'We'll start our day as soon as somebody is available to escort us across borders,' he said to Elle. 'Tell Celeste. We'll wait back at our cabin.'

15

OREN

'How does P make it hot?' he demanded an hour later, looking at his toast. 'It came out of the toaster hot, but by the time I butter and eat it, it's cold. What am I doing wrong?'

Sage shook her head. Hers was dry, the mound of butter on top refusing to melt and soak in.

There was a knock at the door.

When he wafted it open on a gold mist, expecting to see Gabriel, he was surprised to see a pretty blonde female standing there, holding a lidded dish wrapped in a tea towel. She looked maybe a couple of years older than Sage, and her wide smile dripped with all the confidence that Sage had lacked when they'd first met.

'Good morning,' the werewolf gushed, stepping over the threshold and holding up the dish. 'Paella.' She put it on the counter next to the sink. 'I overheard Sage say last night it was your favourite, and that she's not the best cook.'

She threw Sage a smile that was nothing short of simpering.

He glanced at Sage. Her neck was blotching with indignation. He suppressed a grin.

'Estelle, right?' she asked coldly.

'Estelle Dubois.' She held out a hand in his direction, still smiling that radiant smile. It was one he'd seen many times over the decades – an offer, if he was interested. He wasn't interested, but he stood and took the outstretched hand anyway. Usually, he'd ignore such a greeting completely, but he knew it would enrage Sage even more. And he was still a bit miffed she hadn't even realized he'd waited up for her last night. 'Celeste took me in, when I arrived as a small child. Raised me alongside Gabriel.' She clapped her hands together. 'Anyway, just wanted to introduce myself. Do let me know if you need anything. Enjoy!'

She breezed out of their cabin as quickly as she'd arrived.

He looked at Sage, and the expression on her face said that if he even so much as suggested that paella was better than anything she'd cooked, it'd be the last thing he ever said.

He snorted into the dregs of his tea as Gabriel arrived in Estelle's vacated doorway.

'The rest of the livestock has been found.' He sounded relieved. 'Celeste said you needed an escort?'

He didn't like Gabriel.

He didn't like how he smiled at Sage. He smiled at her like Estelle had just smiled at him.

Family trait, huh?

Sure, their initial meeting had been one of shock and confusion, but he'd heard them chatting outside the cabin last night before she'd finally come back in. He'd expected her to be stony and bad-tempered, given the way the mood dropped when he'd shifted into that hall. That was why he'd waited up for her. But she'd been smiling. Then she'd simply wished him goodnight and gone to bed.

He hadn't actually cared that much for the details when he'd asked her how her night had been – but now, with that friendly look on Gabriel's stupid face? He was more interested. Maybe he would ask her about it again later.

Or maybe he was just being stupid.

He was Oren Rinallis.

He wasn't jealous of this werewolf, was he?

Was he?

He shook his head. He really was being stupid.

The sun had risen over the mountains now and the small village was starting to come alive. There were a few furtive glances in their direction. He didn't care. But he knew Sage was watching.

'We don't eat our livestock, so we don't overly breed them,' Gabriel was droning on. Oren rolled his eyes and followed as Gabriel led them down a different path to the one they'd taken that morning to the paddocks. 'We mostly keep them for milk, so losing even one makes a big difference to us.'

He let Gabriel's voice fade out as he observed their surroundings. They walked alongside some vegetable patches. A couple of werewolves stood about, pulling on wellies or examining gardening tools. A few of them looked over, looked at Sage for a moment longer than was natural, but as soon as they saw him watching they looked away quickly.

'How did you get all of these cabins up here?' He tuned back in to Sage asking something he'd wondered himself.

'We made them.' The corners of Gabriel's mouth twitched at her surprised blink. 'That's what we do.'

'You . . . make cabins?'

'Each pack has their own trade. It's how we all survive up here. The Meute de Dubois are carpenters. The back half of our land houses workshops.' He gestured somewhere off to the left. 'Then, we sell them. In the cities. Markets. Shops. Online. That's how we pay for food and supplies.'

'What kind of things do you make?' Oren forced himself not to feel disgruntled that Sage actually appeared interested in what Gabriel had to say.

'Well, there are some older guys who run their own artisan kitchen company. Bespoke designs, build them here, transport them across the country to install. Humans think they're a small family business. Brothers. Then another couple, Anna and Noèmie, they make picnic baskets with matching cutlery sets, which are sold in a chain of homeware shops in Paris. Estelle hand-carves nameplates for children's bedrooms. Sells them on Etsy.'

'You're serious?' He watched her put a hand on his arm.

'Of course.' He grinned at her amazement. 'How else do you think so many of us survive up here?'

Oren had known that the wolves of the Jura mountains had cultivated a thriving trade of their wares to survive. Why hadn't he been the one to think to tell her that? To be the cause of the awe glittering on her face now? That privilege had just gone to Gabriel.

No.

That was unfair of him, to be annoyed she was interested in what this young wolf had to say. He knew that. He'd reminded himself more than once since meeting Sage and P that he'd lived their lifetimes multiple times over. They still had so much to learn about and wonder in. And the Jura mountains were a one-off. There was no other werewolf colony in the world as advanced, self-sufficient or sophisticated as these packs. She didn't even realize just how lucky she was as an outsider to be allowed in to see it. A once-in-a-lifetime opportunity.

He knew the idea of pack mentality bothered her. But he was watching her in real time, seeing now that these wolves had far more choice than she'd supposed. This here, what Celeste Dubois had built: this was a real pack. He watched her beginning to understand more than ever that

Michael MacAllister had failed not only as a father, but as an alpha too. He knew he should be pleased for her, not annoyed.

'So.' Gabriel straightened, like he finally remembered he had a job to do outside of buddying up to Sage. 'I'm taking you to the gate that crosses into Meute de Monreau. They voted to invite you here, so you won't face difficulties. On their other side is the Meute de Bassett, who abstained from voting.'

'Are you coming with us?'

'Not today. I'm first on the patrol rota down by the river. But I'm also down there tomorrow, so I can take you to speak to the witches then, if that works for you? A handful come to the bank every morning to wash cutlery and such after breakfast, so we'll time it with that.'

'I thought you said they won't speak to anyone?'

He chuckled. 'Let's see what happens once they see you, eh?'

They followed the pathway through dense forest. For mountains that were supposed to be getting cramped, there was a lot of uninhabited space. Gabriel assured them that halfway up there was a gate guarded on both sides by a small group of patrol members, who allowed or denied passage through.

Ha.

Let them try.

But when they arrived, he was almost surprised to hear

laughter from the small congregation. Werewolves stood on either side chatting over the top of the gate, cups of something steaming in hands.

'Ah, here she is!' A guard on the other side of the fence looked Sage up and down. He was short, swaddled in a thick coat and scarf. Oren slowed, hanging back, and watched. 'We've heard about you.'

'Good things, I hope?'

'Not all,' he said brazenly. 'You're a werewolf, eh?'

She didn't miss a beat. 'That's a bad thing?' She frowned. 'You shouldn't be so down on yourself. It's none of our faults what we were made into.'

He had to stop himself smiling. It was a choice to be combative, but she'd taken a calculated risk and decided to see where it got her. He was proud of her.

The werewolf looked at her for a moment, his brow twitching at her audacity. But she didn't break his gaze. Then he shrugged. She'd passed the test apparently, with this guy at least. Though it didn't show on her face, he felt a flash of relief down that weird new tether between them he didn't quite understand yet.

'How did you convince the captain of your Arcānum?' the guard asked.

'I didn't. I'm here because my captain is hoping a fight breaks out big enough to get me killed. I won a bet I was supposed to lose. You lot are my punishment.'

The werewolf snorted, but he nodded slowly. Assessing

her. Making his mind up as to whether she really was nothing more than a traitor for working with the enemy – the enemy being anyone but their own kind, it seemed . . . or simply just young and naive.

'She convinced me,' Oren said at last. 'That was all she needed. Everyone else usually falls in line after that.'

The Monreau werewolf who'd been content to pretend Oren wasn't there as long as he lurked quietly in the shadows jumped at being addressed directly. He dropped the cup of what smelt like coffee. Oren let the corners of his lips curl as he watched the man who'd been so confident moments before swear, diving to pick it back up, flustered.

Sage glanced back at him too. Grateful for the back-up, but a warning not to go any further. Let her see what she could do.

His nod was barely perceptible. Fine.

'He keeps me alive,' she admitted.

But it seemed like the cat had caught the werewolf's tongue. And he didn't answer her again.

'This is Thomas of the Meute de Monreau,' Gabriel said into the awkward silence. 'This is Sage and Oren of the Arcānum. This is where I leave you. I'll find you again this afternoon.'

She thanked him and watched him back away.

'Well, Thomas.' She turned back to the guards now standing silently, any fledgling attempts at cordiality apparently evaporated. 'Will you let us through?'

The sound of bolts chinked and scraped, and he pulled the tall wooden gate open and stood back for them to pass.

'I thought the packs didn't get along?' she asked as they followed Thomas away from the gate, setting off through more thick trees, leaving the rest of the guards behind, hushed conversation starting up again in their wake.

Thomas made a non-committal sound. 'We don't all get along. But friends who support different football teams don't get along sometimes, right?' Surprisingly, he appreciated that analogy. 'There are old rivalries, and some newer ones too, and some wolves just . . . don't like each other. Like all people. At the moment.' He made a dramatic shrug not only with his shoulders but his hands too. 'We're united in a single cause.'

'The witch's curse?' He couldn't help the dripping sarcasm again.

But Thomas didn't even have time to answer before Sage was gasping.

In front of them were bright tents in all shapes and sizes, embroidered with swirling patterns, hung haphazardly between the trees, the spaces above them a maze of ropes and pulleys. A monkey's dream play park. The tents fitted into the natural gaps, rather than the pack felling trees to make gaps that worked for them and their tents. In the centre was a tall round tent, the roof sloping up as a rope as thick as his forearm pulled the centre into the treetops. The fabric had been stained a dark blue, and was embroidered with stars and the moon cycle.

'It's beautiful,' she whispered.

'It is something,' Thomas agreed, 'when you see it for the first time. Come. Sacha is waiting.'

16

OREN

Thomas pulled back the flap of the large tent and stood aside so that they could pass. Inside was warm, whatever fabric they used thick and insulated. The floor was covered in woven rugs, cushions and knitted throws, and in the centre was . . . a giant beanbag.

Waiting for them was a tall man in loose-fitting canvas trousers, a tie-dyed T-shirt and no shoes. He had greying hair, a wild, untamed beard, and a face far too jolly for Oren's patience. In one hand was a sheaf of notes and in the other a long pipe that was smoking at the end.

All very hippy.

Sage glanced at Oren and he could see that she was trying not to burst out laughing. She already knew that nobody was going to convince *him* to lower himself on to a beanbag.

'*Bienvenue*. Welcome, welcome.' He beckoned them across the tent. 'My name is Sacha Monreau. Celeste sent word you'd arrived. *Merci*. Thank you.' He took a long drag of his pipe, the tip glowing red and hissing. 'We heard you're a werewolf. I bet that caused a ruckus in the Dubois, huh?'

'But it won't cause one here?' Sage asked, shaking his outstretched hand.

Oren made sure he hung back far enough that Sacha Monreau didn't even try to stretch a hand in his direction.

The alpha shrugged, gesturing at nothing in particular with his hands. 'You're young. All kids act out. This is just your . . . how you say? *Act of rebellion*, eh? You'll come round.' He let out a loud boom of a laugh.

Oh, he could tell by her face that Sage wasn't impressed by that sweeping statement. He stopped himself from laughing aloud again. But she'd obviously decided she wasn't going to be too combative twice in one morning. She introduced them. He almost admired how well Sacha Monreau managed to turn his flinch into another drag of his pipe.

'The tents,' Sage said. 'They're beautiful. You make them all yourself?'

Sacha nodded and gestured for them to follow him back outside. 'We do most of the processes ourselves. Our livestock is llama, alpaca and sheep. We harvest their wool, then hand-weave everything on giant looms, very little is wasted. And at the very back of our camp' – back outside he pointed in a vague direction – 'we breed silkworms, to make threads for our embroidery, and use only natural components for dyes.'

'Fascinating,' she admitted. 'I . . . I love it.'

'Then perhaps we would be the pack for you, if you were to stay.'

'Perhaps you would,' she agreed. 'What kind of things do the other packs trade in?'

'Some produce meats, cheeses or wine. There's carpentry in the Dubois, as you know, and another works with pottery.'

'And you all trade with each other?'

'Some packs get along better than others.' Sacha sounded like he was trying to be diplomatic. 'Meute de Garnier, the cheese makers, are more than happy to trade with us, and the Dubois, for example. The Meute d'Egli are the most difficult. The oldest. They keep themselves to themselves. And their alpha drinks too much of their produce.' Sacha imitated drinking from an imaginary glass of wine. 'I doubt her attitude is helped by her hangovers, eh?'

Sacha led them between tents, not seeming to mind that his bare feet were walking over sharp twigs and dried leaves. He spoke conversationally, with expressive hands, smoking his pipe, and telling Sage about the fabrics and the designs as they passed. Each one had its own story, and he knew them all. Oren resumed his place behind them, at this point little more than Sage's glorified bodyguard. He watched her soak up all the knowledge, watched her look genuinely excited as Sacha offered her the opportunity to try her hand at weaving before they left.

He smiled bitterly to himself. *I want to see you live*, he'd told her as he'd refused to let her die. And this was exactly what for, wasn't it?

Sacha was an inquisitive man, asking many questions about her life in Downside too. Her life underground in a world carved out by magic was as alien to him as all this was to Sage. And when she told him about P, he openly laughed in disbelief: *a real-life poltergeist?* He admitted it was something he would love to see in his lifetime, in a way humans might hope to visit one of the Seven Wonders of the World.

But while he outwardly appeared fascinated by how they lived, Oren knew that Sacha was humouring her. Knew he believed that the longer she stayed in the mountains the more likely she was to see what her life was supposed to be. It was what all the werewolves there thought when they looked at her.

That annoyed him. Because all of them underestimated her, saw her as a naughty, rebellious teenager who'd grow out of this Arcānum phase soon enough.

Or maybe it was just his fear that it could be true.

They soon found themselves before paddocks of fluffy black sheep and long-necked alpacas trotting around wide, open spaces, trees felled to make room for them. They seemed unperturbed by the slopes and dips of the land, munching on bales of hay tied around the fences. In the centre was a large, wooden barn. Evidently Dubois carpentry.

'I can't let you enter,' Sacha told them outside the doors, but he did flick a latch on a window for them to see through. The smell hit him like a train. Sage actually gagged before clamping a hand over her mouth and nose.

Sacha nodded with a grimace. 'Disease has spread. The sick have been quarantined here.'

Oren peered in through the window, blocking his own sense of smell with magic. There were about fifty inside: sheep, alpaca and llama. Most of them lying down, some giving pathetic, half-hearted whines. Eight werewolves were in the barn too, wearing bodysuits like the forensics team in that show P loved – *Silent Witness*, maybe. Masks covered their mouths. They worked between the animals, shovelling away manure as others gently poured water into their mouths, stroking their necks and their sides, trying to comfort them in any way possible.

'We've lost nearly seventy so far,' Sacha admitted as he closed the hatch again and beckoned for them to return to the path. 'They were too sick. We had no choice but to slaughter them. A third of our animals are gone.' He shook his head, his voice thick with grief. 'We have no idea what it is, we've never seen a sickness like this, and we are very careful to treat our animals well in return for what they give us.'

'When did this start?' Oren frowned. He was pissed off. It could all still be explained by a series of coincidences but . . . this was worse than he'd expected to find.

'Three weeks ago.'

'Has anything else happened that's out of the ordinary?'

Sacha looked like he was about to shake his head, then he paused. 'Last night, as one of the farmhands arrived to do the evening rounds – extra checks, you know, if another animal falls sick we want it isolated as quickly as possible. As he came to the first paddock he realized the gate was unlocked. It was lucky. None of the animals had pushed the gate further open. But then he went to the next paddock, and it was the same. All three main gates were unlocked. Had we not been performing the extra checks, the animals would've escaped at some point.'

Sage looked at him. He gave her a small nod. That was too much of a coincidence.

'And nobody saw anything?' Sage asked.

Sacha gave her a withering smile. 'An intruder would've been immediately detected. We would've smelt them. You know that.'

She nodded. She did. 'Anything else?'

'Not here, *non*. But I have . . .' Sacha paused, and pulled out the notes that he'd been examining when they'd first entered the large tent. 'These are reports from other packs. The Meute de Bassett.' He held up one letter. 'Our neighbours have forbidden you to enter their land.'

'Forbidden it?' Oren echoed.

'Forbidden, yes,' Sacha repeated, but realized how it'd sounded as he held his hands up. 'Not just you. Everyone.

Their trade is their meat, with packs on both sides suffering livestock illness, so if their livestock dies they have nothing. They have put themselves into a quarantine to hopefully limit the spread.'

'And if we need to speak to their neighbours on the other side?' Oren demanded. He was rapidly losing patience. 'We will have to pass through to get to them.'

Sacha held up the other letter in his hand. 'On their other side is the Meute d'Egli, who will be evasive and unhelpful, anyway. But on *their* other side is the Meute de Garnier. They voted for you. Elodie Bassett sent a wolf around Egli land into the Garnier to get this report. The trek is long and difficult on two feet.'

Oren understood it for what it was. A peace offering from the alpha of the Meute de Bassett for refusing them entry into their land. He could force his way in regardless, but he knew that Sage would object to that. And he was still adjusting to the idea that not everything had to be achieved through sheer power and threats. P had taught him that.

Sage took both reports with thanks, opened the first folded piece of paper and looked down it, apparently written in English since she frowned. She looked back at Sacha. 'Have you had spoilt crops?' she asked. 'This says the Meute de Garnier found the first spoilt carrot and within twenty-four hours, everything was dead. Absolutely nothing left.'

Sacha shook his head. 'And thank God.'

Sage folded the note and looked down the other. This

time she nodded. 'The Bassetts also report cabin fires the night of the last storm. The Dubois have reported the same. And they say they could not find the source. Generators intact.'

Sacha's expression was serious. 'The only qualified electrician in the mountains, trained before he was turned, is a member of the Meute de Bassett. All packs pay for his services. If he has checked everything and found no faults?' He pulled a face to say he trusted that opinion.

That was interesting information. And not in a good way. Not for his assertion this whole thing was bullshit, anyway.

Sage nodded, tucking the reports in the back pocket of her jeans for him to look at later.

As Sacha took another puff on his pipe, turning to lead them back towards his camp, he frowned. 'A few nights ago, some of the younger ones were out in the trees around the far end of our land and are convinced that they saw a dark mass.' He said it almost as an afterthought. 'Like a fog, creeping between the trees. Apparently.'

'A dark mass?' Sage repeated blankly. Sacha nodded.

'What did it do?' Oren asked.

The alpha shrugged. 'They didn't hang around long enough to see. They ran. And were overheard talking about it in the silk sheds the day after. That's how word got back to me. They didn't initially report it.'

'Did you send someone out to look for it?'

'No. In all likelihood, it was only the smoke of whatever they themselves were smoking,' he said, glancing at his own pipe blandly. 'It was very dark. Probably nothing.'

Probably. Oren rolled his eyes. If wolves of this pack were as high as their alpha, they could've imagined they'd seen anything.

17

OREN

The next morning over breakfast, Sage called P and Hozier and filled them in on their trip so far. But all the pair really wanted to talk about was the mystery French accent they'd heard the other night.

He scowled at his cold toast. It was like them fawning all over Kane again.

He called Gabriel something under his breath, but as if that'd magically summoned him, the door clicked open, and his head popped in.

'Are you ready?' Gabriel's face was bright. 'You've got witches to argue with.'

Sage groaned.

'*Show us that man, right now!*' a voice hissed out of the phone still in her hand.

When Sage looked back up to see if he'd heard, Gabriel was staring at the phone too, his brows raised. He'd heard, and she couldn't pretend otherwise.

She sighed. 'Gabriel. Would you be so kind as to say hello to my housemate, P?'

The corners of his mouth twitched.

Oren threw the remains of his toast crust down and stood to take his plate over to the kitchen counter and away from the girlish giggling. They were pathetic. All of them.

'The poltergeist?' Gabriel asked, walking into the cabin.

'You told him about me?' P's voice asked.

When she held the phone up to Gabriel, who had come to a stop behind her chair, his face contorted in confusion.

'You can't see her,' she told him. 'Ghost.'

'Oh.' He blinked. And then jumped as Hozier's face appeared, taking up the whole screen.

'That's our other friend, Hozier, she's staying over while we're here.'

Hozier plastered on her most indulgent smile, and Oren noticed that she'd changed out of her pyjamas in record time – split-seconds she was off screen, in fact.

Coos and titters erupted as the pair of them said hello and asked Gabriel how he was.

He spluttered politely, but Oren saw the moment he realized this was an ambush, and the girls had already been talking about him before he'd turned up. He raised a brow at Sage, and Oren saw her cheeks flush a deep, blotching red.

It was lucky the toast plate wasn't still in his hand, or it might've exploded.

Five minutes later, Gabriel was leading them back through endless, mind-numbing trees until they found themselves at the edge of a river with a couple of other guards – one of them he recognized from the other night in the hall when he'd shifted in, who had sat opposite Sage stuffing stir-fry and glaring at her with apprehension. But at least he'd greeted her with a neutral hello this morning, and he could tell that Sage was trying not to look relieved.

All of them stood there in silence and watched as thirteen witches emerged from between the trees on their side, some of them with piles of dishes and plates in their hands.

Tall, and beautiful. All of them.

Deceptive. Like sirens who tricked sailors.

He'd had enough dealings with witches. They were vicious, and they were cruel. Not long before he'd met Sage he'd been sent to Ireland. One of the few Cariva requests that'd been submitted to Roderick since his extended leave of absence, but because he was the only assassin living permanently in the British Isles he had to go. A coven had trapped, enslaved and eventually eaten a group of human hikers. Oren had executed them all. It'd earnt a small article on the back pages of *Downside Daily*, although it hadn't named him personally. And it was one of the very few times he'd left a scene with injuries of his own. Only a small scrape across his bicep from the talons of one witch while he was distracted by four others, and it'd healed in a day or so. But it was testament to their skill.

Some of these witches looked young, far younger than Sage, even. But like the warlocks they aged differently. Not quite as ageless as warlocks, but longer-lived than humans like Sage. None of these witches would be younger than thirty. Their hair, all colours of blonde and brown and flaming red, were decorated with coloured feathers or beads which he knew were significant to them and their coven.

'Hello.' The river was calm and there was no wind; Sage's voice carried easily.

As expected, none of the witches answered. Seven did step closer, though, halting at the edge of the river to face off against the five of them: clearly intentional.

Not that numbers really mattered.

Not while he was there.

'Where's the witch mother?' Oren demanded; his patience felt thin today. And as he glanced at their escort, he knew what was irking his temper. 'It's her we've come to speak to, not any of you.'

The witch in the middle, a tall blonde with black raven feathers at the bottom of her long plaits, gave herself away. Her eyes flickered towards him, making it obvious she'd understood. Again, none of them replied.

He was done playing games. With their continued silence, the leash on his temper snapped. And only the gods knew some of the things he had done when that happened.

Without warning, he took Sage's hand in his and shifted them across to the other side of the river. He held on to her until she righted herself, shocked by the unannounced shifting. But she knew better than to tell him off for it until they were back in the privacy of their cabin later, and he took advantage of that fact.

Now they were standing behind the witches, Gabriel and his two guards gawking at them across the river. He didn't care. P would roll her eyes at this little display of temper, but let them see it.

'I won't ask you again,' he growled. 'Where is the witch mother?'

Thirteen witches whirled. Hisses, and snarling teeth, and talons started to grow from nail beds as soon as they realized what'd happened.

He almost laughed. 'Ah, ah, ah.' He shook his head.

It all happened so fast, as was the nature of witches and their volatile tempers. But he was quicker. The blonde witch in the centre lunged, elongating fangs halfway down her chin and razor-sharp. The flick of his wrist was so slight that it was almost lazy, and he slammed a wall of magic into the witch so powerful that it knocked her out cold.

She was lucky. It was only Sage's influence that had stopped him using such force it would've broken every bone and killed her outright. A couple of years ago, she'd have been dead before she hit the floor for daring to lunge at him like that. Her limp body slipped ten paces back across the forest floor, past her sisters, stopping just at the water's edge.

They howled in fury, eyes flashing as they readied to lunge.

He grinned, revelling in how easy it was. Energy

thrummed through his veins. A century ago that knowledge had him drunk on power. And something inside him purred when Sage glanced at him. Something about his cruel smile that he knew was handsome, arrogant and obnoxious all rolled into one always made her cheeks burn. Far more than any werewolf kid's twinkly smiles did.

His was the smile he usually saved just for her.

But today it was also the smile that, as the rest of the witches suddenly realized they couldn't move to defend their sister's honour, confirmed it was his magic holding them still.

'My name is Oren Rinallis,' he told them. 'I want to speak to the witch mother, and you will not stop me.'

He released the magical hold over all of them. But none of them moved now. Frozen only by his presence.

As it should be.

'We'll be back,' Sage said, and again he felt that flash of pride that her voice did not shake, even though he could feel her anxiety flickering. 'Tell her to be here.'

'If she isn't, I will come looking,' Oren warned. 'Accept this offer if you don't want us to enter your camp.'

In all honesty, that was a last resort, if they wanted to keep the situation from becoming too hostile too quickly. Their reaction would result in at least a few fatalities just to regain control. Without another word he held out his hand this time, and waited for her to take it before he shifted them back across the river.

Gabriel and his guards were still gaping as they re-appeared, his golden magic dissipating on the warm air as he let go of her hand.

And then his phone buzzed in his pocket.

Sage looked around, confused. When he pulled his phone out and swore under his breath, she tutted. She knew who it was from his reaction.

'Roderick wants to know if I'm dead yet.' But the hand she put on his arm was a quiet reminder not to be too angry, that it didn't matter, they were here now and there was no point dwelling on it.

He gave her a bitter look. 'I'll only be a few minutes.'

He excused himself, striding into the thick trees and out of earshot, mostly so Gabriel didn't hear whatever heated words he was about to exchange with their captain.

18

SAGE

'He doesn't like your boss?' Gabriel asked, his shoulders relaxing as soon as Oren walked away.

She huffed under her breath. 'That's an understatement.'

'Because that man doesn't like you?'

'He's hated Roderick since before I was even born. But that too, I guess. Oren actually helped me get this job specifically because he knew it would piss off Roderick. He said the look on his face would make his decade.'

Gabriel started to laugh, and she would admit that she liked how it lit up his face.

'So that's why he keeps you around?' Patrice, part of the river patrol that'd met them at the waterside, asked. She ignored the jibe that she knew was hidden under there somewhere. 'Why would you not want to live somewhere like here? In a pack, as part of a community?'

'I do live in a community,' she told him. 'It just looks different from yours.'

'I mean—'

'I know what you mean.'

Gabriel chuckled. 'It was worth a try, though, *eh*?'

She was about to quip back with something equally as cheeky when Gabriel's face went slack. And Patrice stiffened beside him. The other guard still hanging back froze too.

She blinked, confused by their sudden shifts. Then a shiver rattled down her own spine.

She didn't know what it was. She couldn't see anything out of the ordinary. But . . .

She tuned in her ears, flicked on her wolf senses and listened even more intently than usual.

Nothing.

And that was the point. That was what they'd all sensed shift in the atmosphere around them. No crack of a twig underfoot or rustle of leaves. In fact, the silence was so loud, like a blanket had been thrown over the forest, and that scared her even more.

'What's that?' Patrice asked.

'What?' But she could already hear it as the word left her lips. Faint singing. Or . . . no, it was more like chanting.

From between the trees on the other side of the river where the witches had just disappeared, more of them started to edge their way back out. The original thirteen, the blonde witch Oren had knocked cold awake again and among them, and even more. At least another half-dozen. And all of them had their eyes turned downstream, in the direction of the river flowing towards them from the Meute de Monreau camp.

Patrice swore.

There, creeping over the surface of the water, was a black fog.

Sage's heart stuttered in her chest.

The chanting grew louder as the witches came further into the open. In their hands were small pots of powders that they were sprinkling on the ground at their feet, and bags of herbs they were throwing into the air in front of them.

Patrice hissed. 'They're doing it! They're summoning that fog, they're casting a curse!'

But Sage was watching, and those witches, their eyes were wide. Wide with fear – and it was real. She knew it as the chanting became more frantic, more fierce.

'No.' She swallowed, staring at the black mass Sacha had dismissed getting closer and closer across the water. 'That's not a curse.'

'Then what are they doing?' Patrice demanded, fire dancing in his eyes. 'What else if not a curse!'

She didn't know. It looked like . . . maybe they were creating a protective spell? Maybe a shield?

The fog was moving slowly, rolling and twisting, tendrils wisping and flailing at the corners, like a blind creature searching for something it couldn't see. Fingers reaching for something it couldn't quite grasp. It kept low. Flat over the water, growing and spreading until it covered the whole width of the river.

She had no idea what to do. Did they . . . did they run? Did they just leave it there?

She'd just about decided that they probably had no other choice, some part of her knowing that that fog could not touch them, when it seemed to react to something invisible. It recoiled, the edges curling in on itself like a slug that'd touched salt; it came into contact with the witches' spell at last. It jerked, the whole roiling mass shivering and quaking.

That didn't feel good.

It felt . . . angry. Annoyed that something was getting in its way. And as the fog rallied itself, it turned on the witches like a wounded animal defending itself from a predator, taking a stand against the magic that'd attacked it.

Its advancement was still slow, creeping and sinister, and the blonde witch, who Sage now realized was somewhat of a leader, given her position again in the centre and ahead of the rest, hissed something to her sisters, low and urgent. The witches fanned out, trying to cover every angle of the riverbed and block the fog from passing through the trees into their camp.

The fog mirrored them, stretching itself to face off against the barricade of witches still chanting and throwing herbs and powders to repel it.

Don't touch it. Don't touch it! Sage found herself chanting under her own breath, in time with the witches, knowing in her heart that this thing would kill anything it touched. *Push it back, push it—*

A witch with mousy brown hair slipped.

'Chloé!' One of her sisters gasped her name and Chloé righted herself almost at once, but it was too late. In that second, when the witches closest to her turned to catch and steady her, when chanting had paused and powders stilled, the fog erupted.

It had been flattening its whole body out across the water, unable to push itself up thanks to the magic of their spell. But now it had the chance to become whole. The fog grew taller, drawing itself up until it was like a dark spectre hovering over the surface of the water, perhaps two metres tall as the edges still wisped and snapped.

Sage hadn't realized until that moment just how much the witch magic was holding up against the fog, until it'd found a crack in the armour. It whipped a furious tendril out for Chloé, lurching, ready to wrap her in its translucent darkness and drag her within.

Sage's heart thundered in her chest. This was it. She knew that witch was dead.

And then a shrill voice screamed out in fury.

That voice was full of such authority it made Sage's bones shudder. Even the fog seemed to stutter and recoil just a little. The witches spun in unison as another body stepped out from the tree line. Older, face lined and hair greying and wild. In that hair was braided feathers and beads in all the various colours the other witches wore. Sage didn't need the whisper from Gabriel to know that this was the witch mother.

The tendril that'd been ready to engulf Chloé only managed to twist itself around her arm.

There was a blood-curdling scream. And everything went to hell.

The witch mother howled. She threw out her hands and magic erupted. Forks of bright white light shot from the woman's fingertips, and the crack as white magic hit black fog was so deafening she thought her eardrums might burst.

The fog recoiled at once, shrinking away from the light.

And like that, it was gone.

So fast Sage didn't even see where it went, or whether it simply dissipated into the air.

It was only then that Sage realized her chest was heaving.

But the screaming didn't stop. And as her eyes adjusted again, the flashes of light still burnt into her eyelids, she realized that Chloé's arm had gone too.

Gone.

From the elbow down, nothing but blood and a torn joint.

One of the other witches doubled over and vomited all over the floor.

Others were screaming.

The witch mother was panting, her face grey and sweating as she keeled over. The force of the magic she'd had to use to expel the darkness must've almost knocked her out.

'Oren,' Sage breathed. She looked at Gabriel. 'He can save her.'

'What?' He looked sceptical.

She didn't have time. She refused to stand and watch that witch die in front of them.

'Oren!' She screamed his name into the trees. He couldn't have gone far, she knew he'd hear the screaming. 'Oren!'

And like that he was there. Close enough he hadn't even bothered to shift. He erupted from between the trees he'd disappeared into, a long, sharp dagger already in his hand at the sound of her yells – she momentarily wondered what he thought had happened. Whether he had summoned that blade expecting to kill witches or wolves. And then he saw the chaos across the river, and blood spraying everywhere.

'We have to help her,' she said. She knew he would hesitate to get involved, but if they didn't, it would ruin any chance they had of cooperation. 'Please, Oren.'

In seconds, the blade was gone and his arm was wrapped around her waist as he shifted them back across the river.

She stumbled as her feet touched solid ground again.

'Move,' she heard him demand before she could even right herself – one of the first times he'd ever let go of her before she'd found her balance.

The gold casing of his magic that encircled Chloé began to grow like a balloon, and every witch that was surrounding her, touching her or screaming wildly into the air was pushed back as the boundary of the magic made space for him and her alone to pass through.

Sage moved through the barrier like walking through a thin veil of silk, and almost at once the noise from outside was muted. The only sound now was the witch moaning.

She had already lost a considerable amount of blood, the floor at her feet blackened with it. She was on her knees cradling her elbow in her hand; her face was so deathly white Sage was sure she must be moments from death. The other witches howled furiously, hammering on the thin golden wall. Claws scratched against it like nails against glass.

Oren held Chloé's stumped arm in his hands, the gold of his magic hissing in a way she'd never seen. She wondered if that was what her chest had looked like when he'd saved her.

'There's not enough skin,' he muttered, frowning. 'There's not much I can use to knit together over the wound.'

'Can you stop the blood at least?' she asked desperately. 'Perhaps with care the skin can grow back naturally?'

'It's the best I think we'll be able to manage.'

'Can you keep a wall around me if I go to the witch mother?' she asked.

'She can wait.'

'We need her on our side, Oren,' she said. 'You've not seen what I've just seen.'

He glanced up. 'What do you mean?'

She swallowed. Her heart was still thundering in her chest and she knew he could hear it. 'Those stoner wolves were right. A black fog came over the water.' Her throat was dry as she tried to describe it. 'It touched her, and . . . I dunno? Evaporated her arm?' He stared at her. 'I'll explain properly later. Just . . . cover me, OK?'

He looked at her for a moment, then nodded.

As she stepped back through the bubble surrounding Oren and Chloé, a second bubble enveloped her, moving with her as she walked. She could see the lips of the witches around her moving, still shouting and hammering on the wall of the first.

The witch mother was slumped over a rock, her hand over her chest.

When Sage reached her, Oren's shield dropped.

'Sybil Crows-Caw?' she asked.

The old woman looked up. Those eyes. So white. It made her feel suddenly homesick for Berion.

'Your witch will survive,' she told her, crouching to her level. She forced her voice to be as calm and sure as possible. 'My partner stemmed the blood flow and is trying to close the wound the best he can, but it will need time for the skin to heal properly. He will ensure she lives.'

The white eyes gave little away. She blinked. She was so different to Berion. There was no warmth there. No friendliness.

'How?' the woman croaked, confused. 'Witches are natural healers. Not warlocks.'

'His mother was a healer. She taught him, as a young boy.'

'Before she was killed?'

Sage flinched, shocked.

The witch mother smiled through crooked teeth. 'You didn't know?'

Sage blinked. 'She was executed,' she said coldly, standing again to look down on the witch mother. 'I know exactly who and what he is.'

'Does he know what you are?'

She blinked again. She didn't know what that meant at all.

Then Oren was by her side, staring down at the witch mother too.

She looked over at Chloé, her sisters around her now. The golden barrier was gone. The witches were inspecting her wound and wrapping it in bandages Oren must've magicked for them.

'Are you cursing the werewolves?' he asked bluntly.

The witch mother laughed as she pushed herself unsteadily to her feet. She looked exhausted. A few of the witches sensed the movement, turning to watch carefully. Two rose and edged closer, but the witch mother held up a hand. Even if it was painful to stand, she wouldn't have her witches help her up in front of them.

'There has been a series of unfortunate circumstances

over the past couple of weeks,' Oren went on. 'All of the werewolf packs have experienced them and are convinced it's not a coincidence. If it truly isn't to do with you or your witches, surely you have also experienced strange happenings?'

'Oh,' she hissed. 'You mean other than one of my witches just losing an arm?'

The witch mother looked at them both, looked them head to toe and raised an eyebrow, her lips still curling at the edges. Then she glanced back at the rest of her witches, the injured one now seemingly asleep on the floor as another gently brushed her hair out of her face.

'Last week, one of our witches went missing. We have searched our lands thoroughly. We have found no body, no trace. We don't know where she's gone. I tell you this only in payment for saving Chloé's life today.'

'We can help you,' Sage offered. 'Where did you last see her? Could she have left – was there no note?'

Sybil's lips curled back over her teeth as she snarled. 'Witches don't *leave* their coven.'

'You're saying someone took her?' Sage asked.

The blonde witch, the ringleader from the start, could contain herself no longer. She broke away from the crowd and came to Sybil's side. 'Ask the rest of your dogs.' She nodded across the river. 'It's not like they've not done it before.'

It was only the surprise of this accusation that stopped

Sage reacting to being called a dog for the second time that week. The go-to insult for werewolves, apparently.

'Enough, Louise,' the witch mother hissed sharply.

Louise replied in French, her tone angry, but her voice was also thick with some fresh emotion. And perhaps it was because of this that when Sybil replied her tone was softer, and she placed a withered hand on Louise's shoulder. Louise nodded. Then Sybil took a step back and surveyed them both.

'We don't need your help,' she said. 'Now get off our land.'

19

SAGE

Oren shifted them back across the river and sent a pale-faced Gabriel to tell his mother that they would be waiting for her in the hall. And that she *would* join them.

'What kind of fog?' Oren pushed as she told him what she'd witnessed. They made their way towards camp, leaving a shaken Patrice and the other guard with strict instructions not to engage with the witches again, no matter what else they saw or was said.

'What kinds of fog are there?' She tutted impatiently. 'It was thicker than the mist of your magic. Dense enough I couldn't see through it. It was more solid than P. And the edges were wispy. It wasn't a solid form, and it could change shape.'

'I have no idea what that is,' he muttered, frowning.

'Well, it has to be something. It's just taken a witch's arm off!'

He puffed air out of his cheeks and didn't answer, and she knew he couldn't think of any way to explain it.

But something else was bothering her too.

She didn't raise it with Oren, though. Instead, she pulled out her phone. And she didn't ring P this time, but Hozier.

'Back so soon,' Hozier crooned. 'Does the hunky French guy want to chat?'

Hunky. She snorted. Then quickly looked away from Oren's glower.

'No. You're in work, right?'

'Unfortunately,' Hozier sighed. 'But I'm finishing early.' Her voice brightened. 'We're going to a glass-blowing lesson tonight. A new studio just opened across town. Two bugbears, the guy does the workshop at the back and his wife runs the shop out front—'

'Hozier,' she cut in. 'Actually, that sounds amazing, and I really want to try it out when I get home, but I need your help ASAP.'

'What is it?' She could practically hear Hozier straightening up. 'Are you OK?'

'Yeah, listen. I just heard an exchange between a witch and the witch mother. It was in French but I'm sure I heard a name in there. *Kalinka.* I'm not fluent but I'm sure that's not a word. But that's all I have. Other than that, going off the context of the conversation we were having, I *think* she went missing at some point. I was wondering if you could find anything? There won't be anything online since it's supernatural, but I don't know, maybe in the archives?'

Hozier sucked in through her teeth. 'Not about anything

that happened in another country. Can't you ask one of the wolves?'

'Whoever I ask will be very one-sided. I'd rather have an unbiased account first. Whatever happened with this witch, it doesn't sound good.'

Hozier *hmm*ed, thinking. 'Let me see what I can do. Make some calls. But no promises. I'll text anything I can find.'

'Thank you, thank you!' she gushed, relieved.

As she clicked off the call, Oren looked at her. 'You think that was a name?'

'I guess we'll see.'

'But you feel this is important?'

'Maybe,' she hedged. Something just nagged her about that whole exchange. The strange accusation. But . . . she still felt like she wanted his approval too. 'What do you think?'

'It's your call.'

It was an important shift in their working relationship. He'd led her through their first major case – the case that'd won her a position at his side. Things had changed between them since then. A respect that'd been earnt. Oren didn't know how to express himself in any meaningful way, but moments like this, where she was his equal, was his way of acknowledging that shift.

'Let's see what Hozier comes back with first.'

He nodded as they climbed the steps into the hall.

Celeste was already in there, hurrying towards them. Benoît and Gabriel were waiting too.

'Gabriel's just told me something happened down by the river.' Celeste herded them towards the meeting table. The sleeves of her shirt were rolled up and there was a faint smell of pepper. She must have been preparing lunch.

By the time Sage was explaining how the fog had lunged for the witch, Chloé, there was silence. Then Benoît finally looked at her.

'An arm . . . disappeared? Where did it go?' he spat, almost as if he thought she was lying.

'Into nothing.' She didn't even know how to describe what she'd seen. She looked at Oren for help. 'It was just . . . gone,' she finished lamely.

'The wound was clean,' Oren supplied curtly. 'It looked how wounds often do when a limb has been taken with a very sharp blade. Quickly but cleanly. Straight through bone and tissue.'

The beat of silence. She knew they were all thinking the same thing. How he'd come to know those kinds of wounds.

'And you're sure this wasn't the witches?' Celeste asked seriously. 'A trick to throw the scent off them?'

'No.' She was absolutely sure. 'It wasn't until she tripped and the rest of the witches got distracted that the fog seemed to regain some of its power. Their chanting was holding it back. They were trying to keep it from entering their land.'

She looked at Gabriel for back-up, the only other witness.

He looked unsure, and said nothing. Her jaw dropped open.

'Gabriel!' she insisted. 'Tell them!'

'But what if . . .' he said awkwardly. 'What if that was part of the trick? What if that was just to make it look to us like they're being attacked too?'

'Oh, come on!' She threw up her hands in disbelief. She couldn't believe what she was hearing. 'They'd nearly kill one of their own witches just to trick us? That witch would have *died* if Oren hadn't saved her!' She shook her head. 'You saw them when they couldn't get through Oren's barrier. Heard their screams. Would you let one of your pack die just to trick the witches?'

The look on his face said enough.

No.

'Exactly,' she said. And at least he had the grace to look apologetic.

'Witches are bound by their own magic too, Gabriel,' Celeste said, her tone considered, thoughtful. 'Just because they don't have pack loyalty doesn't mean they'd sacrifice a life in this way.'

'Besides, Sacha Monreau told us that some pack members reported witnessing a black fog,' Sage said. 'It'd been dismissed since it was dark and they were up to no good to begin with. But we have other witnesses to this phenomenon in a place no witches were present to cast it. It can't have just been a show for our sake.'

'Really?' Celeste asked. 'Sacha's pack has seen this?'

She nodded. 'It didn't touch anyone. They just ran. Nobody was hurt.'

'Then, I agree with Sage,' Celeste said. Relief rushed into her. If Celeste believed her, Gabriel would fall in line. 'In fact,' Celeste continued, 'from what we've seen, I'd argue that the witches are just as fiercely protective of each other. Look how they still hold grudges, after all this time. I don't think they'd sacrifice one of their own for a deception.'

'The witch mother told us that recently one of their witches disappeared. They've not found her,' Sage said. Celeste's eyes went wide at the news. 'We offered to help. They declined.' She decided not to mention Kalinka. Not yet. See what Hozier came back with first.

'So what are you suggesting?' Benoît asked. 'That this . . . thing? This fog, has something to do with it?'

'Well, it's a logical possibility, *non*?' Gabriel asked. 'If it can make an arm disappear, it can take a whole body, if it has a chance to engulf it?'

'If that's the case, then how do we protect ourselves?' Benoît asked. 'How do we secure borders? How do we stop a *fog*?'

Celeste shook her head. She had no answer.

'Do you think it's . . .' Sage made a face. 'Eating them? I mean, for nourishment, or energy, or something?'

'Probably.' Oren shrugged. 'I want to check something. I won't be long.'

Without another word, he shifted away.

Sage sighed. 'Sorry. He does that. Usually when he's bored.'

But the table only seemed to let out a collective breath of relief. She started to laugh.

Celeste gave her a knowing smile. 'You truly are safe?' she asked. 'You *want* this partnership? This life? Because we will protect you, if you need us to help you get out.'

'He's my best friend,' she told the alpha.

She really did appreciate the offer, though. That they would be willing to face off against him and take her in despite who Oren was and the potential consequences. Wolf loyalty would compel them to do that. She'd realized these last few days that everything that'd repulsed her about MacAllister and his pack was only their personal failing. This was real pack life. Wolf life. And she didn't hate the idea of it nearly as much as she had before they'd arrived.

Celeste looked at her for a minute, and she was sure the alpha still didn't quite believe her. Maybe they thought he'd used his magic to alter her thoughts, or trap her at his side.

Gabriel cleared his throat. 'I'm concerned about Patrice. The guards witnessed what happened, but Patrice was particularly angry. As the fog approached he was certain it was summoned by the witches. We can't let that story spread.'

'I'll speak to him this evening at dinner. Remind him that we don't tolerate gossip here.'

Everyone nodded. There wasn't much else to say. Not until they knew more.

'Stay vigilant.' Celeste stood, then looked at her. 'Let's keep communication open.'

It was subtle, but that offer to keep building a bridge was still there.

20

SAGE

Her mind was whirring as she left the hall. Gabriel had offered to walk her to her cabin, but she was still a bit irritated he hadn't initially backed her up. And God knows where Oren had got to. She wouldn't be too surprised to find him lounging in that cabin, his shift just an excuse to leave.

She was thinking about P, wanting to talk the whole thing over, when her phone buzzed.

She pulled it out to see Hozier's name flashing across the screen.

'It's either very good or very bad news, if you're getting back to me this quickly,' she said, pausing outside the cabin door and sitting on the step for a few minutes to let the spring sunlight warm her face while she chatted to her friend.

'Bit of both.' Hozier sighed. 'I got through to my French counterpart in their archives. A helpful warlock called Lucas. He had a look for me. That is a name and it was a witch. There is a file on her, Kalinka Crows-Caw. She went missing about seventy years ago.'

'That's . . . a long time ago.'

'Uh huh,' Hozier agreed. 'And get this. Kalinka was the youngest birth *daughter* of the witch mother.'

Sage gasped. 'Her actual daughter? Not just a coven witch?'

'Yep. She was found a couple of days after she went missing. And then she died not long after.'

'*What?*'

'Yeah. Doesn't say how or why. That's on you to find out. The witches weren't very forthcoming with details, apparently.'

'Surprise, surprise.'

Hozier huffed a small laugh. 'There are coordinates for where she was found, I'll text them over, but even those are only a rough estimate provided by a third party. Witches found her, but a skin changer heard the commotion and was able to provide the general direction.'

She shuddered. Even the name gave her the creeps. 'That skin changer will be dead now, though, right?'

'They have pretty similar to human lifespans. So probably, yeah.'

'OK. Well, thanks anyway.' She sighed. 'Send me those coordinates.' And she clicked off the call.

As expected, Oren was lounging on the sofa.

'Where'd you go?'

'To visit the Baba Yaga.'

She physically recoiled, horrified. 'You did *what*? There's one here?'

Because there were three sisters, that weirdly all shared the same name. And who either helped or hindered any that were brave enough to approach her cabin.

He nodded. 'I felt her presence. She's old. Very powerful. I could feel her the minute we arrived.' He shrugged. 'I had a run-in with one, about ninety-five years ago. And another, about fifty years ago. And they never forget a smell.'

She kicked off her trainers and came over to the sofa, throwing herself down and twisting so her back leant against the arm as she faced him.

'And?'

'It was the first one.' He grimaced. 'I was hoping it might be the third one. The one I've never met. She told me to . . . well . . .' He rolled his eyes. 'I was leaving almost as soon as I arrived. She won't speak to me. But if anyone knows what lives in these mountains, it would be her.'

'And you wanted to ask her about the fog?'

He nodded. It was a good idea.

'If she won't talk to you, then I'll go?'

'No,' he said sharply. 'You don't go near her, Sage. I mean it.'

She flared. 'Why not?'

'Don't start.' He knew why she was being pissy. 'It's nothing to do with what I think you're capable of. I've stood back and let you deal with pretty much everything since we got here, because I know you can. But the Baba Yaga is *old* magic. Far darker than anything you're used to. Creatures like her, sure, they might help you if they feel like it, but they just as easily delight in cruelty and torture. Trust me, death is better than being her prisoner.'

'You could come and get me, though.' She jabbed him on the arm with a finger. 'You'd just rescue me. Or are you saying she's more powerful than you?'

'Of course not.' He tutted. 'But if I killed her, she has two sisters who will seek revenge. And it's more hassle than it's worth.'

'Why has nobody ever just killed all three? Why haven't you?'

'Why do we not kill all spiders? Because as unappealing as they are, they keep other insects at bay. Neither wolf nor witch will have any real comprehension that their boundaries have been kept so safe all these years by the Baba Yaga that lives here.'

'Kept them safe how?'

'Well, she eats pretty much anything. I think it's probable she set up camp in that exact spot knowing how alluring the werewolf and witch colonies are. Knew it'd bring an endless feast passing by her door.'

She surprised herself in realizing she was impressed by the Baba Yaga's way of thinking. Only in the kind of way you could be impressed and horrified all at the same time.

Sure, she could have one good night making her way through the packs, or she could restrain herself, position herself as their unofficial guardian, and enjoy years of the ripe pickings of every passing monster that hadn't had her foresight.

'Besides . . .' he carried on. 'Old magic doesn't die in the same way. They come back. Eventually.'

She stared, taken aback. That was news to her. 'They can't be killed?'

'They can. They just resurface. It could be decades. Centuries. Depends on how powerful they are. Nobody quite knows where they go, exactly. Another realm? Another dimension?' He shrugged as if he didn't quite believe that. 'But every time they do reappear, they're stronger than before.'

'Right.'

'Exactly.' He read her horrified expression correctly. 'So don't go near her.'

They sat in silence for a few moments. 'Do you think this fog could be connected to what's been going on here? The real "curse", as it were.' She quoted the word with her fingers this time.

'Do you?' he asked. 'You're the one who saw it.'

She contemplated for a moment. 'Maybe. Black fog isn't going to be easy to see in the dark, even for a werewolf. So if it is creeping about causing chaos, it'd explain why nobody's noticed it.'

'It's something to consider,' he agreed. 'Without knowing

what it is, who knows what it's capable of. And if it is old magic, a creature like the Baba Yaga, it'll be capable of a lot.'

'And it's sentient, to a degree. I mean, why did it eat Chloé's arm but not any of the livestock in the paddocks? So it's got a purpose, right?'

Oren shook his head, frowning. Something to think on.

'Hozier called me back, by the way. Kalinka was a witch. She went missing seventy years ago, was found, but then died not long after.'

Oren, who had been rubbing his eyes with the palms of his hands, looked at her with interest for the first time since they'd arrived. 'Well, that explains Celeste's comment about the witches holding long grudges,' he said. 'Did you notice that?'

She nodded. 'That was a slip-up. I don't think she meant to say that in front of us at all.'

'Exactly,' Oren said. 'If they know there's a long-standing grudge here, something causing heightened animosity, that would explain why they jumped to believing they were being cursed so quickly. Why haven't they mentioned it before now?'

'I don't know. But I also don't think the werewolves are involved with this missing witch,' she said. 'The recent one, I mean. Despite that being what the witches were implying. I do think that fog took her, got hold of her and just gobbled her up.' Even thinking about what she'd just seen made her heart pound. 'Because when it arrived . . . I felt it before I saw it. I felt a shift in the atmosphere, then I heard the witches chanting, and then I saw the fog last.'

'The fog wasn't a surprise for the witches?' She loved him for how quickly he always understood her.

She shook her head. 'They were already prepared. They had herbs and powders to repel it. And that has to come from experience, right? I think they've seen it before, and knew what it was capable of.'

'Why not just tell us that, though?'

'I think they'd rather fling accusations.' Sage shrugged. 'Piss the werewolves off even more. If there is a long-standing grudge, they won't wanna help us, so if they can lie and further tensions with the werewolves in the process? Bonus, I guess.'

Oren *hmm*ed his agreement.

Before he could answer, her phone pinged again.

She looked at it, then back at Oren. 'If you won't let me go to the Baba Yaga, will you do this with me instead?' She showed him the coordinates their friend had just texted her. 'It's where they found Kalinka. Roughly.' She opened the map that appeared in gold mist on her lap. She circled the area on the map with her finger. It was on the wolf side of the river . . . but miles away.

'That skin changer will be long gone, Sage, you know that, right?'

'I know. But I want to see the place anyway.' She looked up at him. 'Please, Oren.'

He looked down at the map a moment longer and sighed. 'It's getting late, and the dinner hall will be opening soon.' But he held out a hand, an offer to shake on it, a promise. 'If you can wait until morning, I'll shift us up there.' When she put her hand in his to agree to the terms, she felt the familiar callouses and memories of that kiss flashed in her mind again. Rather than let go, she curled her fingers between his. Rather than let go, he squeezed hers back. A promise. Wherever she went he would go too.

21

SAGE

'Why don't you come eat in the hall with me this evening?' she whined as he opened cupboard doors, stared inside, then closed them again with an irritated huff, uninterested in her bland-looking bolognese. She'd put that stupid paella in the fridge and refused to touch it herself.

If she was honest, she missed him. She saw him every day, lived with him still, but the laughter and the chatting they shared over mealtimes with P was something she'd taken for granted back home in Downside. She didn't realize she would miss it until it was gone.

'I have plans tonight.'

'Sure,' she huffed.

'I do,' he said over his shoulder, walking into his bedroom. She could hear him opening and closing the drawers full of his clothes. Was he changing? Did he actually have plans? 'Don't wait up.'

She froze. Something uneasy settled in her stomach. Had Estelle managed to corner him again when she'd been distracted with Gabriel? He'd taken Flora for a drink once, that'd started her obsession, so she knew he wasn't averse to taking random women out.

She wondered how many times that'd happened since they'd met. She supposed she had no idea what he was actually doing when she and P went out socializing and he refused to come. She was pretty sure he wouldn't be able to sneak anyone home past both her wolf senses and P's hospitality senses, but . . .

'Where are you going?' she asked carefully. 'Do you want me to come?'

'No, Sage. I definitely do not.' He appeared in his bedroom doorway, some black trousers in his hands, threw her a delicious smirk, and closed the door in her face.

She refused to probe further. She knew it'd give him some kind of satisfaction if she asked any more questions, and she was too stubborn. But . . . why so secretive?

'Well, maybe I'll make plans of my own.' Pettiness got the better of her as she rifled through the cutlery drawer. Even through the closed door she knew he'd hear her.

His tut was scathing. 'Oh, well, tell Gabriel I said hi.'

She could feel his eyes rolling through the walls, so she called him something that only made him laugh obnoxiously. Her decision to not give him the satisfaction of knowing she was irritated at being kept in the dark failed at the first hurdle. She stalked out of the cabin, slamming the door behind her.

But when she walked up the steps and into the hall to

find Gabriel, she knew immediately something was wrong.

There was a new tension in the air.

Everybody sat in their usual places, mixing and chatting stretched over three long tables, but that was the thing about wolf ears. If they wanted, tuned in at just the right frequency, they could pick up anyone's conversation.

And that's what they were doing.

Everybody was pretending they weren't. But they were. They were listening to Patrice telling a small group sitting around him about what they'd seen at the river.

She looked around.

Gabriel wasn't there yet and neither was Celeste. The conversation was in French, she couldn't understand it, but the tone of his voice was accusatory enough. And the looks on some of the other surrounding werewolf faces said enough.

'Here she is.' Patrice switched to English and gestured as he spotted her. 'Tell them.'

'Tell them what?' she asked slowly, and she headed for their table.

'About the witches, the curse!'

'They weren't casting that fog, Patrice. That wasn't a curse.' She couldn't stop herself sounding exasperated. 'They were trying to slow it down. You saw what happened once they stopped chanting, how it attacked? One of them lost an *arm*!'

Patrice made a sound, a mixture of dismissal and

disgust, furious she wasn't backing him up. He made a gesture like Benoît had when they'd met, like he was brushing her away. Another werewolf smirked.

That pissed her off.

'I suggest you stop, Patrice,' she warned. 'Right now. You're stirring up trouble and scaring everyone half to death in the process!'

'You can't tell him what to do,' the smirker cut in.

'Actually, I can. I'm not a pack member. I'm with the Arcānum.' She looked down her nose. 'But I don't need to. You should find Celeste and see what she has to say.'

Patrice flared at once, drawing himself up, ready for a fight. 'Celeste—'

'Is not stupid.' She was rapidly losing her temper too. 'You think I've not discussed this with her already?'

She was ready to walk away. She'd rather sit on her own in the cabin. After all, she wasn't one of them, and some of them had just been reminded of that.

As she turned, she heard the scraping of wooden bench on floor.

'You're meant to be on our side.' Patrice's voice was loud enough this time for the whole hall to openly hear. 'You're supposed to back us up.'

She stopped still.

Every werewolf turned to look. And every one of them had the same question in their eyes. She knew what came out of her mouth next mattered. Knew it wouldn't make the remainder of their time any more comfortable if she didn't say exactly what they wanted to hear. But she was Arcānum. She was there with a job to do. She knew what Oren would say. Knew what Hozier and Berion would say. Only P would understand how she felt.

God, she missed P.

She put her food down on the table beside her and turned back.

'I'm on the side of the truth.' She lifted her chin defiantly. 'There may well be a curse, but that thing we saw today, that wasn't it. If you want to start a fight with the witches, at least have the balls to be upfront about it. Don't hide behind what you know is a lie.'

'You're a traitor.' Patrice spat the word at her.

The room gasped.

She was surprised to realize that it didn't hurt. Not in the way that he intended it to, anyway. He meant for it to cut deep, in a wolf way: in a loyalty way. In the way that such a comment would floor any member of their pack. But these wolves didn't understand her. They didn't understand Downside.

They didn't understand her life at all.

'A traitor to what, exactly?' she demanded. 'It's my *job* here to be reasonable, and look at both sides—'

'That's enough.' The voice that spoke was so quiet it would've been easy to ignore.

But every other werewolf in the room knew that voice

and was bound to its command.

Celeste stood in the doorway of the hall, Gabriel behind her. He looked thoroughly uncomfortable.

She knew the conversation that was about to happen between alpha and her pack was not a place for her. She picked up her food. She'd eat in the cabin tonight. Ironic, really, the one night Oren wouldn't be there to eat with her like she'd wanted.

She managed to make it about twenty paces before Gabriel caught up with her.

'Come on.' He nudged her arm with his elbow. 'It's a clear sky tonight. I know where we can eat.'

She knew that Celeste had sent him after her, whether to keep relations friendly or keep an eye on her, she didn't know. But she was grateful enough he'd followed her that she couldn't quite bring herself to tell him how much she hated to look at the moon.

22

SAGE

Twenty minutes and a small hike later they were perched on some rocks at the edge of a little clearing, their feet dangling over a cliff that disappeared into darkness. It made her feel queasy, and she refused to look down. Yet up in the sky to their left was a crescent moon, and looking at that made her feel queasy too.

The small issue of the moon aside, she couldn't deny that the rest of the view was spectacular. An endless carpet of trees stretching out over jagged mountains, towards the tallest mountain of them all in the distance, its bare peak just visible to her human eyesight. Witch territory, Gabriel told her as they settled down, and sometimes, if you came in daylight, you might spot a broomstick or two shooting just over the treetops.

If she were here with Oren, she knew there was every chance he would shove her off the edge and use his magic to catch her, just for a laugh. She told Gabriel this, and his laughter echoed off the mountains around them.

'Would he really? That's some power trip.'

'His ego is unrivalled,' she agreed. 'Suppose it comes with being one of the most powerful warlocks on the planet. Other than the Elders.'

He didn't answer. But she knew he probably had a comment he was keeping to himself. It was clear Oren and Gabriel had a dislike that was mutual.

'I brought these for dessert.' He held up two chocolate bars. 'A peace offering,' he admitted. 'For not backing you up before.'

She couldn't help smiling as she took the chocolate. She knew it wasn't much, but up here, in these mountains, she also knew it wasn't that easy to get hold of. Any supplies they got from the human shops would have to be rationed.

'Are you sure?'

Instead of answering, he gave her a lopsided smile and bit into his burrito. She assumed it was now as cold as her spaghetti, but neither of them complained. She realized she just . . . enjoyed sitting with a companion. She'd started to feel so homesick for P every morning she woke and the ghost wasn't there, and having at least one friend who didn't look at her with intense apprehension was a comfort.

The fact he was cute helped.

She wasn't sure if her attraction to Gabriel was simply because she was still trying to fight off her desperation for Oren, and he was just a welcome distraction. Or whether his hazel eyes and floppy hair were what she'd decided she liked for now.

She didn't know why she felt a little bit guilty about it all. Could she be interested in two people at once? Maybe. Could it be that she just liked it when Gabriel openly flirted with her? Definitely. Did enjoying time with him stop her thinking about that kiss with Oren every waking second he was in her line of vision? No.

Ergh. She hated all her mixed-up, confused, awkward feelings.

She wished she could tell Gabriel how she felt about her wolf. So far it was a secret she'd kept from everyone except Oren and P, and she wondered what that said about him. She knew it'd hurt him in a way that only mattered to wolves like him, though. For a pack wolf like Gabriel the notion of her disliking it would be outright offensive. And that was one thing Oren had never made her feel ashamed of.

'Why is there' – she squinted through the darkness, then turned her wolf eyesight on, just to be sure – 'grey smoke rising from that mountain?'

The tall peak in the distance, the highest point of witch territory, she now realized, was smoking at the tip. And with her wolf eyes enhancing her sight, she was sure she could just see the tiny black pinprick of a cave.

'Ah.' Gabriel smiled. 'The witches call that the Häxgrotta.'

'What the hell is that?'

'We don't really know what it is. They sing, celebrate solstice there, leave offerings. They burn their dead on pyres at the foot of the mountain. You can hear their songs sometimes, if the wind is blowing in this direction. It's their . . . goddess, for want of a better word. It sounds like worship, anyway—'

'You mean some lucky monster happy to pretend to be their deity to get free food,' she scoffed.

'Oh, one hundred per cent.' He grinned.

'But you think there's definitely something in the cave?'

'For sure.' Gabriel nodded. 'Some days the smoke that rises is thick, especially after they've left fresh offerings. And then some days there's barely any smoke at all. I suspect whatever really lives up there is just having a good old time eating all the food they leave it as it keeps warm over a toasty fire.'

She thought about Oren's assertion that the Baba Yaga had been smart to position herself where she had – in a spot that was most advantageous to food landing easily on her doorstep. She supposed this didn't sound much different. God, maybe that was just another one of her sisters up there.

'But nobody accuses the Häxgrotta of being part of this curse?'

Gabriel leant in and whispered conspiratorially, 'Don't give anybody ideas. No,' he added seriously. 'The Häxgrotta is a very old tale. Whatever's up there is benevolent, so we leave them to it, I guess.'

She grimaced at the thought of all these monsters living

and thriving in their own ways, hidden in this endless canopy stretching out before them. She missed Downside. At least she knew what lived there.

'Can I ask you something?' She decided if she was going to ask anyone, it was going to have to be him. 'And tell me the truth.'

He looked at her, puzzled. 'Go on.'

'Tell me about Kalinka.'

He paused, surprised. 'How did you hear about her?'

So he did know.

'The blonde witch made a comment, just before Oren shifted us back over the river.'

He sighed, scrunching up the foil wrapping of his burrito as he looked out across the darkness below.

'All I know is that she was a witch who lived here, a long time ago. One day she went missing. And when she was found she was miles away, across the mountains. Beaten, tortured and left for dead. She was found on our side, so the witches accused the werewolves of snatching her.'

'And did they?' she asked.

Gabriel pulled a face. *Who knows.* 'There were accusations. But other things live in these mountains too. Minotaurs. Skin changers. Cockatrice. Griffins. And the Baba Yaga.'

She shuddered.

Gabriel chuckled. 'She's OK, if you leave her in peace. And keep the kids away. But that's the problem with living so long. The witches remember it happening. Most of us weren't even alive then. It's a grudge we can't relate to.'

'But she's the reason you all think the witches are cursing you, isn't it?' she asked. The guilty look he gave her was confirmation. 'You should've told us from the start. It makes so much more sense now.'

'We worried it would make it seem like we deserve it.' He sighed. 'To be cursed.'

She rolled her eyes. 'You're not cursed.' She was starting to sound like Oren. 'What do you think happened to her?'

Gabriel shrugged again. 'Who can say? Perhaps she just couldn't see a life for herself in these mountains.' He looked at her sideways, and smiled. 'Like you.'

She smiled back. 'You're going to have to get over this, Gabriel.'

'I could still change your mind, yet.'

And . . . yeah. Something about him *was* flirtatious. And she did like it.

The way he smiled at her wasn't the way Oren smiled at her. Oren's smile was cruel and cold and arrogant. But it still took her breath away for its beauty. Gabriel's smile was cheeky, and warm, and didn't make her wonder how many times it'd been the last thing people had seen before they'd died. Polar opposites. Two very different kinds of futures.

'Legend has it that grey smoke rose over that mountain for a week after Kalinka died, they left so many offerings for safe passage to the afterlife,' he told her at last, this extra information obviously another kind of peace offering. Like the chocolate bars. 'There's a wolf in the Meute de Monreau who is eighty-nine. If anyone remembers anything, it would be him. But enough for tonight.' Gabriel waved away the memory of the long-dead witch. 'Let's talk about something else.'

They chatted for a while longer, and though neither said it, she knew they were wasting time before they had to go back, where Gabriel would face his friends, who had seen him follow her rather than stay with them. But the night wouldn't last forever. When at last he rose, he offered her a hand to pull her up beside him. No callouses.

'I won't push you off,' he whispered into her ear as he held on to her hand for a moment longer than necessary. 'I promise.'

23

OREN

He ignored a distant raven call as he stood in the shadows of the trees.

The moonlight illuminated them as they sat on the edge of a cliff looking out across the mountains. He wondered what'd brought them out here, rather than eating in the hall. The moon was visible in the sky, and he knew that Gabriel probably assumed this was all rather romantic. Had no idea, hadn't even noticed that she'd refused to look up at the sky the whole time they sat there.

Huh.

If it were them, he'd shove her over the edge and catch her with his magic. She'd scream and punch him and call him all the names under the sun. But she'd still let him wrap an arm around her back and pull her close and shift them home. She never stayed mad with him for long.

She was laughing now, though. Laughing in a way he hadn't heard for a while. Not since *before*.

Sometimes, she complained about a gulf opening between them. Little things that reminded her that there had been so much time for him before she even existed. He saw the kind of look she got on her face sometimes, like the morning Kane turned up and she'd heard him speak in his mother tongue for the first time, and the gulf had cracked open.

It never bothered him in the same way. His life before her and P was dark and violent, and he was grateful they hadn't been there for any of it. But this . . . this was the first time *he* felt a gulf opening. She was bothered by the thought of his past without her, but him? He was more bothered than he'd ever realized by the idea of a future for her without him. Especially now they'd agreed to share one in at least some kind of way.

Maybe not exactly the way he wanted, but he'd already settled into the idea of a future that had both of them in it.

But this, her sitting there with Gabriel, this was how her future would look, wouldn't it, if she'd never met the world's most dangerous assassin? A quiet, peaceful life with someone just like her. A pack. That's what she was giving up, by choosing this life in the Arcānum. He wondered just how much she'd come to resent him for it at the end of all things. If she didn't settle, would she consider it a wasted life, once it was lived? Once she was dying, old and frail in his arms.

And if that day eventually came, he would not be able to save her.

The weight of that future was heaviest. The hardest of

what ifs. The likely, inevitable future for him without her. The weight of what would come for a pair when one was immortal, and one wasn't.

He backed away and looked down at the blade in his hand. It was dripping with blood. He'd already killed a chimera that'd jumped for him out of the darkness. And a basilisk that'd burst out of the ground, grabbed his ankle and tried to drag him into its tunnel.

This was the life he offered her. Danger and death.

The blood disappeared in a fine gold mist, and he slid the dagger back on to the sheath at his hip.

He hadn't let her come tonight because he knew it'd be dangerous. He knew she'd explode if she discovered that he'd been out hunting without her. But until he knew what that fog was, he wouldn't risk it.

He heard her laugh again somewhere behind him as he set back off through the trees, and despite the jealousy at seeing her happy in the company of another man, the sound made him smile.

24

P

Hozier sat opposite P in Northern Psyche, grinning. It was supposed to be a hand-blown glass paperweight with an autumn leaf motif inside.

P didn't think it looked like that at all. But Hozier was proud of herself regardless. P was proud of herself too — at least her paperweight in the shape of a pear, her favourite fruit when she was alive, looked like an actual pear.

The bright yellow restaurant was buzzing. And not just from the vivid insect wings of the fairies that waitressed Downside's most popular grilled cheese spot. The smell made P yearn for the time she could still eat. P was good at grilled cheese, but she couldn't figure out how to get it as good as this place. She was sure there was a secret ingredient she was missing. Maybe she'd sneak into the kitchen and see . . .

Hozier had ordered a whole load of extra sides, eyeing P as she asked whether she wanted a bowl of her own to just hold something in her mouth and taste, even if she couldn't chew and swallow. It was a sweet gesture, and not one anyone else had ever actually thought to offer — not even

Sage. But she knew it'd look weird. She shook her head and settled down to watch her petite friend stuff enough food for three grown adults into her tiny body.

The glass-blowing class had been amazing. They'd spent the first twenty minutes trying not to *die* at the back of the group, because the little opening into the furnace the molten glass went into to be fired was called a *glory hole*! And the more everyone else kept saying it with a serious face . . . well, it just made it worse and worse.

The teacher bugbear – a giant, lumbering beast that usually hid in caves and ate naughty children – almost lost his temper with their relentless bouts of silent laughter. She'd have been worried he'd try to eat them too for being naughty, but he had explained that he was a vegetarian, so eating children simply wasn't his deal. His parents were deeply disappointed with his decision to pursue his passion for glass-blowing rather than continue the family line of child consumption.

She wondered how much it'd cost to set up her own studio to practise at home. Maybe build a little workshop at the bottom of the garden. Oren tolerated a lot when it came to what he called her 'phases', but she reckoned this suggestion might push him over the edge. Especially since he financed most of it.

P's phone lit up.

'Which one is it?' Hozier asked, her eyes flicking towards the light.

'Oren.'

Hozier sent a faint red bubble around them to sound-proof their table. 'That means Sage isn't there, or they'd call off her phone.'

P *hmm*ed. She didn't know whether this was going to be a personal therapy session or something else, but as she clicked the green answer button and put him on speaker she made sure she opened with, 'Hiya, Hozier and I are both here, just eating out!' So he didn't say anything he wouldn't want anyone else to hear.

He grunted a greeting. 'Where are you?'

'Northern Psyche.'

He practically whimpered. 'I'm telling you, P, Sage is a terrible cook. No matter how enthusiastic she pretends to be on the phone. She knows what she cooks is *bad*.'

'You could try and cook for yourself, Oren,' she pointed out.

'Why?' He rolled his eyes. 'I'm more than happy to shift to a restaurant and pick up food for us every night. That's what I did before I met you. But she's adamant she wants to try. And all of it is crap.'

Hozier snorted as she dipped a mozzarella stick into some ketchup. 'We just went to the glass-blowing class. Sage will love it.'

'Oh, yeah?' He couldn't have sounded less interested.

'Hozier's paperweight looks like it has a massive reddish-brown poop in the middle.'

Hozier exploded in indignation, snatching up her

paperweight and holding it to her chest as if trying to comfort it from P's painful accusations. She snorted.

'So where's Sage?' P asked. 'Where are you?'

'She's eating her dinner with Gabriel.' He spat the name. She looked at Hozier, who smothered a grin, putting a finger over her lips to imply they mustn't laugh.

'That sounds nice,' she ventured carefully, hoping he couldn't sense her smiling.

'Sure.'

It was kinda funny to hear him, this century and a half of warlock, the world's most feared assassin, sulking over some guy Sage had only known for a matter of days.

'I can hear you rolling your eyes down the phone, Oren,' Hozier said.

'He's an arse, what can I say?'

'So what's wrong?' P asked. 'Or is this just a social call out of boredom?'

'No. I'm in the forest. Listen . . .'

And he embarked on a long story, starting with a couple of werewolves seeing something strange in the dark. Then an encounter Sage had had that morning at a river's edge between witches, werewolves and a mysterious black fog. By the time he described his arrival and a witch with a missing arm, all Hozier's food was discarded and forgotten as they both gazed in horror at the phone.

'Just . . . gone?' P repeated slowly.

'Gone,' Oren repeated. 'Clean off. Just dripping blood all

over the floor.'

'What the hell was it?' Hozier demanded. 'I've never heard of anything like it. Have you, Oren?'

'No,' he agreed. 'I have no clue what it is. Whether it's a sentient being in itself, or is it, I don't know, being sent to do someone else's bidding?'

'But what?' Hozier frowned. 'Surely that's old magic? A one-off creature? I can't think of any modern magic that's even remotely similar.'

'Perhaps,' Oren agreed. 'If it is, that means I can't just kill it. Well, I can, but you know. It'll come back.'

'Though it becomes a problem for another decade,' Hozier pointed out. 'Maybe even century.'

'That's true.'

P wasn't sure what they were talking about. But it was rare for Oren and Hozier to be on the same wavelength like this, so she let it carry on uninterrupted.

'That could explain why we've never heard of it,' Hozier hummed thoughtfully. 'If it was killed, went . . . wherever they go for a few centuries, and has only just resurfaced? That'd explain why we've never encountered it before.'

'That was my thought process,' Oren agreed. 'But that means someone killed it once, right?'

'Right?' Hozier sounded like she wasn't sure exactly what he was getting at.

'Then there has to be a record somewhere. If not in the

archives, then perhaps in the libraries across Downside. P. You've never failed yet. Can you help?'

Hozier's eyes met hers. 'Up for the challenge?'

25

P

Hours later, P was annoyed.

She'd been to the central library in Downside. She'd combed all the sections on the known creatures of old magic. She'd looked up fog, mist, steam and smoke. She knew that she needed more time, but there weren't even any early indications of direction. Nothing that sounded *anything* like what Oren had described.

And the problem with old magic was that each creature was individual. It wasn't like a whole race of werewolves or warlocks or whatever else: an entire group that shared the same traits and limitations. Old magic was mysterious. Dark. It could be anything. Do anything. If it wasn't one of the most famous or notorious creatures of old like the Baba Yaga or Medusa, who knew what it was and whether anyone had made a record of it at all.

Downside libraries were archives of a sort, but they recorded . . . everything. Every story. Every detail. Everything that wasn't what she was looking for, that she had to sift through at the same time. She needed something like the Arcānum's archive, where specific incidents were logged. That would help her narrow the search. But Hozier's archive only contained Downside. Not the whole of the supernatural world.

She threw herself back down on the sofa in a huff. Then immediately sat up, the lightbulb of an idea blinking away.

But . . . should she? Could she?

She picked up her laptop and tapped a few keys to light the screen. She googled the time difference. Three hours ahead. She looked at the time in the top corner of the screen. Four-thirty. Kane had told her he worked in a bank, and surely bankers got up early to go to work, right?

Seven-thirty? Was that too early?

Kane had taken her phone number before he'd left a couple of days ago, with the promise to keep in touch. She'd seen his disappointment that Oren had left without even saying goodbye, and had held out this olive branch so that he went away feeling like there was something to show for his efforts. Even if contact was only ever going to be through her.

Just as he'd said he would, he'd texted her a picture of the Eiffel Tower that night, all lit up and glittering. They'd exchanged a few messages and the next evening, from the airport, he'd sent her pictures of everything he'd eaten at two different restaurants that day. She hadn't even asked. But she'd secretly been thrilled he'd realized even from their briefest of meetings that this was what she was going to be most interested in.

So . . . were they friendly enough for her to ask a massive favour?

She flicked through her phone, clicked 'call' and listened to the tone connect.

It rang and rang; maybe it was too early, or maybe he hadn't saved her number either and hadn't recognized it. She tried not to feel too disappointed.

She clicked off with a sigh. Maybe if she texted him and he had the time to help, he could call her back later. She'd just started to type when the phone started to buzz in her hands.

'P?' That familiar – very sexy-accented – voice came through the speaker. 'Is everything OK?'

She was surprised to find he sounded concerned. Maybe the early call out of nowhere did look like an emergency. But he did know it was her, so at least he'd saved her contact. She grinned.

'Oh! Yes, Kane, of course, everything is fine. I'm sorry if my call startled you!'

Why were her cheeks burning?

She kinda wished she'd FaceTimed, so if he'd FaceTimed back she could get a sneaky look at that face, so like Oren's but more bearded and . . . less cold.

He breathed a sigh of relief and chuckled. 'Only because it's so early!'

'I hoped you might be getting up for work.' She tried to make sure she sounded guilty.

'It's my day off,' he admitted. She cringed. 'But you weren't to know that. So what's up? You know I'm not in Paris any more, I can't order certain dishes for the pictures on request, I'm afraid.'

Oh my God, P. Stop it. She could feel the girly giggle rising up her throat.

She cleared it.

She told him everything she could. About what Sage and Oren had found in the mountains, and about the fog. About how badly she was doing. Her first big research failure.

'It's only been one night, P!' He laughed. 'It's a little early to call it a failure.'

'I'm not used to it taking this long to find out one piece of information,' she admitted. 'I don't sleep, do I? I have all the time in the world.'

'Never?'

She shook her head. Then remembered he couldn't see her. 'I don't even get tired.'

'Wow.' And as if on cue, he stifled his own yawn. She cringed again.

'The reason I rang . . . well, you live in Al-Khazneh, don't you? Where Oren is from?'

'And you want me to look in the archives here?' he guessed correctly.

The Stone City, as it was otherwise known, was the oldest supernatural city in the world. The capital city, where the Elders who ruled over them all resided. It was the one place Oren swore he'd never return to. The reason he'd allowed Roderick to pretend to have control over him for all these years: to avoid the Elders and their orders. He'd sworn his vow of lifetime service to the Cariva, the elite assassins who answered to nobody else, at a very young age, and that vow could not be broken. But service was service, and they allowed him to stay where he was as long as he at least served something. Oren had chosen the Arcānum – the lower-ranking police force. And he'd had to agree to accept Cariva orders if there was ever a case so severe that only he could deal with it quickly and efficiently. He'd told P that they'd only asked him three times in the last eighty years.

One of those times had been Amhuinn and MacAllister: the extermination of their magical hybrid wolves.

The archives in the Stone City were unrivalled. Endless and ancient. They didn't just record their city, they recorded the world. If this fog was recorded somewhere, it was there. Honestly, it would be her dream to see it.

For now, she would have to settle for seeing it through Kane's eyes. She didn't think Oren would take her there any time soon.

'I know it's a big ask,' she breathed.

He whistled. 'You have no idea.' She cringed a third time. 'But it is my day off. I can have a look, but I can't make any promises. Like you, I might need longer than a night.'

That's all she could ask for. She told him exactly what

she was looking for while he noted it down.

'Thank you so much,' she gushed, relieved. 'You'll be a massive help to them.'

'And what about you?' he asked. 'Are you OK? Is it quiet with them gone?'

She blinked. She realized nobody really asked her that any more. As a ghost, she guessed most people assumed she was always OK, because what could hurt her now? Sage asked her. But for now, she was gone.

'Hozier's staying, just until they get back.' She slumped back on the sofa again, putting her feet on the coffee table, even though she'd flay Oren or Sage alive if they dared do the same. But her feet wouldn't dirty it. 'She's still in bed. It's not even five a.m. here.'

'Sounds exhausting.' She could hear him smiling.

She smiled too. 'I don't like it when it's too quiet,' she admitted. 'I like noise. And Sage and Oren winding each other up provides enough of that.'

He chuckled, then he sounded more sombre. 'I can't imagine Oren allowing anyone to wind him up. Let alone entertaining it.'

She sighed sadly. She couldn't help feeling sorry for him. 'He . . . can be quite good fun, in fact.'

'I suppose we'll have to agree to disagree,' he said after a pause.

'I suppose we will.'

'I'll call you tonight with anything I find?'

'Thank you.'

When the call ended, she shook her head, embarrassed at how girly and giggly she felt.

26

SAGE

Oren had come home an hour after Sage had got back and she couldn't scent anything on him. No perfume – or anyone else at all, in fact. She'd refused to ask him again where he'd been. His obnoxious smirk would only make her want to punch him.

She knew she'd spent her evening with Gabriel, but at least she would be honest if he asked her. And they'd only ended up alone because of the argument in the food hall. P would tell her she sounded like she was making excuses, and she couldn't be mad if *he* was with someone if she was out with Gabriel, but . . .

Whatever.

She still felt annoyed.

So she'd stayed in her bedroom and pretended to be asleep.

Then made sure to hammer on his door at six the next morning as the watery spring sunlight crept over the treetops, and remind him of his promise to take her out to visit those coordinates Hozier had sent over.

They shifted out to a spot surrounded by trees, thicker than anything around the wolf camps. The canopy overhead was so dense that their surroundings were still dark and gloomy, despite the time of day. The floor sloped upwards, the ground was covered in knotted roots, ivy, moss, and other bracken and brambles.

'Up or down?' Oren asked.

'That way.' She pointed up. The higher they were, the more they could see.

'If it looked like this seventy years ago, it's a miracle she was found at all,' Oren grumbled as he tugged on a vine that was trapped around his ankle.

She *hmm*ed in agreement, shivering. The lack of sunlight made the air cold. 'How far do you think we are from the nearest camp?'

He paused to turn and look around, and then a map was in his hand again. He shrugged. 'If the packs are all as equally spaced out as the Dubois and Monreau, I'd say . . . twenty kilometres, maybe?'

'Gabriel admitted last night that this missing witch is the reason they believe they're being cursed—'

'Of course he did,' Oren muttered, his eyes rolling. 'But we know it's not a curse. That's their paranoia. There's a long-standing grudge and in the face of some unexplained bad fortune, they've assumed it's the witches taking revenge at last.'

'Yeah,' she agreed. 'She was found beaten on the wolf

side of the river. Gabriel said there were rumours, but they never found a definitive culprit.'

Oren sighed heavily through his nose. 'Well, at least it all makes a bit more sense now.'

She nodded. 'We still can't deny that something is going on here, Oren. Sure, you were right, there's no witch curse. But unless we can figure out why crops are dying, and livestock are getting sick, and everything else, this won't end. The wolves will keep on believing there's a curse no matter what rationale we present.'

He nodded too, though it was resentful. 'We do still have to find out what's going on,' he agreed. 'But I don't know, Sage. There's so much animosity here, so much underlying history, most of it bad, that I don't know if we will ultimately fix anything at all. Both sides of the river will still go on hating each other. There will always be a tension, of sorts.'

'Well . . . that's why we're here,' she admitted. He gave her a look. Once again understanding her without even having to speak. 'Please, Oren,' she said. 'Let me try. Just on the side, it won't interfere with our real job here.'

'Sage,' he said quietly. And he closed the gap between them in three steps until he was right in front of her. He pushed a wisp of her hair behind her ear. 'You don't need my permission for anything. I'm your partner, not your boss. And there's nothing wrong with wanting to give a mother some peace,' he said. 'If you want to figure out what happened to Kalinka, then try. But be aware, it could fix something – or it could make everything worse. Consider very carefully the risk.'

'I know,' she said. 'Maybe I'll just make some small enquiries for now, and then back off if it looks—'

It happened so quickly that she didn't even see Oren move as he threw a golden shield around them.

'What the—'

The foliage ahead of them started to shudder and vibrate. And whatever was disturbing it was travelling at an alarming speed and coming towards them. She acknowledged that Oren did her the courtesy of not pushing her behind him, even though a small dagger had appeared in his hand.

Then he groaned in a way that said he knew what it was.

'What is it?' she whispered as it got closer.

Twenty paces now.

Fifteen paces.

'Bergsmed.'

'What was that?'

'It means *mountain smith*. They're usually found across Scandinavia. But they've been known to travel further afield, and we're not far from the Swiss border.'

'Oh. And are they . . . safe?'

Ten paces.

Oren's only answer was to lower the shield to their knees.

Then everything went still.

'Hello?' she ventured uncertainly. 'Are you still there?'

No answer. She looked at Oren, confused, but he simply tapped his ear with a finger.

She tuned in her wolf ears, and listened again.

And yes, there it was. Faint, but it was chatter. Whispers. Tiny voices. It wasn't in a language she understood, and she was quite sure too that it wasn't the French she'd become accustomed to hearing around the Dubois camp.

'My name is Sage,' she tried again. 'We're not here to harm you.'

Another beat, and then a head popped out of the ivy.

She blinked.

It was the ugliest thing she had ever seen.

It reminded her of the pukwudgie outside his joke shop back in Downside. A bent old man, but even smaller, with a beard so long he'd braided it and wrapped it around his head like a hat. His skin was grey and wrinkled and sagging, and he wore only a pair of brown leather shorts roughly sewn together and fraying at the hems. In his hand was a tiny pickaxe. The topmost point of his considerable beard-hat came to just under her knees.

He said something in that same language, deep and guttural. It was clear the tiny man was shouting up at her, yet for all his effort, he still sounded quite quiet.

'Do you speak English?' she asked uncertainly.

'Even if he could, he'd refuse,' Oren tutted. 'Bergsmed

are stubborn. And proud. If he understands what you say in English, he will still answer in Bergsmouth.'

The dagger evaporated from his hand, and he flicked a finger. A trail of golden mist floated to her face and welded itself to her ears and lips. She jerked back instinctively.

Oren gave her an exasperated look, and shot a tendril of the same magic into his own face to make a point.

She blinked. 'What does this do?'

'Translates.'

Was he telling her that they were staying in a place where English was not their first language, and he hadn't decided to get this party trick out at any point?

He shrugged.

'Who are you?' she could hear the bergsmed spokesman shouting.

She introduced them, and now as she spoke she could see her breath, like the fog that comes on a very cold winter morning, only this time it was shimmering gold. Whatever the tiny creature heard, he understood.

She heard more muttered whispers and knew there were more hidden out of sight. The dwarf disappeared back into the ivy to confer with them.

Oren shifted his weight, and thrust his hands into his pockets, bored.

But when the bergsmed reappeared, he brought more with him, their heads popping up one by one. Some wore their beards like hats too. And some wore them wrapped around their bodies like clothes. One had his stuffed into a satchel slung across his chest.

Then they did something else she didn't expect. They clambered on to each other's shoulders. Tier by tier, up and up, the structure grew, until they'd formed a living, breathing pyramid. And then they started to heft something else up there. A delicately carved, albeit tiny, wooden, throne-like chair, which was then rested, a leg each, on the shoulder of the four bergsmed at the top.

She watched, bemused, as one last bergsmed scrambled up, propelling himself higher and higher, stepping on the shoulders of all the dwarfs below him, until he settled himself on the throne, his face level with Oren's.

He looked no different to the others – at least, she couldn't see anything that particularly singled him out as more important than the rest of them. His beard was braided and wrapped around his neck like a scarf, and he too wore only a pair of shabby leather shorts.

'We felt the vibrations of your footsteps.' He looked between them. 'Nobody has walked over our tunnels in decades. The Arcānum has not been here for nearly a century.'

They were brave, she conceded, for creatures so small, to come out and confront them so readily. And she wagered that here might be one of the very few places left on this earth that had never heard of Oren Rinallis.

'I'm looking into an incident that took place here nearly

seventy years ago,' she told them. 'Or nearby. Involving a missing witch. We were told this is roughly the area where she was found. Do your people have any memory of this? Of a search?'

She had no idea the lifespan of bergsmed, or indeed whether there were any who would remember it.

The bergsmed leader frowned. And then as quickly as the pyramid had been constructed, it started to dismantle itself.

'Oh,' she stammered. 'No, please, wait—'

But they were already back under the foliage, and she could hear them whispering between themselves again. She looked at Oren again, bewildered. He seemed entirely unsurprised.

Then, discussions apparently over, the pyramid began to rebuild.

'Uh . . .' She watched the throne ascend again, but this time, a second bergsmed clambered to the top alongside the original spokesman, who settled himself back down on his little throne. 'You don't have to . . . I can kneel?' she offered, somewhat lamely.

The bergsmed was utterly disgusted. 'A king will not be looked or spoken down upon,' he told her. 'You will look me in the eye or not at all.'

Oren suggested he could do something else under his breath.

'This is,' and he made a sound that she knew she would

never be able to repeat. Whatever the name of this second creature was would forever remain a mystery. 'We know the story of which you speak.'

'Great—'

'For a price. A gift for a gift.'

Her heart sank. What did they have to offer that these strange little creatures would want?

Oren waved a hand, and then in it was a Swiss army knife, and with another puff of gold, it shrank down to half its size. He offered it to her. 'See what they think.'

'Um.' She pulled out one tool to show them – a screwdriver end. That didn't look too enticing, so she pulled out another, a small saw. 'Lots of . . . things in one place.'

The second bergsmed, who had scrambled to the top of the pyramid with the king, took it and started to pull out all the different tools. He looked at his king and nodded enthusiastically. He was happy with the exchange.

Thank God. She'd thank Oren for his quick thinking later.

'I was on guard duty the day a witchling passed through here. And her companion.'

'Her companion?' she asked. The bergsmed frowned at her. 'Sorry,' she said, gesturing for him to carry on.

'Another female. We stopped them not far from here. We patrol a few kilometres' circumference from the entrance to our tunnels.'

'Another witch?' Oren asked.

The bergsmed shrugged. 'We didn't know or care what either of them were as long as they didn't try to enter our tunnels. We only learnt that one was a witch after, when a search was underway in the area by her kin.'

'Can you remember what the other one looked like, the other female?'

He shrugged again. 'Brown hair.'

Unhelpful.

'We felt the vibrations of some commotion through the earth less than a day after we had spoken with the pair. And then all went quiet. By the time they found her two days beyond that, she was still alive. We could feel her breathing. It made the ground below where she lay hum. We don't know what happened to her after that. Or where her companion went.'

Her breath caught in her throat. She didn't understand what she was hearing.

'The commotion, the one right after you spoke to the pair?'

'Screams. Thuds. We felt the ground shake. It felt like when two wild beasts are fighting for scraps.'

She stared at Oren. He looked back at her grimly.

'And you didn't think to go and help her, if she lay there for two days after?' she asked.

'Not our business. Not our problem. We have work to do.'

'What work is it that you do?'

'We tunnel,' he said simply. 'We smith. We dig.'

He offered no further explanation. Why did ants tunnel through dirt? It was just what they did, she supposed.

She nodded. 'Thank you for your time.'

And as quickly as they had come, they disappeared. One Swiss army knife richer, they dismantled their pyramid once more, and in a rustling of bushes they left, vanishing back down into their holes.

She stared at Oren. 'Did that just happen?'

He scoffed. The gold around his ears and lips dissipated, and she guessed her own did too. 'Weird little creatures. They mind their own business. You won't ever get much help from a bergsmed.'

'The companion, though?' she asked.

He nodded slowly. 'That is interesting.' He thought about it. 'Keep it to yourself for now,' he suggested. 'Likely a second witch. And if so, why didn't she tell the coven what happened?'

27

SAGE

When they shifted back into their cabin, they found a note on the small table in the living area. It wasn't signed, but something about the angry, hard capitals pressed so hard they indented the paper suggested to Sage that the author was Benoît.

It told them to meet Celeste in the hall at their earliest convenience.

So they did. And she was surprised to find not just Celeste and Benoît, but a decent-sized gathering of wolves in the hall, faces full of frowns, and some passing looks of concern.

'This doesn't look good,' she muttered to Oren as they crossed the varnished floor towards the crowd. Gabriel smiled a small greeting. She smiled back. And saw Patrice roll his eyes at the exchange.

'Ah.' Celeste spotted them. She said something to the crowd around her, and it started to disperse until only she, Benoît and Gabriel were left.

'A messenger arrived about forty minutes ago. I took the

message for you,' she said apologetically. 'But your cabin was empty, and they had a long journey back around the Bassett and Egli land.'

'A messenger?' Sage repeated. 'From where?'

'The Meute de Garnier has reported a black fog seeping out of one of their outbuildings. It was spotted by the early shift heading to milk their dairy cows,' Celeste said. 'They didn't even know about the fog, or anything that happened yesterday, but they were so alarmed they sent word. Like Patrice, they thought it was a curse sent by the witches.'

'Did it touch anyone?' Oren asked sharply. 'Any injuries?'

Celeste shook her head. 'I was already heading towards Egli land by the time they got there. But all the milk they had stored in that building ready to be churned for cheese had soured. Every last drop. Nearly a hundred churns.'

She looked at Oren. He nodded grimly. If it was spoiling milk, it could wilt crops. Could it also make livestock poorly, or unsettle them enough to stop producing milk altogether? Probably. It felt like a sickness. A disease. A darkness that consumed anything it passed over.

This was it. It was their curse. Not a witch curse. But the fog was the thing causing all of their problems. She was almost relieved. Relieved it wasn't a separate issue they had to solve before they could ever go back home.

'I want any sightings reported to me immediately,' Oren said. 'Time. Location. Map reference, if possible. I'll shift straight there. I need to see how it reacts to my magic first.

Then we can figure out how it can be contained, if at all.'

'We were just organizing messengers as you arrived. To the other packs. To warn them to keep clear if they see it and report any sightings.' Celeste gestured towards the doors the other wolves had just left through. 'And Gabriel has assigned extra guard patrols.'

Gabriel nodded curtly. 'I've doubled the numbers at the river and at the border crossing, and extra patrols up and down the border lines. There are extra eyes out there now. We'll see it if it comes back in daylight.'

'But not in darkness,' Benoît cut in. 'I suggest a curfew. Inside cabins, doors locked by nightfall for everyone who doesn't need to be outside.'

Celeste nodded her agreement. 'Go spread word. Curfew starts tonight. Nine-thirty p.m.'

As Benoît left the hall, Sage wasn't entirely sure locked doors would make any difference. But she didn't think it was worth saying it out loud.

'You said it was headed for Egli land?' Oren asked.

'Yes,' Celeste said. 'They won't report anything even if they do see it. But we've sent a messenger that way regardless. And they won't let you search their land.'

'Oh, they will,' Oren growled. 'Once I've paid them a visit.'

Sage looked at him, startled. Not because he planned to visit a pack. But she knew that tone of voice. It was the Oren he never brought home. It was the cruel, arrogant Oren who issued execution orders, and knew how clean wounds made with a blade looked.

'You stay here.' He gave her a look when she opened her mouth. 'I need to search the whole land, and I'll move quicker in shifts.'

She knew that was an excuse. She knew he just didn't want her to see him become the monster he had to be to instil fear. The person he was grateful to not have to be in front of her and P. And it was only because of that that she relented.

'I've got some paperwork to do anyway,' she said. When he smiled back, she knew that he understood that meant probably calling P to chat.

Back outside the hall, Gabriel sighed. 'How do you contain a fog?'

She shook her head. She had no idea. She knew Oren would say that if it couldn't be contained, then it would have to be killed. But she didn't think telling him that would make Gabriel warm to her partner.

She'd decided to walk down to the river with him. He was about to start a morning patrol shift, but it was something to do until Oren returned. She'd be able to make her own way back and chat to P on her way.

'So, dinner tonight?'

'I'm not sure I'm welcome in that dinner hall,' she huffed as they made their way between the trees. 'Not after last night. And we'll break curfew eating anywhere else.'

'We'll sit in a corner.' He nudged her shoulder with his. 'Come on.'

'I'll think about—'

He put a hand on her arm, and groaned.

They'd cleared the last few trees before the land dipped down towards the riverbank and, yep, there, at the water's edge, was a group of the border guards who'd just been in the hall with them.

At least eight wolves – the old guard and the new who'd just arrived to relieve them.

'What is this?' Gabriel demanded, hurrying down the bank and pushing his way to the front.

Across the river a couple of witches stood watching, but their ringleader, the argumentative blonde witch, Louise, she was on *their* side of the river, on the werewolf bank, long talons already sprouted from her fingertips. A redhead was beside her, a warning arm on her shoulder, but her expression was livid too.

Patrice was hissing furiously, and a few other werewolves she didn't know by name were hurling insults. This was about to descend into chaos, and quickly.

'Enough!' She rounded on the gathered wolves, forcing herself between them all, and held up her hands. 'This ends, now!'

The witch behind her laughed. 'Why? Someone like *you* would never side with us—'

But you know what, she'd had enough of hurled accusations.

The wolves had already turned on her for *not* siding with them. She couldn't win either way, could she? Blood thundered through her ears. Slowly, she turned to the witches, pointing a finger at them. And she could see her own claws starting to grow from her nail bed. A small droplet of blood dripped to the floor.

'Be very careful,' she breathed.

She could feel her wolf sticking her nose towards the surface. Had to force her back down.

'We have been more than fair since we got here. We tried to work *with* you. You weren't interested in even a conversation.'

Another werewolf shouted something else, but she didn't understand it. The witch did, though, and her cheeks started to blotch. Whatever was said wasn't helping. But she knew she had to hold her nerve or lose any remaining credibility. Even as her heart felt like it was about to fall out of her chest, she refused to let any of them see it.

Yet . . . she didn't know what to do next.

And this was exactly how Roderick had expected her to fail.

She knew how Oren would deal with it.

He'd threaten both sides into submission and not care what either thought. But she didn't have the raw power to back it up. She had nothing but words. And both sides had talons and claws and magic.

'I thought your witch mother commanded that you don't cross the waters,' she said. 'Why are you on this side?'

'Rules change.' The witch shrugged. 'We can cross now, if we think there is a threat to our safety. Say, if we think we see a dark fog and need to flee?'

And there it was. An easy excuse. One they'd twisted to their advantage as soon as Patrice and his cabal had provoked them.

'Well, I see no fog now.' She looked around pointedly. 'So go home.' She turned to the crowd behind her. 'You too. Disappear.'

None of them answered her. All of them were staring at her hand. Claw tipped and dripping with blood. She grimaced. She'd lost her temper, and they could see she'd nearly transformed. That wasn't professional at all.

'Now,' she repeated. And hoped to God she sounded like she had even a scrap of authority.

There were a few uncomfortable glances. Nostrils flared. But bodies did start to move, to turn back in the direction of home. She let out the breath she'd been holding.

Then a few eyes went wide. And she knew.

Whatever was going on behind her, it wasn't good.

She barely heard the sound of the footfalls, but as she turned to look, three more witches who had been watching were now landing next to their sisters. She hadn't realized they were able to jump the whole distance. Had no idea just how easy it was without their witch mother's command holding them back.

Snarls erupted.

As did more talons from the tips of the witches' fingers.

The red-headed witch tipped her head back and let out a high-pitched cry, shrill and as bone-chilling as a magpie's. And then it was almost drowned out by the ripping flesh and cracking bones that was the sound of transforming werewolves.

Memories of that nightmare night last year came flooding back. The terror. For the second time in her life she was surrounded by furious werewolves, and once again, Oren wasn't there.

'No!' she screamed, holding up her hands again. She looked desperately to Gabriel, the only one besides herself who hadn't transformed. He was yelling too, putting himself in front of the wolves closest to him, but they were already snapping dripping, furious maws.

A black wolf dived, and so did the witches. And a flash of terror rippled through her as talons slashed, and red blood sprayed. More fur moved as they lunged for his rescue, and more witches jumped the river. Witch blood sprayed too, and suddenly, the air was thick with screams and howls.

'You need to transform,' Gabriel breathed, dragging her out of the way of the bodies hurling themselves at each other. 'It's not safe as a human, not now.'

'No.' She struggled from his grasp.

'You stand a better chance—'

But whatever he thought she stood a better chance of didn't matter, as her vision was obscured by more red mist, and she felt the razor-hot burn of something sharp raking down the side of her face, nicking on the curve of her ear. Everything seemed to slow as the force of the blow took a few moments to register. She saw Gabriel's face distort in horror, and then fury. But she didn't even need to turn to see who had sought her out.

She knew.

And she felt *her* then. Properly. The wolf. Not roused from a slumber, groggy and irritable. But awoken with a jolt of rage. She turned to face the blonde witch just as she resolved to let *it* out of her cage at last. Like she had done to Flora back in Downside. Because she was going to *skin* this bitch alive. And this time, Oren wasn't there to stop her.

The witch was grinning ear to ear as she raised her hand covered in blood, and licked it clean off her nails.

Sage snarled. The first bone in her neck cracked. Her spine started to shudder. This witch would probably kill her. Would definitely kill her. But she would do what she could to take her with her.

Howls echoed around them. And more magpie-like screeches. She could hear the footsteps of more bodies arriving. Werewolf and witch. More joining the fight.

And then there was a bang.

So loud the floor shook beneath her feet.

So loud she yelped out in shock.

She didn't see him arrive, and she didn't see him move. She didn't see the weapon explode from his hand, or see it swing.

All she knew was that where the witch had been standing moments before, now she was on the floor screaming, the back of her dress ripped wide open and a deep, dark gash exposing the bone of her spine.

Oren Rinallis stood over her, the golden mist of his shifting floating away on the soft breeze, the sword in his hand dripping with black witch blood. The rage was real.

Her bones clicked back into place as her own wolf hid from the sight of him, and the white-hot fury radiating off him in pulses.

He didn't even breathe as he stood there, glaring at the witch he'd floored with a single blow. She'd wondered what he really looked like in those moments he could barely bring himself to talk about. She'd imagined it. But she'd never really understood.

Oren's head rose slowly, his eyes landing on her. Assessing her face. Taking in the blood she could feel rolling down her neck.

Then she realized nobody else around them was moving. Not just a pause in the fighting to see what was happening; once again he'd used his magic to freeze them mid-lunge, mid-bite, mid-attack. Every single one of them other than her, Gabriel and the blonde witch at his feet.

'Get up,' he said quietly.

It took her a second to realize he was talking to the witch. She didn't, but it wasn't for lack of trying. Her shaking arms tried, but between the whispers and the blood oozing from her shredded back, she couldn't.

'Get up,' he repeated.

'Oren,' Sage said. 'Don't.'

His eyes didn't even flicker in her direction.

He turned instead to look at the crowd still frozen around them.

'The next time something like this happens,' he raised the bloodied weapon for them all to see, 'every single one of you will die. From both sides. No matter who started it.'

Silence. He must've frozen even their mouths.

'Out of respect for my partner, I have stood back and watched her try and keep the peace between pack and coven with honest intentions. Today, because of this, that changes.' He turned to look down on the witch, who had managed to roll over on to her side to gaze up at Oren with pain-filled eyes. 'It is out of respect for her compassion that you still have your head,' he said softly. 'The next time Arcānum blood is spilt I will walk into the offending pack or coven and remove it from existence. From the young to the old. I swear it to whatever gods you worship. Not one of you will survive me.'

She didn't think the witch could do much more than whimper.

He stared at her for a moment longer.

And then she noticed movement. The witches at least had begun to move again.

'Take her home,' he told the women who moved on unsteady legs as the feeling returned to their limbs. 'Take her now and get out of my sight, before I change my mind. Warn your witch mother, I had better not see her face at this water's edge again.'

They didn't need telling twice. Nine in total made to leave: four of them running forward to lift the blonde witch so that they half-carried, half-dragged her back through the water to their side of the river. And even as they disappeared into the trees on the other side, she could still hear the cries and whimpers of her pain.

When the sound died out at last Oren's sword evaporated again, and he strode through the blood at his feet to inspect Sage's face.

She could see the panic behind his impenetrable wall as his fingers, ever surprising for their gentleness, cupped her face and turned it to the side.

'What about—' Gabriel started, gesturing to his pack still frozen mid-fight around them.

'Don't' – Oren snapped, then caught himself – 'even speak,' he finished quietly.

'Oren,' she said again.

'No, Sage.' She could feel his fingers shaking as he forced himself to control the urge to lunge for the werewolf. 'You were in his care.'

'Imagine a scenario in which I didn't need a carer,' she hissed. 'I certainly didn't ask for one.'

'Yeah,' he retorted furiously. 'Imagine that. I think it would look like our home: somewhere we weren't stuck because our captain wants you dead. But here we are, Sage, so forgive me for trying to minimize the possibility.' He saw her expression and relented . . . slightly. 'I know you don't need a carer. But Roderick sent you here because he knew it could be *this* dangerous. I'm not giving him the satisfaction of letting you die.'

'Only because you want to avoid a shitload of paper-work,' she snapped.

'Exactly.' He let go of her face at last. Inspection apparently complete. 'I can heal this when we get back.'

'I can take her to the medical—'

'I think you've done enough.' Oren didn't even look at Gabriel. He turned to the remaining werewolves. 'If you think any of what I just said was a show in front of those witches, try me.'

The magic disappeared, and limbs began to move again.

Oren looked at Gabriel at last. 'Close this down. Now.'

Before Gabriel could answer, he put an arm around her shoulder and guided her out of the clearing back towards their cabin.

28

OREN

The healing took longer than expected. He'd had her lie down, her head resting on a cushion on top of his lap as he slowly pinched and fused her skin back together, trying not to lose his still-short temper with her hair.

Why had he never realized how thick it was? And why did she have so bloody much of it?

He hadn't even said goodbye to Sacha Monreau when he'd felt her flash of pain and anger. He'd shifted through three or four likely places until he'd found her at the river's edge, and saw the blood running down her face.

At once he'd been transported back to those moments of soul-crushing terror as she'd lain on the floor of that storage room, blood pouring from her chest.

All his nightmares came back to haunt him.

He'd numbed the pain so Sage wouldn't feel any of his tugs at her skin and sent a soothing wave of warmth down her body, and within twenty minutes she'd dozed off. He coated her with more magic, sent her into such a deep sleep that she wouldn't wake again until she was fully rested. It'd be at least a few hours.

Good.

He didn't want her to see how angry he still was.

He wished P were there. She'd understand everything he was hiding from Sage.

He'd call her when he was done. Magic Sage into bed and call P and tell her everything. He was just mulling over whether the whole thing might actually scare her when there was a light knock on the front door of their cabin.

He expected that Gabriel would turn up at some point to try and apologize, or at least see how she was. But he wasn't in the mood.

He was about to say so when he looked up and saw it was Celeste, not her son, in the doorway.

'How is she?' the alpha asked, closing the door behind her.

He knew the matted blood in her hair and still crusting across her skin looked bad.

'She'll be back to normal by this evening.' He forced himself to sound even. 'My magic will ensure she's fully rested.'

'She's lucky the hair will cover most of the scarring,' Celeste said. 'That'll leave quite a mark.'

He huffed under his breath. 'You haven't seen her chest scar.'

Celeste blinked, confused. 'No?'

'She was stabbed, the evening of the last moon ball, by a blade made of silver. Right in her chest. The scar is . . . something to behold.' Celeste looked faint when he glanced up at her silence. 'It's black,' he explained. 'With shoots branching off, like small forks of lightning across her chest.'

'And it was you who saved her from this?' He understood why she sounded so perplexed. It was impossible for a wolf to survive that kind of injury. Or so the world thought, so he had thought, until that night.

At first he didn't answer. Their story wasn't any of her business. But this wasn't just his story, was it? And he knew that Sage didn't keep her entire life a secret like him.

So he nodded. 'As far as we can tell, she's the only known survivor of a silver wounding.'

'I was told you were a monster, you know,' she said after a while.

'Oh, I am,' he replied softly. He didn't look up.

'Then why do you repeatedly save her? Find yourself a stronger warlock to work with. One who'll last longer. Let her live out her life peacefully.'

'Where? Here?' He couldn't help his lip start to curl into a sneer. 'What exactly is it that you see her as?' he asked. 'A damsel? My prisoner? What if I told you she stays with me out of choice? What if I told you she sees herself as my equal?'

Celeste's expression didn't flicker. She knew what he meant. 'She's not a monster.'

'No,' he agreed. 'She isn't.'

He was still waiting for her to figure that out. For all that grief and self-loathing to realize her sins could never outshine his.

'And the stories. They didn't change her mind about you?'

'She knows other stories too.'

'I can see that.' So this was the reason she'd come, to assess the truth of their partnership – whether their bond was real or obligation. She was quiet again for a moment, then said, 'I'm happy to assign a set of guards to follow wherever she goes. Older wolves, who can be trusted not to be goaded. Would this be something you're interested in?'

'That would surely irk some of the other alphas if she appeared to need a guard to enter their land,' he pointed out.

'Gabriel told me what . . . warnings were given today, and I see clearly that you meant every word.' She looked down at Sage again. 'Despite any tension between the packs in this mountain, I would not see any of them obliterated. I offer this for as much for their safety as for hers.'

He bowed his head, the closest he would get to thanking anyone. 'She won't accept. And I won't force her.'

Celeste nodded again. She still didn't move.

His brow twitched. 'What else is it you really want to say, Celeste?'

He watched her throat bob. 'Gabriel tells me that Sage nearly transformed down by the river.'

He knew that. He'd turned up just in time to put a stop to it.

But that . . . that wasn't what she meant. Something else had happened before he'd arrived and Gabriel had spotted it. She'd *partially* transformed. He could see it in the carefully controlled expression on her face. He glanced at Sage's hands; there, just on the tips of her fingers, was dried blood. She'd grown claws.

And they'd all seen it. The supposed impossible.

He knew he'd have to be careful here. So careful.

'Who sired her?' the alpha asked. Just like MacAllister had.

'She doesn't know.' Just like he'd answered the first time.

He knew the next question on her lips, even if she didn't voice it. Did he know?

'The Elders will call for her one day, to get a look at her. The first werewolf in the Arcānum.'

'I know.'

'There is . . . safety in numbers,' Celeste said casually. Too casually. 'Safety here. To anyone who needs it.'

He didn't answer. He wasn't going to admit anything to anyone, despite the fact Celeste knew as blatantly as Michael MacAllister had that something wasn't . . . normal about Sage's wolf. But still, he would remember the offer.

She seemed to know there was no point pushing it, because she shrugged and turned for the door at last. With her hand on the handle she looked back.

'There are three of you, I think she said. There's a ghost too?'

He pulled a considering face. 'Five, I suppose. Two other warlocks who are . . . within their confidence.'

'But not yours?'

'They are within my protection,' he said instead. 'By virtue of their loyalty to Sage and P.'

She looked thoughtful. 'The moon magic that forms the bonds of pack is old magic. Older than yours. It plays by different rules. Ones that sometimes don't make sense, and can't be changed.'

He nodded. 'We have exceptions in the law for it.'

'Not many realize that when one wolf offers the gift of loyalty, it doesn't need to be another wolf that returns it. If the intent is true, if the love is strong enough, the magic ties all those together tightly, no matter the race. So closely you can practically feel each other.' His ears pricked, his attention renewed. 'You become each other. It's almost never seen this way, since wolves so rarely form such tight bonds outside of their own kin. But it has been known to happen.'

'What's your point?'

Celeste shrugged. 'Were you all there the night she was wounded with silver?'

'Yes.'

'Maybe it really was the magic of the most powerful warlock alive that saved her. Or maybe it was the desperation of you five, tied together by the bonds of old moon magic, that willed her to live. I think likely it was the unique combination of both.' Celeste waved it away as if it were a silly thought. 'Who knows, *eh*? But, as they say: the strength of the pack is the wolf. And the strength of the wolf is the pack.'

The lump that rose in his throat as the door clicked shut behind the alpha was unexpected. And it remained there until he had finished healing the wound, and carried Sage to bed. Silently, he leant down and kissed her gently on the forehead. Then he slipped from the cabin into the dense trees, and called P to tell her everything.

29

SAGE

It was dark outside her bedroom window by the time she woke. Her fingers traced the side of her head but . . . nothing. He'd fixed her again. She could hear him moving about, clattering in cupboards, and the soft sizzle of a frying pan.

She sniffed.

Her stomach growled.

He must've shifted out of camp while she slept to buy the bacon she could smell, because they hadn't had any in their fridge that morning. She looked at the little clock on her bedside table. Nearly eight-thirty. She'd slept most of the afternoon.

While she'd acknowledged – and appreciated – that Oren had used his magic to take the blood from her matted hair, he hadn't removed the blood staining the front of her T-shirt. Typical. Berion would've thought to do that for her, and Hozier.

She pulled it off and dragged on an old sweatshirt she usually wore for bed that'd once been his. Then she tied back her hair and went in search of bacon.

'You're not eating in that hall tonight,' was his greeting, barely looking at her as he moved the delicious-smelling meat on to two slices of bread.

For the first time, she didn't want to. She dragged out a chair and sat cross-legged, accepting the plate he handed her with a grateful hum as a knock sounded on their cabin door.

From Oren's growl she knew it was Gabriel. The door opened by itself on a haze of gold to reveal the werewolf standing awkwardly in the doorway, a package in his hand.

'This arrived for you at the boundary gate,' he said, stepping into their little living area and handing her something soft wrapped in brown paper and string.

'What is it?' she asked, confused.

He gestured with a hand to open it, the faint smile on his lips suggesting they wouldn't know until she did. Oren's eyes hadn't moved off Gabriel's face, his cold fury barely under control. Gabriel seemed to think the best course of action was to not look at him at all.

She peeled back the paper to find a folded chequered blanket, beautifully woven in shades of pale and dark blue. It was wrapped in a silk ribbon with a card pushed into the fold. She pulled it out and opened it.

The guard will be doubled on our side of the river. Get well soon.
Sacha Monreau

'My mother went herself, this afternoon, to tell him what happened,' Gabriel said. 'They're the only others bordering the witches, so I think she wanted to make sure they understood.'

What they needed to understand hung in the air between them all. Those threats Oren had made, that he would kill *anyone* who caused trouble like that again. 'I think he wants to make clear he will not cause any trouble for you.'

'Have messages been sent to the other packs?' Oren asked quietly. 'About the extra guard watches?'

'Yes,' Gabriel said curtly, but he didn't take his eyes off Sage. 'They've been instructed to report any sightings of the fog to you immediately.'

Oren's expression was pointed. He looked at Gabriel, and then the door. *You've said what you needed to say. Leave.*

'Sage,' Gabriel said, not moving. 'Can we talk? There's half an hour until curfew.'

She looked up at him, his hazel eyes wide and full of apology. She felt sorry for him.

It hadn't been his fault, it really hadn't. They'd been nowhere near the river and he'd been the only one to try to stop the altercation. The only one who hadn't transformed and who'd stayed human at her side. Oren was just . . . Well, she understood him too.

Why was this all so difficult?

But Gabriel's pleading eyes made her feel worse than Oren's furious ones.

She nodded and began to get up.

Oren stood quicker, and the stare he gave Gabriel said everything even as he said nothing at all.

'Oren!' she hissed. Both men were looking at each other and entirely ignoring her.

'It's OK,' Oren said after what felt like an eternity of silence. 'He understands. Completely.'

They walked through the trees.

Gabriel tried to apologize, but she told him to shut up. There was nothing to apologize for. Apparently, Celeste had forced the truth out, and even though the witches had been the ones to cross the water, it had indeed been Patrice who'd started hurling insults at them first. Still convinced the fog he'd witnessed, that he'd heard had been spotted in neighbouring lands, was a curse sent by the witches.

As punishment, he was dismissed from the guard and placed under house arrest. He would be escorted anywhere he needed to go until she said otherwise, and would have all other privileges confiscated.

If she was honest, she knew they were all just scared of Oren. Had thought they'd known, but hadn't really understood until he'd lost the leash on his temper in front of them. And now they had to look like they were sorry.

She ate her bacon sandwich as they walked, and she

knew without asking that they were heading back to that quiet spot they'd escaped to last night, where they'd eaten their dinner overlooking the mountains.

'I . . . wanted to say that, although it's been short, I've enjoyed this time we've spent together,' Gabriel said, after they'd sat down, and he'd let her digest her food. 'But I think . . . I think it should end.'

She blinked at him, surprised. 'What do you mean?'

It was only that morning he'd been trying to cajole her into dinner with him again.

'My mother assigned me as your guide and, of course, I will still escort you wherever you need to go. But this?' He gestured between them, and then around them. 'Spending time together, chatting, eating dinner, hanging out.' He shrugged. 'I don't think—'

The sinking feeling in her stomach as she watched their budding friendship fizzle out. She knew what this was. He'd told her at the start, hadn't he? *Now I know he isn't your boyfriend and won't behead me for even speaking to you.*

'Gabriel, Oren and I . . . we're not *together* like that.' She refused to acknowledge the feeling in her stomach even saying those words. 'We're not— I don't—'

She didn't even know what she was or wasn't trying to say any more. She was so sick and tired of every confusing, painful feeling. No matter what she felt for Oren, she was still allowed to have other male friends. And Oren would never tell her she couldn't either. Gabriel was wrong.

He looked awkward. 'I don't think any of us realized that your . . . companionship was real, until today.'

'But I told you. When your mother asked if I needed rescuing. You all thought I was lying?'

'We thought, perhaps, you weren't in full control of that decision.'

She could barely contain the snarl that rumbled up her chest, temper flaring as she realized he'd seen her as a pathetic weakling, held against her will, all along. Some poor girl in need of rescuing.

'At the river, he was . . . so *angry*, Sage.' Gabriel looked shocked at the memory of it. 'Not angry at what any of us had done: breaking the rules or starting fights. *Merde*, I think he'd quite like us to fight to the death and rid him of the hassle. No, he was only angry you were hurt. He couldn't take his eyes off you.'

'I'm his partner.' She could feel herself getting more and more annoyed. He was backing her into a corner, making her feel like she had to justify why Oren might care about her.

'I'll be honest and admit that I like spending time with you.' He was looking over her shoulder rather than meet her eye. 'I thought . . . I thought that you'd see that this is where a werewolf is meant to be. I thought that . . . pack loyalty would . . .' For once, it was his cheeks that were starting to burn. But there it was. That old sticking point she hated about pack life. The automatic assumption that they, their alpha, their way of life, was best; nothing else was ever as important. 'I don't know.' He sighed. 'See what happened when it was time for him to leave.'

'Gabriel. I—'

'I heard you in the hall last night too. About where your loyalties lie. I thought that was part of however he'd trapped you. But it became clear today that your loyalty is mutual. Is real. I can see now that I would always be second best.'

'Second best?'

He held up his hands and shook his head. 'When your time here is complete you will go back, with him. And I accept now that this really is your choice.'

She flared up at once. 'Don't say *him* like that, it isn't fair. Downside is my *home*. It's where my friends are, it's where P is. Gabriel, it's where my parents are buried. It's all I have left of them. You think so little of me that the only reason I'd go back is for *a boy*?'

At least he had the grace to look apologetic. He swallowed. 'Then I would still be second best, if I suggested you leave all that behind and settle here.'

Settle there . . . with him? Was that what he was outright saying?

They'd spent time together, and she'd enjoyed it. She really had. And, *fine*, she supposed she liked him enough that had he leant in to kiss her as they'd sat on that cliff edge last night then, yeah, probably, she'd have let him. But as a holiday-romance type thing. A fling. Yes, a distraction. But upending her life and staying here forever was never on the cards. She had told him that.

'I'm sorry.' It was all she could think to say. And she was. She wished they could remain friends, even if she didn't see a future for herself in the mountains.

'There are no hard feelings.' He smiled. 'Goodnight, Sage.'

He walked off, leaving her to stare after him in a daze of confusion that all they'd been building over the past couple of days was over. Another friendship. Gone.

She was grateful Oren wasn't in the cabin when she got back. She slammed the door behind her, threw herself on to her bed and tried not to cry.

30

P

All day Kane had been texting her pictures of the archives in the Stone City.

It was breathtaking. Beautiful. And the ancient building, carved into the stone, was magnificent.

Hozier had asked her more than once why she was smiling into her phone, and when Berion had turned up for dinner, Hozier hadn't been able to contain herself.

She'd told him over her slow-braised lamb shanks that P had been texting a fancy man.

P's face had exploded so badly Berion had exclaimed that her head had gone almost entirely opaque.

She'd refused to answer any more of their questions. Floating back into the kitchen to get more boiled potatoes, but not before snatching up her phone so none of them could sneak a peek.

When Berion had left, and Hozier had finally gone up to bed, she'd called him back at last.

'What time is it there?' he asked.

'Ten-thirty.' She made the quick calculation in her head.

It was gone one in the morning for him. She cringed for the millionth time.

But his voice was still bright and awake, and as she settled on the sofa, leaning back to lie across it, her head propped on some cushions, she barely registered that nearly forty minutes had passed without them even starting to discuss the archives.

They just . . . chatted.

It felt surreal. Outside of her group of friends that mostly consisted of two categories – embarrassed geeky teenagers or centuries-old crime fighters – she'd forgotten what it was like to just chat and laugh with someone who was happy and intelligent and carefree.

'So tell me, the necklace Sage wears,' Kane asked. 'When did Oren give that to her?'

'The moonstone?' P blinked, surprised. 'Why?'

'Humour me.'

'Her birthday, not long before Yuletide.'

'Her *birthday*?' He whistled through his teeth again, but he was laughing. 'Who'd have thought he was capable of being romantic.'

'I don't think so. He told her he found it somewhere or other. It's probably old junk but she still wears it every day.'

'That necklace is a very old family heirloom, P. It once belonged to my grandmother,' Kane told her. 'The last time I saw anyone wearing it was nearly a hundred and fifty years ago. We've believed it to be lost. And yet there it was.

The last place I ever expected to see it – around the neck of a werewolf on the other side of the world. Oren must've taken it with him when he left.'

'What?' Her eyes were wide as she shot upright again. His maternal family. Attaia. Not Rinallis. She knew at once somehow that this was an intentional distinction on Oren's part. A gift that was not a link to the infamous name and everything that came with it. 'Will you tell them?'

'I don't think so,' Kane said thoughtfully. 'He has no sisters to claim it. It was his by rights once Sonja died.'

Sonja Attaia. She'd never heard Oren's mother's name before.

'What was she like?'

'Kind,' Kane said. 'And she loved her son. She was unusually gifted – not many warlocks are skilled at healing anyone but themselves. But Sonja was known for it here in the Stone City. Nursing is not considered a profession for families like . . . Well, warlocks rarely need the services of a hospital, since we can heal ourselves, so she went down into the city to heal other races that did need her help.'

Another titbit of information about the woman Oren had never spoken of. Another piece to his puzzle. It fascinated her. She didn't think Kane even knew that Sonja's son had inherited that gift, so powerful that he'd been able to save Sage from a silver dagger. She'd researched it and couldn't find a single case of a werewolf surviving any injury caused by silver, whether bullet, blade or powder. It was supposed to be impossible.

But somehow, against all the odds and the impossibilities, he'd saved her.

'P?'

'Sorry,' she said quietly. 'I was just . . . thinking about something.'

'It's an unlikely love story, huh?'

'You've got no idea.'

No idea what was to come for those two. Either a life where Sage had to hide forever or face execution, or a life where she would age and die. There were no winners. There was no happy ending.

'What's wrong?' He was perceptive.

'Nothing.' She forced herself to sound brighter, even if she didn't mean it. 'So tell me about your day. Did you find anything?'

'I don't think you're going to like my answer very much.'

She groaned.

'I know.' He sighed. 'Now I know how you felt when you first rang me, eh?'

'So there was nothing?'

She could hear some rustling paper as he looked at some notes. 'Well, I found a kind of mist in the Sahara Desert that eats the flesh of anything it touches. But that's made up of a very specific, carnivorous type of tiny flying carbuncle. And it glows red and green. So . . . not that.'

'Not that,' P agreed.

'And I found one beast called the Vinegaroon. It is old magic. A giant scorpion that sprays an acid-type substance that also dissolves anything it touches. But the records showed the last sighting of that was seventy-six years ago.'

'This isn't good, is it?'

'No,' he agreed. 'But the archives are endless, P. Huge.' He tried to sound encouraging. She smiled. 'I'll go back tomorrow.'

'What about work?'

'I actually have the whole week off after my work trip overseas,' he said sheepishly. 'I didn't want to say in case I didn't like the job you offered me.'

She found herself starting to laugh. 'Charming. After I kindly made you that packed lunch too!'

He laughed. 'It's good news for you I enjoyed myself. And that steak baguette. I'll go back tomorrow. Believe in us, P! We might still figure this out yet!'

She lay back down on the sofa. She liked the idea of 'us' and 'we' facing this behemoth task together. She wondered if that was what it felt like for Oren and Sage.

31

OREN

Oren spent the night in the forest to continue his hunt for the fog. If any monsters attacked him, he reasoned, he could chop their heads off and pretend they were Gabriel.

He'd seen Sage and Gabriel only once, almost as soon as he'd entered the dark shadows of the forest himself, wandering near the tree line. She'd been smiling, and he was laughing quietly at something too.

He personally didn't find Gabriel all that funny.

Whatever.

He'd turned and stalked off into the darkness, his favourite blade materializing in his hand as he went.

And he'd decided not to go back. He'd set a magical barrier safely around himself and settled down on a camp bed, extinguished all light around him to lie in the impenetrable darkness. And he listened. To every rustle. Every soft breeze. Just to see what came near him.

But . . . no fog. All night.

When he got back to the cabin it was dawn, and Sage was sitting at the table, a mug in her hand, glaring at him.

'You're up early,' he said.

She was still wearing the same clothes she'd been wearing last night – his too-big sweater with an old stain even P couldn't get out. That's how it'd ended up as her bedwear. There wasn't a second mug discarded by the sink, and he couldn't scent anyone else, so . . . she'd come home alone and . . . sat there all night waiting for him?

'Trying to sneak in without me knowing?' she asked tightly.

'Something like that,' he muttered. That was preferable to whatever this ambush was.

'Where have you been?' she demanded. 'I've not been able to sleep all night, not knowing where you are, or *who* you're with.'

Ah. Estelle and the untouched paella were still bothering her, then.

'I stayed out.' He walked over to the kitchen and turned his back on her to flick on the kettle. He wasn't sure why he hadn't just told her already that he'd been stalking about the forest at night, entirely alone, looking for the fog. He was nearly a hundred and fifty years old and he knew that letting her suspect he was with some other werewolf was a petty, childish retribution for his jealousy over Gabriel. 'I thought you might . . . I wasn't sure who would be here when I got back. So I made my own bed for the night elsewhere.'

He'd spent his night listening to the sounds of the forest, but he'd also spent it dwelling on Sage and Gabriel. The rational voice that'd driven him most of his life told him he was reading too much into it all. But the irrational voice that he wasn't too familiar with, which was a new feature in his life, still whispered to him late at night. Warned that she would come to resent him. That he'd ruin her life in the end. That she'd be better off somewhere like here, with her own people, and he should let her explore that possibility if she wanted.

'Gabriel ended our . . . friendship, actually,' she said stiffly.

His head whipped around to look at her before he could control the urge, but thankfully she didn't notice. She was staring down at the half-drunk mug in her hands.

'Why? What did he say?'

'It doesn't matter.' When she put her mug back on the table it banged louder than she'd intended. But suddenly he felt a flash of her embarrassment.

She stood quickly, trying to hide her face.

'Sage—'

She shook her head, turning from him towards her bedroom. 'It was true, anyway.' He heard the small crack in her voice. 'But it doesn't matter.'

He knew she would get to the room before he could stop her, and he wouldn't force his way through a closed door into her private space, so he shifted into the doorway before she could get there.

She jumped when he appeared, her hand already moving

to wipe away a tear she'd hoped he wouldn't see.

'Sage. Wait.' She tried to push past him, but he put his hands on her shoulders and held her back. 'Why are you upset?'

She stopped shrugging out of his grip and looked up at him. This close he could see her eyes were ringed with red; she'd been crying for some time.

She opened her mouth like she was going to say something, like it was right on the tip of her tongue, then she closed it again and shook her head. 'I don't know. I don't know why I feel like this,' she admitted. 'The smallest things, it just comes out of nowhere. Sometimes I just feel so sad. And then I feel so angry I want to scream. Then some days I feel fine. I don't know what's wrong with me.'

He gazed down at her.

He knew what Berion would say it was.

He'd known she was having irregular mood swings, that was obvious enough, but this was the first time she'd admitted anything *and* wanted to talk about it.

'How long have you been feeling like this?'

She shrugged. 'I dunno. The last few months.'

'Have you felt anything else?' he asked, but even he knew it sounded too casual not to be probing. He cursed himself under his breath as her face contorted.

'Like what?' she demanded.

'You've not felt dizzy, or faint, or anything else out of the ordinary?'

'I'm not *sick*, Oren.'

She flinched away from him, and he saw the flash of temper across her face. And he was sure he saw a flash of yellow for a moment, her wolf eyes peeking out behind the brown.

'All right.' He held up his hands. 'I'm not saying you are. But you have been through a lot recently, never mind everything that's happened since we got here. The witch fight. It's my fault if I've expected you to deal with things like I would.'

'You're saying I'm not up to the job?'

'No,' he said evenly. 'I'm saying I'm a bastard. And anyone else would need time to deal with some of the things that happened over Yuletide. I've been neglectful as your partner for not seeing you needed time.'

'I'm over it,' she said sharply, looking down instead of at him. 'All of it.'

'It's OK to grieve for the bad things that happen to us, Sage.'

She shook her head and wiped a tear with her sleeve.

He sighed and pulled her into his arms. He still shuddered at the thought of it – not the holding her part, but the tears. That level of emotion was so alien to him and he wasn't used to it.

'Nothing happened last night,' he said into her hair as she leant against his chest. 'I was in the forest. All night. I didn't leave and go anywhere else, or stay with anyone else.

Just so you know.'

'It's none of my business where you spend the night,' she said curtly.

'Yes, it is.'

'How is it?'

Exasperation got the better of him at last. He pushed her back gently, to look into her face. 'Listen, Sage. The only body I've had in my hands recently is yours. And sometimes it's covered in blood while I desperately try and keep you alive, and sometimes you kiss me. The rest of the time both of us pretend neither of those things have happened. Both of us act like any of this between us is normal, but it isn't.'

She seemed to deflate in front of him. 'You're the world's deadliest assassin and I'm the first werewolf arcānas. We were never going to be normal, were we?'

'No,' he agreed. 'Yet here we are. But if all this has become too much for you, Sage, if Gabriel has ended your friendship because of me, and that isn't what you want . . . if you'd rather stay somewhere like here, in a proper wolf pack, then tell me and I will go and tell him the truth. That our life together might be complicated, but that nothing has ever happened between us. Not really.'

She shook her head. 'He said that he knew he would always be second best,' she admitted at last. His heart gave a little jolt. 'And staying here wouldn't make me happy again, anyway.'

'Then what will?' he asked. 'Because I've rarely seen a

real smile in months.'

He realized now that's what had pissed him off so much about Gabriel. Some of her smiles for him had felt real.

'It doesn't matter,' she said. 'It'll never be. No matter how much I wish for it, Oren, I will get old and die while everyone I love stays young without me. There will come a day when you and P will be my carers, not my friends. And Berion and Hozier will visit me in my bed because I'll be too old and weak to go to them. And you'll all gather round one final day and wait for the inevitable. Comfort each other and wait for my frail old ghost to come back.'

He stared at her.

He didn't need the flashes of her feelings to know what her heartbreak felt like. Because when she spelt it out like this, explained the vision of what bothered her so clearly, he felt nothing but horror too. He felt the endless well of despair he'd lived with for so long, that'd started to disappear only after he'd met Sage and P, open its gigantic maw again.

He brushed a finger across her cheek. Her eyelashes fluttered at the touch.

'There are so many things . . .' He could barely whisper past the lump in his own throat. 'I wish—'

'I know,' she said, and she put a hand on his chest, a request that he stop talking. 'I know.' She couldn't talk about it any more. 'Me too. And that's what counts. So we don't need to keep torturing ourselves with *what ifs*.'

He swallowed, and nodded, and let her squeeze past him into her room and close the door behind her.

He didn't move for a long time, even after he heard a second door click, and then the hiss of her shower turning on.

He wished he'd been brave enough to kiss her this time.

32

SAGE

'Wait.' P's voice came through the phone as Sage lay on her stomach on her small cabin bed, wet hair wrapped in a towel.

'She's getting a notepad.' Hozier huffed a laugh, munching her toast down the phone propped up on the kitchen island back home. 'Hang on.'

'This is the kind of mystery that needs a notepad,' P's voice tutted as a pen and some paper floated back into shot. 'Maybe even a picture wall,' she added with a laugh.

Hozier snorted. 'Oren would freak.'

Sage smiled to herself at the memory of Oren's constant disgruntled expression in those early days. When P's Silver Serial Killer picture wall had slowly expanded. They hadn't even really been friends back then. He'd thought she was insane.

'Well,' P said after a few more minutes of a pen scribbling in mid-air on its own. 'Who was the companion with Kalinka? That would be my most important question.'

Firstly, Hozier had filled P in on what sparse detail she'd

got from the guy in the French Arcānum archives, and then Sage had told them both about the visit to the spot where the witch was found, and the encounter with the bergsmed.

'There was no mention of another person in the file,' Hozier said.

'Gabriel didn't mention a second person when I asked him about it either.'

'Do you think the witches know there was another?' P asked.

Sage shrugged. 'They wouldn't tell us if they did. But . . . I don't think so. The bergsmed didn't say that she was scared, or bound, or there against her will. I'm not quite as sure as the witches are that she was taken. So maybe she was leaving of her own volition. She was a blood daughter of the witch mother, remember. Perhaps she was tipped to be the next? What if she didn't want it? What if she decided to leave and another witch was secretly helping her?'

Hozier sucked in through her teeth. 'That would be a *big* risk.'

'How so?' P asked.

'For all the rivalry going on in those mountains, witches are more like werewolves than they'd admit. In terms of loyalty, anyway. Perhaps even more fiercely so. Witches don't just go off and live in general society like some wolves do. Like you have, Sage. They are *always* part of a coven.'

Sage hummed thoughtfully. Sybil had said the same, hadn't she?

'And if another witch helped her, she would almost certainly be killed by her own sisters in punishment for doing so.' Hozier shook her head. 'If a second witch did help her leave, she would never have been able to admit it. Even if she witnessed something happening to Kalinka and escaped herself. No, that witch would've had to play along with whatever theory her sisters settled on. Let the were-wolves take the fall for all these years, even if it was nothing to do with them.'

'But she could still be there now?' P asked. 'With the real truth?'

'Maybe,' Hozier said. 'Most probably. Though I doubt even Oren could force it out of her. She'd rather die at his hand than face her coven now after all this time.'

'You don't think . . .' P said slowly. 'I mean, they said she died of her wounds, but it's their word, right? Would they have killed her themselves as punishment—'

A knock on her bedroom door, and Oren's head popped in. 'Messenger,' he said urgently. 'Meute de Duplantier, furthest pack. Fog sighting.'

The Duplantiers didn't want them there. But it was interesting that they had decided to report the fog. It must've scared them.

'I'm going now,' Oren added. 'It'll probably be long gone; the messenger will have taken so long to get here. But I need to try . . .' He shook his head. She knew his search yesterday had been fruitless, and he'd told her last night that until he caught up with it he couldn't assess what it was or what to do with it. Witnesses said it seemed like it was searching for something, but for what, they weren't sure. There was nothing but storage in the sheds it went in and out of, one after the other. She knew he was getting frustrated.

She nodded. And then he was gone.

'What're you going to do, then?' P asked when she turned her attention back to the phone. She hadn't told them about Gabriel. She couldn't face going over it all, and she hated talking about feelings as it was. She didn't want to examine her confused thoughts about Gabriel in real time in front of them.

'Dry my hair?' Sage suggested. Then she made her good-byes, and clicked off the call.

She did know what she was going to do, in fact, and half an hour later, with dry hair and wrapped in a hoodie against the brisker chill today, she set off through the trees. Gabriel had told her he would still escort her anywhere she wanted to go. Being her escort was still his assigned duty. But it felt too awkward now. Especially without Oren there.

When she reached the border fence into Monreau land, Thomas wasn't on guard today. This lot were a surly bunch. On both sides. She recognized a few faces from the river's edge yesterday. So not everyone who'd been involved in the fight had been punished. From the silence when they spotted her, though, she could guess what they'd just been telling their neighbours about.

None of them greeted her.

Fine.

She picked one at random, a female guard on the other side of the fence, and addressed her directly. 'I'd like to speak with your alpha, could you take me to him?'

The guard ignored her question and sniffed. 'Why are you working for the Arcānum?'

She was relieved that someone had finally just outright asked her, rather than skirt round it with pointed comments or sly questions. 'Because I want to stop bad things happening to people,' she said honestly. 'Because I don't think anyone should ever have to feel afraid.'

'How old are you?'

'Nineteen.'

'How long have you been a wolf?'

'About eleven years.'

The wolf tilted her head as she looked at her: more feline than lupine. 'They killed your whole family? The wolf that changed you?'

Sage nodded. This wolf might be the first one in the pack to get even halfway to understanding.

'I'll take you to Sacha.' The female werewolf unlatched the lock on the gate with a swift movement, and pulled it open for her. 'Come through.'

They walked in silence. This werewolf wore shoes, not as

carefree with the soles of her feet as her alpha, and soon enough a familiar sea of tents came into view. A few werewolves milled about, some of them sat outside smaller tent flaps scribbling in notebooks, tapping calculators and looking over papers, but most of them, she assumed, were working.

'Sacha,' her companion called.

He was outside the main tent, chatting to two men in overalls, his pipe in his hand. When he spotted her, his eyes went wide. He excused himself from his workers and hurried over.

'*Merci*, Anna.' He dismissed her chaperone, who nodded and set off back the way she'd come. 'Are you well?' he asked, peering at the side of her face.

'Oren healed it quickly,' she told his confused look. 'With magic. Barely a scar.'

He whistled through his teeth. But it didn't exactly sound impressed. More, *rather you than me*, for letting his magic work on her wounds.

If only he knew. The scar on her chest let out a dull twinge.

'Your partner is not joining you today?' he asked as he looked around, but not for Oren. He got the attention of one of the women with clipboards on the other side of the clearing and made some kind of hand gesture. She didn't know what it meant but apparently the woman did, because she rose, and went to a green tent embroidered with wildflowers.

'He's visiting the Meute de Duplantier. They reported a sighting of the fog.'

Sacha led her towards some tree stumps, gesturing for her to sit down. 'You've seen it for yourself?'

She nodded. 'I saw it take a witch's arm off. Down by the river.'

'And you think this fog is the cause of so much trouble?' he asked. 'The sickness. The dead crops. Everything?'

'I do think so, yeah.'

'But why?' he asked. 'What is it? What would be its purpose?'

She hadn't quite got her theories on that straight yet. So for now she shook her head. 'I have no idea.'

'Ah!' The woman returned and Sacha stood to take from her a wide, wooden chopping board, thanking her with a grateful smile. She backed away politely. As he sat down again she saw that it was an extravagant cheeseboard. Crackers, grapes, some slices of cured meats she guessed might have come from the Bassetts, and of course, a whole array of cheeses. What pack was it that made cheese now?

'Please.' He gestured to the board as he rested it on top of another tree stump in front of them and started to slice brie for himself. 'Eat. It's nearly lunchtime.'

She didn't need telling twice. 'My housemate, back home, this would be her dream,' she admitted. 'She loves to cook. Well, hosting is her real passion. A well-presented cheeseboard like this . . .' She popped some mature cheddar in her mouth and hummed.

Sacha grinned. 'Then you must take some back for her, what's her favourite cheese? We'll send word to Matthieu Garnier. They have everything. Whatever she could want.'

'Oh, well.' Her face fell as it always did when she had to admit her greatest sin. 'She's dead. She's the poltergeist I mentioned.'

Sacha gaped, horrified by his accidental misstep. 'She cannot eat the food she cooks? What does she do with it?'

'We eat it. Or she gives it to those most in need,' she said. 'Oren allows her to buy the ingredients on his credit card. He complains endlessly about how someone who can't even eat can spend so much.'

Sacha's small laugh was incredulous. She supposed the thought of Oren Rinallis funding a ghost's charity work was quite a funny notion. 'She is a gift.'

Her throat was suddenly tight. 'We know. We're incredibly lucky.'

'I'll send for some cheese anyway,' Sacha said. 'To feed as many as she can.'

She smiled at him, and perhaps he could tell she needed a moment. He busied himself wrapping a small cube of cheese inside a slice of chorizo rather than look at her.

'So,' she said, when she was confident the lump in her throat was gone. 'The reason I came.'

'This wasn't just a social call, you mean?' Sacha threw her a wry smile. 'You haven't come to ask us if you can stay.

A tent of your own?'

'Not today.' She smiled. 'But you do sound like Gabriel.'

'Ah.' Sacha's eyes twinkled. 'That young wolf causes a stir every time he comes to my camp. But not as handsome as your warlock, *non*?'

She chose not to answer that, and his chuckle said he knew it. 'I've been told that the oldest werewolf in these mountains lives in your pack,' she said instead. 'Would it be possible to speak with them?'

'With Eugene?' he asked, surprised. 'He's not in trouble?'

'No.' She shook her head. 'It's a side project I'm working on. I'd like to use his memory.'

'He's been here a long time – I'm not sure what he can tell you other than the goings-on in these mountains.' He got to his feet. 'But you're welcome to ask. Wait there, I'll bring him to you.'

She was banking on him knowing exactly what happened in these mountains.

33

SAGE

Sacha returned with an old man linking his arm, a walking stick in his other hand. Eugene's face was wrinkled and covered in liver spots, his hair candyfloss-thin, and he was wearing an apron covered in bits of sticky tape, the front pocket filled with pens and markers.

'Eugene sits in our office and oversees the packaging labels for our online sales,' Sacha told her as he helped the old man sit on the stool he'd vacated. 'He cannot speak English, I'll have to translate.'

'That's fine,' she agreed. '*Salut*, Eugene.'

The old man was more interested in the half-eaten cheeseboard, leaning forward to pick up the small bunch of green grapes neither she nor Sacha had touched in favour of the meats and cheeses. He held the bunch in one withered hand and started to pick off the small fruits with the other.

'How long has Eugene lived here?'

Sacha started to answer, but he paused to confirm with Eugene. 'Seventy-four years. He was changed in his early teens. He travelled across France to live in the mountains.'

She puffed out her cheeks. 'That's a long time.'

Sacha nodded. 'Our elders are greatly respected; they have contributed to our existence the longest. It's an honour for Eugene to live with us.'

'I wanted to ask him about Kalinka Crows-Caw.'

Eugene's eyes snapped up to meet hers for the first time. 'Kalinka?' he repeated. Then he said something else.

'He says he hasn't heard that name in a very long time.'

'But he does remember her?'

Another exchange.

'She died a few years after he arrived,' Sacha translated. So he *had* been here. He did remember. Her heart quickened excitedly.

'Do you know the story?' she asked Sacha.

'We all do,' he said. 'But especially here, and in the Dubois. We're the only packs to border the river. Our patrol guards have it spat in their faces a lot more than the other packs.'

She told them of her growing belief that if she could solve the mystery of what happened to Kalinka alongside the fog that was plaguing them, it would dampen some of the ongoing animosity between both sides of the river.

Eugene shook his head. He looked annoyed, gesturing towards her with his gnarled hands as he spoke to Sacha.

'Eugene says it doesn't matter,' Sacha said after a moment. 'It was too long ago now to start dragging up the past. Let sleeping witches lie.'

'But it isn't sleeping,' she pointed out. 'The witches still hold a grudge, and you all jumped to the conclusion you were being cursed because of it dangerously quickly. Fights have already broken out. It's a slow-burning pot about to bubble over. And it'll land on your doorstep first, Sacha. Yours and the Dubois. Are you willing to let your pack fight it out over a witch none of the rest of you even remember?'

Eugene remained defiantly silent even after the translation, frowning down at his grapes rather than look at her. So Sacha asked him something instead, a question she hadn't posed. Apparently, he understood Eugene's silence better than her. The old man nodded.

Sacha sighed. 'Eugene finds it hard,' he said carefully. 'Although you are a wolf, you are law enforcement, you are not part of a pack here. To speak of this to you goes against pack loyalty. Do you under—'

Sacha stopped talking abruptly, his eyes going wide as he jumped to his feet. The cheeseboard still resting on a tree stump between them went flying, what was left of the food scattering.

She jolted so quickly at the shock of this burst of movement that she felt a muscle in her neck zing. She gasped in pain, her hand clamped to her neck as she turned to look for whatever had caused Sacha such a visceral reaction.

And there, behind her . . .

'Shit.'

All the breath left her body.

Black fog was creeping between two tents on the edges of the camp.

Sacha started bellowing, waving frantic arms to three werewolves stood talking, comparing notes between their clipboards – one of them was the wolf who'd brought them their cheeseboard. A woman looked up, spotted it, and screamed as another pulled her out of the way just in time.

'Don't let it touch you!' Sage yelled. But luckily the camp was mostly empty, most of the werewolves out weaving and sewing, and anyone in the vicinity had already started to run.

And, bloody hell, they *definitely* hadn't appreciated just how much the witches and their chanting had held that thing at bay. This time it didn't lie flat, crawling slowly across the floor. It was taller now, at least a metre off the floor as it spread, stretching and changing its shape to accommodate every twig, tree stump, branch and tent rope it travelled over. And it was quick. Wisps flicked out at the edges, like tongues of a flame, as it came towards them.

'Eugene!' She grabbed for his arm. 'We've got to move!' He was muttering, but she didn't need to understand him to hear fear. 'Sacha!' The alpha didn't need telling twice. He was kicking the tree stumps around them out of the way in an attempt to clear their path and make an escape easier.

Both of them linked their arms through Eugene's and practically dragged him backwards away from the rapidly moving fog. The fear in her chest felt like it was going to explode out of her. What could any of them do against it? What cage could hold it if—

It lunged.

She knew she would always look back on that moment and feel guilt. Because her first instinct was to duck and roll out of its path. But in doing so, letting go of Eugene to make her own escape . . .

Sacha's howl reached her ears before she could look up from where she was sprawled on the ground.

The scent of blood hit her nostrils, strong and iron-laced and distinctly pine.

Eugene was gone. Completely.

Gone.

His cane, all that was left of him, rattled on the floor between her and where Sacha had fallen to his knees. The back of his arm, the arm which had been holding on to Eugene, and some of his shoulder, had been taken clean off. Right down to the bones she could see now, white and stark against cleanly sliced flesh and tendon.

And it was only then that she realized the fog was gone. She scrambled to her feet, stumbling over uneven forest floor as she whirled on the spot. She barely spotted the end of the fog disappearing around another tent in the opposite direction from which it had come. As if the fog had just been passing through, and damn anything in its way.

She shouted Sacha's name, closing the distance between them. 'Stay still!' she begged as blood splattered all over the floor around them. The scraps of what was left of his tie-dyed shirt hanging from his neck and other arm were already doused and dripping with crimson blood. But the agony must've been too much. He collapsed forward on to his hands and knees, his ravaged shoulder buckling, and she caught him just before he faceplanted the floor.

She looked around, desperate, *desperate* for help.

She held on to the alpha, her arms shaking under his weight as she tried to keep him upright, even as they both knelt there in the dirt and his blood. Through the howls of pain she only heard one word. He sobbed Eugene's name.

Then the woman who'd brought the cheeseboard was running towards them, screaming, her face wild with panic.

She screamed hysterical words Sage didn't understand. She could do nothing but shake her head and apologize. But the woman was screaming into the air. Screaming for help. Between all the pain, Sacha managed to gasp that she was his sister. And then other wolves started to appear. More shouts went up. Running feet. First-aid boxes were thrown open as Sacha was urged to lie on his front so that they could try and do what they could to stem the horrendous blood flow.

But she knew.

Judging by the terror of the werewolves around her as Sacha's blood flowed too quickly out of his ever-paling skin, they knew too.

Their alpha was going to die.

The weight of it, their horror and their fear, the sounds of their strangled shouts, it reminded her of that storage room. Red flashed in her mind. Pain. Only that time it'd been her lying there dying.

She couldn't breathe, this scene even worse than the witch with no arm. These cries even more soul-crushing than Chloé's sisters desperate to save her.

It was Oren who had saved the witch. It was Oren who'd saved *her*.

If they wanted Sacha to survive, they would need Oren now.

'Who speaks English?' she demanded.

Nobody answered her. Nobody even heard her.

She repeated it again, shouting.

But these wolves only had eyes for their alpha, and his eyes were drooping. His sister looked ready to pass out. She looked around desperately. Did she just run? Did she get back to that gate and just hope that Oren was back from the Duplantier camp? How much time had passed?

Then she saw Anna, the guard who'd brought her into the camp, running with two more patrol guards at her side.

'Thank God,' she gasped, lunging for the guard she knew spoke English, and grabbed her arm. 'My partner can save him. Tell them. Do what they can until we come back.'

'You know the way to the gate?' she asked. Sage nodded. 'Then run.'

Her heart burnt in her chest as she tore through the

forest. She knew it was mostly a straight line, and it didn't matter anyway. She could scent her way towards Oren from anywhere. She tuned in her wolf senses and breathed deeply through her nose, snatching the faint tendrils of the cedarwood aftershave she loved and latching on to it.

When she reached the gate she didn't stop. She didn't answer the calls of the guards on either side of the gate as they saw the dark blood drying into her jeans and staining her hands. She wrenched the gate open and careened through, not even bothering to pull it closed again after her. Maybe she had more in common with that fog than she thought, eh? But what would she do if that fog turned up here? Now?

Well, she'd die, she supposed.

She'd never get to say goodbye to P. She'd never get to tell Oren everything she really felt—

'Sage!' His voice was urgent as she fell out of the trees and into the Dubois camp. She didn't know what'd called him to her but suddenly he was there, running out of their cabin, his eyes already assessing her body for whatever injury could cause so much blood down her front, but coming up short.

'The fog.' She crashed into his outstretched arms. She felt like she was going to be sick. 'Sacha.'

There were more wolves here than in the Monreau camp. It must've been the end of lunch, as bodies started to spill out of the hall at the sounds of her commotion.

She didn't need to say anything else. He understood.

'Is he alive?'

'Just.'

But Eugene? Nothing could be done to save him.

Her chest swelled with grief again, and guilt.

Then she saw Gabriel running down the steps of the hall, his eyes wide with shock at the sight of her still clinging to Oren, gasping for breath and trying not to be sick. She started to shake. She could feel all of her limbs shuddering and tears welling in her eyes as the shock set in. Gabriel was the last thing she needed.

'Tell your mother there's been another attack. Next door. It's close. Any sightings, report to me as soon as I'm back,' Oren snapped at the young werewolf as he got to them, his eyes still on her crusting, bloodied jeans.

A warm rush of familial, comforting magic washed down her spine, and the shaking in her limbs eased as he washed away the shock of everything that'd just happened. And then Oren was gone. Off to see if he could save Sacha Monreau.

But his magic hadn't managed to wash away the tears she could feel spilling over.

'Sage.' *Bloody hell!* She didn't want to start crying in front of them. 'What happened?'

And she couldn't stop it. The tears started to roll down her cheeks.

'*Arrête. Ne pleure pas.* Don't cry.' Gabriel moved to put

his arms around her with an ease she knew Oren would never, ever be capable of. And before, she might have allowed it.

But not now.

Not now he'd looked at her with pity, thinking she'd only ever needed to be saved.

She pushed away from him. Pushed away from the were-wolves still coming out of the dinner hall and watching. She saw Benoît take her in and turn, likely to go and get Celeste.

So she turned too, and ran.

34

SAGE

'P,' she whispered down the phone, her breathing ragged as she gulped in the air she hoped would stop her from having a complete meltdown on her own in the middle of the forest.

'What's wrong?' P said at once, hearing it in her voice.

'I need your help,' she said as she kept running in the one direction both Oren and Gabriel had warned her away from. Her heart was pounding. A mixture of what she was about to do, and what Oren would say if he found out about it.

'What is it?' P asked.

'I'm going to do something really stupid,' she said. 'If I don't call you back in' – she pulled the phone from her ear to check the time – 'forty minutes from now. Tell Oren I went to the Baba Yaga, and that he needs to rescue me.'

'Sage!' P sounded appalled.

'P, please.' She shook her head. She didn't have time for it. 'I'll tell you everything later. But we need answers right now. And she might be the only one who has them.'

'Can't Oren go?'

'He tried . . . they met a century ago and she hasn't forgotten. She won't help him.'

'Why doesn't that surprise me?'

But Sage had stumbled to a halt. And anything P said was forgotten.

In front of her was a wooden hut. The corners were green with moss and damp, and the roof was thatched. And underneath it were two enormous, leathery chicken feet.

'Sage? Are you still there?'

'Uh, yeah,' she said, distracted by the chicken feet that were moving, making the hut slowly revolve. 'I've got to go. Forty minutes, P.'

She clicked off the call before P could say anything else.

The world seemed to quieten, as if the forest itself knew it wasn't safe. No wildlife lived there. No birds sang from the treetops. No small woodland creatures rustled through the bushes. Nothing. And it was cold. Colder than any other part of the forest she'd been in.

As the ancient hut slowly revolved on its feet, she took it in. No windows on the back or sides. A solid roof. No escape routes, if she was really desperate.

As the front came back into view she could see a rope ladder hanging down, swaying gently, from a small porch in front of the door – two murky windows on either side. A rocking chair sat next to an old, extinguished gas lamp. Everything was covered in a thin layer of mould, and under it she could see rotting wood.

She swallowed.

The rope ladder reached her at last. It wouldn't be hard to reach out, grab it and start to climb, but . . .

Now she was starting to second-guess her decision.

Oren was going to kill her if the Baba Yaga didn't first.

She let the rope ladder pass, deciding to allow the hut one more turn while she thought about what to do . . . climbing it felt stupid, right? Reckless. But . . . so was being there at all.

She watched the slow-turning feet, a little voice in her head geeing her up, egging her on, building her confidence. She could do it the next time, she could grab the rope and knock on the door and—

She froze.

It was faint, so quiet she'd nearly missed it. A sound was coming not from the hut – but behind her.

She turned slowly, tuning in her wolf ears.

Now she could hear it clearly. And it was crying.

All thoughts of the hut forgotten, she followed the sound instead. Amplified by her wolfish senses, it was harder to tell just how close the sound was, so she switched between that sense and human, trying to figure out what and where it could be. It was female, for sure: light and scared. She sniffed: faint traces of blood. Fresh blood. Not Sacha's blood still dried on her hands.

'Hello?' she called.

The crying faltered, and she heard a ragged, deep breath.

She called out again, promising whatever it was that it didn't need to be afraid.

To her left: a rustle of leaves. If there was a wounded person . . . creature? Anything, out here bleeding, it'd attract the Baba Yaga soon enough.

She saw a flash of snow-white hair behind a tree.

'Hello?' she called again, her hands already up in submission, hopeful that whatever was injured would not be afraid of her.

She wondered whether she was afraid. She wasn't sure. She knew she should be. What a world away she was from the girl she once had been. Another time she'd take a moment to marvel at it. But not now, because something was injured and she needed to get it away—

She gasped.

Sprawled on the floor was a young . . . woman? She looked barely older than a teenager, and she was covered in blood. Her eyes were closed in pain, and she was slumped against the tree as she shuddered and sobbed.

'Oh my God.' Sage hurried forward. 'It's OK. Let me help—'

She jumped as the girl looked up, opening her eyes which were wholly white. Like Berion's.

She was a witch. A powerful witch. But not the witch mother – far too young. And she'd met Sybil already. None of the other witches she'd met at the river were powerful enough to have white eyes. A million confused thoughts ran through her mind.

'What's your name?' She crouched, careful not to touch her without permission. But she was pretty sure she'd have to find the source of that bleeding and put pressure on it soon. The woman's dress, which had once clearly been white and sewn together at the seams with thin strips of leather, was stained a dark crimson red. Her arms, wrapped with beaded bracelets and more thin leather straps, were covered in dried blood flaking away over goose-pimpled flesh. And there were three long rips down her front over her chest and stomach. Rips like on P's clothes—

She could barely breathe. 'Who did this to you?'

The witch mumbled something in French, but she didn't understand. Not all of it anyway. One part she understood though, and that was enough. *Le loup*. The wolf.

Her heart sank.

'*Le loup m'a attaquée.*' She didn't need Oren's magic translator to take a guess at what that meant.

The witch's white, pain-filled eyes stared up at her, and it struck her that it'd been so hard to read Sybil's eyes with no colour. But this time, she understood completely. The witch was begging her to believe her.

She nodded. 'I will find who did this.' She gestured that she was about to touch her, to help her to rise, and get her to safety. 'Let me—'

Then something else happened, so horrifying that she instantly recoiled, falling on to her bum as the witch rose to her feet, strong and not in pain.

The moment Sage had nodded, the pain, the fear, the sadness, it all slipped from her face. And a wide grin split her cheeks. Wider than it should be. Abnormally wide and revealing. Well, Sage didn't know how many teeth were supposed to be in the average mouth, but it definitely wasn't this many. And all were pointed, and sharp.

Her white eyes flooded with colour, and then red irises were looking down on Sage sprawled on the forest floor. The Baba Yaga herself stood over her.

35

SAGE

Sage's stomach lurched. It'd been a trick.

A long, black tongue slithered out between the razor-sharp teeth and licked them.

Her heart pounded in her chest, but there wasn't time for regrets. She didn't have time to think about every warning Oren had given her that she'd ignored. All she could do was push herself backwards out of the reach of this creature before she dived and devoured her where she lay.

'Are you scared, wolfling?' the Baba Yaga asked, her head tilting so far to the left it looked in danger of snapping off her neck. The face distorted. The young witch she'd thought she'd found might've been beautiful in other circumstances, but this, the enormous mouth stretched thin over too many teeth, the red eyes, and the nose that'd elongated now to a sharp point, made her grotesque. Sage stared, confused and fascinated, as the long white hair turned grey before her eyes, and the smooth silkiness turned ragged and coarse.

Would her answer make a difference?

'Yes,' she said, because there was no point lying. She wondered whether admitting this made her brave or a coward.

The Baba Yaga laughed, and the sound made her spine shiver.

She tried to crawl away backwards, far enough to jump up to her feet and run, but the Baba Yaga lunged, her limbs contorting at angles that weren't human, and then she was on her hands and knees scurrying forward, that wide face still grinning.

Sage screamed.

Or at least she tried. It was a yelp, perhaps, before the monster was on top of her, a hand that was suddenly gnarled and wrinkled and old clamped across her mouth to keep the sound of the scream locked inside. That terrifying face centimetres from her own, their noses touching. Hot breath stinking of rotting meat. She gagged.

The Baba Yaga was still laughing, her red eyes peering into Sage's face as if she was trying to seek out something tiny in a large space. Sage felt her heart hammering so hard she was sure the monster could hear it. She flinched as a warm droplet of saliva dripped out of that carnivorous mouth on to her cheek.

The Baba Yaga was no larger than her – if anything, perhaps a bit smaller. But her frame was solid. And those teeth were too close to her throat. There would be no escape. Not unless the monster allowed it. She'd be long dead before P could tell Oren to shift there to find her, his face wild and furious.

'I know what you've come for,' the monster breathed, hissing through thin lips that were barely able to stretch fully over her endless teeth to form full words. 'I know what you seek.'

Slowly, one finger at a time, the hand over Sage's mouth unclamped. Her invitation to speak.

'What is it?' she breathed. 'The fog?'

'I don't know!' The face distorted again, and suddenly she looked like she was about to cry. The Baba Yaga howled into the sky, her wailing voice echoing around them. Then she froze, the angst slipping away, and she was smiling again. 'Just joking.'

Sage stared. She'd psyched herself up, had known whatever she'd find would be horrifying, terrifying, but she hadn't prepared herself for crazy.

'Well.' The Baba Yaga paused. She leant in and sniffed deeply, and licked her lips again. More saliva dripped on to Sage's face. 'I don't know it personally, anyway. We've never been formally introduced.' She inhaled again, her eyes almost rolling back in her head. 'It's a strange thing, you know, I never felt it arrive.'

'What do you mean?'

'I know these mountains,' the Baba Yaga whispered. 'I can feel them, full of life. Full of . . .' She shuddered. 'Flesh. And magic. Old. New. I know the earth and what walks over it. The wind whispers it all to me. I know everything that enters and leaves. I knew when *you* came.'

'But this thing, the fog . . . you didn't sense that?'

She shook her head. 'Oh, but I can sense its strength now.'

A million thoughts raced through her mind. 'Can it be killed?'

The Baba Yaga nodded emphatically. 'Can't we all, little one? If you find the heart.'

The monster lifted the hand that'd clamped over her mouth, and stuck out one long and gnarled finger. She pulled back just enough to reveal Sage's chest, and pressed the tip of her crooked nail over her hammering heart. 'If it still has one.' The red eyes still scoured her face. 'But . . .' She sighed dramatically. 'I can sense the remnants of an old cloaking spell. *He* will need more than tracking skills to find it. Does he know you're here?'

'No.'

'Maybe I should kill you,' she sang softly. 'Just to see his face.'

'Then he would kill you.' She hoped she sounded braver than she felt.

Her grin widened. 'I'll just come back.'

She didn't miss a beat. 'So will I.'

'It's not the same,' she purred. 'A half-life. Never to touch. Never to love.'

Her stomach squirmed as it always did when she thought about all she'd taken from P.

But the Baba Yaga was wrong in some respects. P *was* able to love. It was P's love that'd saved her. And Oren. It was her compassion and her care that had made their little group into a family. And she could touch . . . most things. Everything. Except her friend.

'Why did you trick me?'

'Witch versus wolf,' she whispered. 'I wanted to see.'

Before Sage could say anything else, the monster lurched back. She turned, and still hunched over, running on her hands and feet like a spider with four legs, she scurried back towards her hut.

Sage stared after her, watched her not bother with the rope ladder, simply reaching up to the wood and dragging her body up and over on to the porch with strength she didn't look like she had in those withered arms. Sage didn't move, watching as the deformed creature scurried through the door and slammed it shut.

And silence fell again. The eerie silence from before.

Her whole body started to shake again as the reality of what'd just happened set in. Her wolf hadn't even tried to get out and save her, but perhaps even it knew that'd be futile. She shuddered a ragged breath as a hand brushed wisps of hair off her face.

The monster had wanted to see what? If she'd help a witch who had been attacked by a wolf? Hadn't that been the question on everyone's mind?

She could see now that her decision to enter that cabin

wasn't just stupid, it was completely insane. But . . . it did seem a waste, now she was there. If Oren was going to kill her anyway, was it worth it if she didn't come away with answers to *all* the questions she'd had lately?

Should she consider it now she'd seen that thing? No.

Should she turn and run as far away as she could from that monster? Yes.

Would she be able to hide from Oren that something was wrong? No.

Would he absolutely lose his mind when she told him? Yes.

She sighed.

If the Baba Yaga was going to kill her, she'd have done it already . . . right?

She almost laughed at herself.

Was she trying to talk herself into going into that cabin anyway?

What should she do?

What should she do?

She looked at the time on her phone. She had twelve minutes before her time was up and she needed to call P.

What would her friends do?

Of course, P would tell her not to be stupid. She'd offer to go herself, because she couldn't die twice, and Sage would almost certainly die if she went in.

Oren would go in there with no fear. But that was easy for the most dangerous warlock in existence.

Berion? Oren had told her once that he was so arrogant that he'd rather die with his head held high than admit that he was afraid.

And that felt to her like the right amount of balance.

She smiled at the thought of the only white eyes that didn't scare her, and she rose on shaking feet.

She stood on the porch, the smell of damp wood overwhelming, and raised a hand ready to knock on the door.

Before she could, it opened on creaking hinges. Of course it did.

Inside was as awful as she'd imagined. There was a bed covered in old blankets and more mould, and she wasn't sure if it was hair or fur, but it was . . . something fluffy. She tried not to gag again.

She refused to step over the threshold. Knew that was pushing her already thinning luck too far. A figure hunched over a hearth to the right, a black pot hanging over it as the bent crone – a different figure completely to the one that'd crawled all over her outside – stirred with a big spoon.

'You won't come in?' said the old woman the Baba Yaga was pretending to be, gesturing to a round wooden table perhaps three paces in.

The room was dark, and she could see dust molecules floating through the air. Things hung from the ceiling but she tried not to look too closely. Things covered in feathers, some of them slowly dripping liquid on to the filthy floor. A wooden tray on a table next to the hearth had an untidy array of knives thrown inside. Not all of them had been cleaned. In pots on the windowsills were long-dead plants. They reminded her of the witches' house back in Downside, all that could be seen through the musty windows and limp netting.

This version of the Baba Yaga had dark, deep-set eyes. Her skin was even more wrinkled than before and she wore a shawl over her head, and her ears were lined with golden earrings. She reminded Sage of the traditional travelling fortune tellers, ready to pull out a pack of cards.

'I had one more question,' she said, still frozen in the doorway.

'You can try,' the fortune teller hummed. She slammed a roughly hewn wooden cup on to the round table and poured black liquid from a dirty glass bottle. When she lifted it and drank, the liquid dribbled down her chin and dripped on to her ragged clothes.

'If you've been here for nearly a century, you must remember when the witch went missing? Kalinka?'

'Ah,' the monster smiled, drawing the word out long and slow as she pulled out a stool from under the table and lowered herself down. 'Little Kalinka, the witch with the white eyes.'

'White eyes?' Like her mother. Like . . . she felt instantly sick. What face had she taken on outside?

The Baba Yaga nodded. 'Not many witch mothers are born with white eyes.' Long fingers started to idly trace the edges of her glass. 'For most, they come with the extra surge of magic when taking the mantle. But, oh, she was powerful,' she whispered, almost to herself. 'Oh, how they loved her. Destined for greatness. If they hadn't left when they did.'

'They?'

'Kalinka and *Mathilde*.' She sang the name. Let it hiss off her lips. As if the sound was delicious. 'The wind told me the day it happened. But it was not my business, no.' She sighed loudly. 'They ran into the wrong people on the path. People who were scared of all that she was. People who didn't trust so much magic inside the body of a dainty young body.'

'Mathilde? That was the other witch?'

She grinned, her black teeth dripping with saliva again. 'So sad. To be bound to one whose lifespan will long outlive your own.'

Sage gritted her teeth. She refused to be antagonized.

The Baba Yaga's eyes lifted to meet hers. 'Moon and magic,' she whispered. 'Which one do you think resented it more? The mortal doomed to die or the one doomed to live on without them?'

'What?'

'But, alas, you know how it feels.' The Baba Yaga gestured with a hand. 'How is it for you and the warlock? Will you come to hate him more than he'll hate you?'

'Mathilde . . . was a wolf?' Was that why Eugene had seemed reluctant to talk? Why pack loyalty made it hard for him to tell her, an outsider, anything about a pack member?

'And whatever she ran into?'

The Baba Yaga shrugged, licking her lips as she looked down at her bloodied jeans. 'Dead now. So I guess it doesn't matter.'

'What happened to Mathilde?'

'Dead now too.' The Baba Yaga sat back. There was a finality about the movement that told Sage the story was almost over. Their conversation, the grace the monster was affording her, was coming to an end. 'Had she lived, she'd have become one of the most powerful witch mothers of all. And they knew it. Oh, how they grieved.' She drew her finger from her eye down her cheek, her lips pulling down in the corners, a sarcastic impression of crying. 'Her funeral pyre was so high it could be seen over the treetops. Even the firebird lifted his head at the sight.'

Sage nodded. 'A wolf told me that smoke rose from the mountain for a whole week after her funeral, they left so many offerings to the Häxgrotta in her memory.'

'Child, nothing rose from the mountain before that day at all.'

'Never?'

Baba shrugged. 'Perhaps they ask for her continued peace in the beyond.'

Perhaps. And with one last look at the sharp teeth behind the Baba Yaga's withered lips, she backed out of the cabin without another word.

36

SAGE

She clicked off the call with a stressed-sounding P as she hurried back through the trees. She'd had three minutes to spare before P called Oren, and she'd just made it away from the chicken-footed hut in time.

She hadn't been gone that long. She hurtled back into the camp and towards her cabin. Wolves stopped to watch her. Gabriel was still standing outside the dinner hall, his face anxious. Probably terrified of what Oren would do if he found out Gabriel had let her run off into the forest on her own, covered in blood. But she should be able to get back in and get washed up and—

'Sage.'

She skidded to a halt, loose stones and dirt spraying underfoot. She didn't need to turn to know that Oren was there. She could see it on some of the expressions of the watching werewolves. He was behind her. Had shifted into the centre of the camp as he'd either heard or sensed her return.

'There's a twig in your hair. And leaves stuck to the back

of your clothes. Have a little rest on the forest floor, did you?'

She gathered her nerve and turned to face him. And he knew. He already knew. She didn't know how. Maybe he could scent the Baba Yaga on her, or just by process of elimination, but she could tell by the fury on his face that he knew she'd gone and done the one thing he'd expressly forbidden.

'I can't imagine you were faced with model hospitality.'

'Just listen—' She held up her hands, closing the distance between them. 'I need to speak to the witch mother.' His eyes narrowed. He didn't need to voice the *why* she knew he was asking. 'Do you trust me?' She asked the only question that ever mattered between them. The question they asked each other only when it mattered most.

She could see his teeth clenching behind his cheeks, holding back the furious answer he knew every wolf in the vicinity would hear. Then he held out a hand.

When they reappeared at the river's edge, the guards that'd been shackled by new and more severe orders from Celeste not to hurl insults were standing, staring silently at the six witches on the other side who were throwing suggestive smirks as they washed bowls and plates in the water.

'Bring me the witch mother.' Oren's command was deadly calm as every set of eyes fixed on their sudden appearance. 'And don't make me ask twice.'

'Sacha?' she asked after she watched the witches look at

each other, and silently disappear into the trees.

'Alive.'

'They told you about Eugene?' She could barely say his name. Could barely look at him. She was back on top of that observatory again, admitting she'd killed P.

And then when he looked at her, saw her face, his expression softened. 'It doesn't matter,' he told her, as he always did. As she told him. 'It's done. I don't care.'

But she cared. 'I sacrificed him to save myself.'

'That's not entirely fair, Sage,' he whispered. She knew he didn't dare reach for her, not with werewolves in earshot and witches watching. 'He was too old. Too slow. He wouldn't have got away regardless.'

But now her adrenaline was finally starting to wear off, the dark well of pain and guilt was opening up again, ready to swallow her whole. Consume her. Maybe this was what it would feel like if the fog took her. Would it rip her limb from limb into nothing but flesh and blood particles? Or would she implode into bone-crushing nothingness? She still didn't think it could hurt as much as the pain inside her now. Another person, dead, because of her.

'Look at me,' he demanded, pushing her to keep her focus on him rather than every other thought trying to make her crumble. 'Breathe.'

Oren's magic brushed down her body, all he could offer her in place of a physical hand, but at least it focused her thoughts again.

She nodded. 'I think . . . I think there's more that the witches aren't telling—'

'What do you want?' An older, yet still annoyed voice cut through the quiet anticipation building around them. 'Have you returned to nearly kill any more of my witches?'

She recognized the challenge that flashed in Oren's eye for a split-second before he turned to look at the witch mother. She was wearing a long-sleeved dress of midnight blue, held together at the seams with black ribbon, and her hair looked as wild as ever. Though she seemed to have recovered from her burst of magic when they'd last met, and she was able to walk without looking like she needed to be held up.

'I don't know.' Oren shrugged, shifting them again across the water. They re-emerged behind the witches gathered on the bank. 'Have you re-established your orders to prevent them crossing the boundary line?'

Sybil Crows-Caw whirled, and the six witches loitering at the river's edge moved quickly, slotting themselves into a tight formation around their witch mother. Sage could see lots of teeth bared in warning.

'What do you want?' Sybil repeated slowly, accentuating the words. 'Now you've *summoned* me here—'

Across the other side of the river a commotion sounded, and Gabriel and five other werewolves, presumably even more of his border patrol, fell out of the trees into the clearing. Did he suspect another fight breaking out? He couldn't have honestly thought Oren would need reinforcements. Maybe this time they were just there as an audience.

'You're incredibly lucky we haven't yet entered your camp,' Oren warned her. 'But if you'd prefer that to a summons . . .'

A couple of the witches hissed, and Sybil's lips pulled back over her own sharply pointed teeth as she snarled at the suggestion. She felt another brush of Oren's warming magic down the back of her neck. *Go on*, it urged. *The floor is yours.*

She took a deep breath, reminded herself of the small, weak girl that she'd been before him, and stepped forward.

'The mountain cave.' She stared down the witch mother's glare.

The old witch wasn't quick enough to hide her surprise. It flashed across her usually unreadable white eyes. But she regained her composure quickly. 'The Häxgrotta? What about it?'

Sage shrugged. 'It isn't a goddess hidden in there, is it? What you're doing isn't worship.'

This statement was greeted with the fiercest hisses yet.

'How dare you,' Sybil growled. 'That ground is sacred. It's where we honour the dead and celebrate the solstice. We leave offerings in thanks for—'

'You see, I don't think that's true,' Sage cut across her. 'I think it's a very carefully crafted cover. I think you've refused to help our enquiries since we've been here because you didn't want us looking too closely at what you really get up to. At what's really in that cave, and what it might be capable of.'

Sound erupted as all the witches flanking Sybil protested Sage's assertion, furious that she dared call their witch mother a liar and insult their deity in the process. She could feel the tension curling tightly like a spring, ready to hurl towards her any second. She could sense Oren's magic igniting, and knew if she turned back now, his hands would be wreathed in gold. Sybil saw it too, and knew that if he intervened this time, her witches would die. She threw up her withered hands, a clear stop sign. *Be calm. Stand down.*

Sage watched on as the bodyguard of young witches did as their mother commanded, straightening and releasing some of the tension in their shoulders. But it didn't quell the fire on their faces. True anger.

And honestly, that wasn't a reaction she'd expected.

'That's interesting,' she said under her breath, her eyes darting between them all, thoughts racing as she regrouped and reassessed.

Oh my God.

'They don't know either, do they?' She stared at Sybil as she reordered all her assumptions. 'I thought it was all of you – but it's just you. They've got no idea what you've done.'

The look Sybil gave her was full of contempt. And for a moment, Sage wondered whether she was considering throwing herself forward. Oren would kill her for it, but perhaps she was wondering whether she could take Sage with her in the process. Perhaps then, the truth would die with them both rather than be confessed.

'I'm trying to be fair, Sybil,' she said. 'I will hear your explanation first, if you have one.'

'Oh, really?' It was entirely sarcastic, spit flying from her lips as her furious face was suddenly so close that Sage could feel her breath on her cheeks. 'Fair, you say?'

It took everything in her not to flinch at the sudden approach. She threw up her own warning hand to stop Oren hurling a magical barrier at the ancient witch. She refused to back down. Had she not just experienced the Baba Yaga, this might've scared her.

Sybil pushed her wild hair back. 'And the punishment? Will that be fair too? Will you judge me the same as you'd judge, say, Celeste Dubois?' Sybil scoffed like she already knew the answer, and spat at Sage's feet.

Furious barks and loud growls erupted across the river at such an act of disrespect in the same breath as their alpha's name. And Sage realized all she could do was laugh bitterly as her own temper ignited inside her.

She was sick of every side thinking they knew her.

Sybil couldn't know just how wrong she was. The wolves didn't. Not once had any of them considered that she felt no loyalty towards any of them at all. They weren't her family. They weren't her priority.

'Last year, we entered the camp of a wolf pack in our own city. They forced us to separate, and then they attempted to ambush and kill him.' She gestured to Oren. 'I killed the wolf that tried.'

She didn't need to turn. She wouldn't look. After that admission, she knew she would never be able to look Gabriel or any wolf here in the eye again. Even the witches froze, appalled.

'I don't change, you know. Other than the full moon. That's a personal choice.' She swallowed. *In for a penny, in for a pound*, she thought. There was no going back now. The next words out of her mouth would cut a betrayal so deep in the wolves that nothing would survive it. 'I *hate* the wolf. I hate to be her a single second longer than I have to be. But I changed that night and I tore the throat out of that wolf. And I would do it again without hesitation.'

'Sage.' Oren's voice was soft. Not a warning. Not anything really, other than a reminder that she didn't need to justify anything to anyone.

She ignored him. 'So when you say that there is nothing you will not do to protect the people you love, trust me when I say that I understand that.' Her voice was barely a whisper now, her throat closed so tightly. 'You accuse me of being loyal in all the wrong places.'

She realized her chest was heaving as she stared down the livid witch mother. But she had not been through so much shit in her short life to have these kinds of accusations thrown at her.

Not when Sybil Crows-Caw had done what she'd done.

'So this is your last chance to tell the truth,' Sage said. 'To try and help me understand why your daughter is a prisoner in that cave.'

37

SAGE

Silence.

Sybil seemed to deflate. Like the accusation was the needle that burst all the tension building up inside her.

'. . . Kalinka?' Gabriel said blankly. His voice trailed away as realization settled over him. 'What are you saying?'

She looked at Oren, who, thank God, didn't look surprised. He'd been the only one following. He nodded his support. *Keep going.*

'*Quoi?*' one of the witches whispered as they glanced between each other, eyes full of confusion.

'*Maman?*'

'*Quoi? Maman?*'

'The legend of the Häxgrotta is nothing but a carefully crafted cover, cultivated over decades. The "offerings" are supplies.' She looked at Sybil. The grey smoke that rises from the mountain is . . . what? Those supplies cooked over a fire? Or maybe she's just trying to keep warm on the cold days. Whatever the reason, Kalinka is alive, and she's in that cave. Am I right?'

The silence seemed to drag on forever as Sage, Oren, all the witches and the werewolves gathered stared at the witch mother for ultimate confirmation.

She crumpled, covering her face with her hands.

Blank shock rippled through the witches, their defensive positions breaking as they turned to gape, confusion and horror etched on their beautiful faces.

Sage didn't understand some of the things they started to ask the witch mother, but she understood the tone. Desperation, begging for this news not to be true. Some of them had already started to cry. How could she have done this? This wasn't the truth? She could not have lied to them all this time?

Sybil's head drooped, and she let out a sob. When she looked back at Sage and Oren, she looked ancient. 'Will you trust that none of my witches were involved, if I tell you the truth?'

Some of the witches had started to cry. *What truth? This wasn't true?*

'That depends on the story,' Oren said quietly.

Sybil looked at him for a moment, then nodded, resigned. 'When Kalinka was born she was special. Powerful. And they were scared of her.'

'Who?' he asked.

'Everyone.' Sybil shrugged. 'One day a young female werewolf befriended her. Mathilde.' Sage's ears pricked at the name – the name the Baba Yaga had told her. And the way Sybil said it sounded like poison. And even through their tears, the rest of the witches hissed. 'We never knew, not until after it happened. Mathilde lured her further away from her home. But it was a trap. Other wolves ambushed her. Tied her up. They stripped her outer layers and beat her bloody. They tortured her and in the freezing cold rain, and left her for dead—'

Had Eugene known this part of the tale too? Was this what he hadn't wanted to confess to a law enforcer of the Arcānum?

Noise erupted from the small crowd of werewolves. 'How do we know any of this is true?' one shouted. 'Now she admits Kalinka lives! How can we trust anything she says? How do we know *Mathilde* existed?'

One of the witches, a tall woman with high cheekbones and long black hair flowing down her back, shot to her feet, her expression contorted with rage.

'When she was found, Kalinka slept for a day and a night,' the young witch said defiantly. Her voice was strong and loud. The complete opposite to her witch mother. 'And when she woke, she would say only one word. *Mathilde.*' The witch accentuated the name. Let it hiss slowly off her tongue and between her teeth. '*Mathilde. Mathilde.* Over and over. Like a chant. Like a *curse.*'

More snarls.

Sage knew the wolves would take that as provocation, and she couldn't let it escalate.

'It's true.' She stepped in quickly. 'I got the coordinates of where she was found. It's close to some bergsmed tunnels. They told me they met her not long before she was attacked, and that she was accompanied by another young woman. Until today I thought it was another witch.'

Gabriel's eyes snapped to her, and they were so cold and alien that she almost flinched.

'You knew I was here to investigate, Gabriel. Why are you surprised that I did?'

He shook his head, and the smile that curled the corners of his lips was cold. 'I'm just surprised at all the sneaking around. I didn't think you had it in you.' The unspoken insult was there. He expected it of Oren, but not her.

'You mean you're surprised I didn't tell you everything?' she snapped back, refusing to let the hurt at their broken friendship show. 'So you could run back and tell Mummy?'

It was his turn to flinch. Had he honestly not expected her to know that every detail he could squeeze out was reported back? She was almost disappointed in him. But she was more disappointed in herself. Every time she realized just how stupid and weak he must've thought she was not to notice anything going on around her.

'Today I spoke with the Baba Yaga,' Sage admitted. Both sides of the river gasped. Maybe the first time they'd been united in something in decades, she thought. 'She also told me Mathilde's name. And that she was a werewolf. She was real.'

When nobody answered, still too shocked by the revelation Sage had survived an encounter with the Baba Yaga, Oren cleared his throat. 'Carry on, Sybil.'

'When we found her, when we brought her home . . .' Sybil's mouth continued to open and close, but nothing came out. Like she couldn't get the words out. She shook her head, covering her face with her hands again.

The sight of it finally broke the rest of the witches.

Two of them moved to wrap their arms around her back, to whisper in her ear and comfort her. It was an interesting thing to witness, Sage thought, watching them forgive her for this monumental bombshell she'd just dropped so easily. Was that genuine, or did their loyalty alter their perception? She looked back at the werewolves and wondered how they'd react if the roles were reversed. Would they hear Celeste out before judging her? She knew they would.

The witch with the long dark hair lifted her chin. 'Though our tonics could start to heal the physical wounds' – she threw another glare across the river – 'the burn marks from the ropes that bound her, and the cuts they'd made to torture her, we could not heal what was in here . . .' She tapped the side of her head with a long finger. 'Kalinka was not what she was before. She was home for three days but she was changed forever. She slept often, but when she was awake, she . . .' She shook her head. 'Her control? Gone.' She clicked a finger, to indicate how instantaneous this change was in their sister. Then she looked at her witch mother. *'Maman?'* she asked. 'Is this what you're trying to say?'

Sybil looked up at her witch with watery eyes and a weak smile, and nodded her thanks.

'I knew immediately her mind was beyond all repair.' Sybil's voice was barely a whisper. Her grief palpable. And Sage was shocked to realize she felt pity. She didn't have children of her own, but she loved her family fiercely. Would she do whatever she thought necessary for P? For Oren? Even if it broke the law? She knew she would. 'Little made sense when she spoke. She just repeated that name. Over and over. Like she wanted us to know who had done this to her. Power exploded in uncontrollable bursts. When one of my witches tried to clean her wounds, she set her hair on fire. When another tried to change her dressings, she threw her back with such force it broke her arm. It was like all her anger, all her pain, was expressing itself in the only way it could, now that coherent speech had left her. I knew that if the world found out what she'd become' – she looked at Oren this time, as if he represented the world she was talking about – 'she would either be taken from us, or executed.'

Oren gave no reaction. No confirmation or denial of what he would've done if he'd been sent to assess a tortured witch who'd lost control of all her power.

Sybil drew in a deep, shuddering breath, and she turned

away from Sage and Oren, and towards her witches. And Sage understood. This was the turning point now. This was the part of the story that changed everything. This was the story they didn't know, and she would tell it to them first.

'I made a decision. Over the first two nights I set about making the cave at the top of the mountain comfortable. A bed, and furniture. And then on the third night I swapped the rota so that I was the one on duty to watch over her. I took her up to the cave and locked her safely inside, invisible to the outside world. I told everyone at first light that she had died in the night. I said that I had already prepared the body, that I had wanted to do it alone, as her mother, and placed it upon a pyre at the foot of the mountain.' She held her hands out apologetically towards her witches. 'It was not her body wrapped in the silk shrouds. I just made it look like that. Nobody knew any different. We lit her pyre at dawn.'

'The werewolves believe you have worshipped a goddess that lives in that cave for centuries,' Oren said. 'It appears that your witches believe the same . . .'

'I used very old magic,' Sybil admitted. 'Powerful magic.'

'Dark magic,' Oren said bluntly. 'Call it what it is, Sybil.'

The witch mother looked like she wanted to snarl at him again, but she nodded.

'Dark magic,' she admitted, if reluctantly. 'It's not illegal. Just frowned upon. But it was the only way to save her. The only way to make her life bearable. To take away some of the pain it was causing her as she struggled to control it. I used a dark spell to siphon out most of her power, and redirected it.' She looked at Oren again. 'You know magic that powerful must be used up. I had to put it somewhere. So I reinforced the spells on the mountain. The tethering spell that kept her from straying too far from the cave mouth, just far enough to collect the supplies we left as offerings. And a concealment spell, so that nobody could see her, even if she stood at the cave mouth building a fire. And I have used the rest ever since to make my witches believe that the cave has always been inhabited by the Häxgrotta. That we have always worshipped and left offerings there. It hid Kalinka better. And it saved my witches from any culpability.'

'Oh, *Maman*,' one of the witches muttered. And Sage wasn't sure whether it was shock, horror, or sympathy. But a sister next to her shushed her with a hand on her arm. *Be careful*, Sage was sure her wide eyes seemed to warn.

'How much does she have left?' Oren asked her to confirm.

But Sage wasn't listening. Something else had snagged her attention.

'Enough to light a fire. Enough to keep herself warm.' Sybil drew in a shuddering breath. 'She still makes little sense when you try and speak to her. Her mind never fully healed. She is' – she seemed to struggle to even say the word – 'insane.'

'When did you last go in there, to try to speak to her?' Sage asked.

Sybil blinked, unsure. She looked down at her fingers and appeared to be counting, trying to figure something out. 'About three weeks ago. She does not . . . react kindly if you try to enter the cave.'

No shit, Sage thought. She'd be pissed off too if she'd been locked up for seven decades, tethered by spells so she could see her own coven, but they couldn't see her. Coupled with other instability . . .

'What did she do?' Sage asked. 'She did something to you, didn't she?'

'No—'

'Yes,' Sage cut across her. 'What happened?'

Sybil's nostrils flared, and the shadow of the cold, cruel witch mother she'd been at the start of their confrontation flashed across her face again. 'She pushed me out of the cave. I fell back. I hit my head.'

Sage nodded. 'And for a split-second you lost control of the magic you were using to open the concealment spells so you could see her?' Sage didn't bother to wait for her answer. She turned to Oren. 'You know what else the Baba Yaga told me?'

He raised a brow, waiting.

God, he was handsome when he did that. But now wasn't the time.

Concentrate, Sage.

'She told me that when we arrived in these mountains, she felt your power. Like you told me you could feel hers, right? But . . . she told me that she never felt the fog arrive.' The grin that split Oren's face was wide. And proud. She smiled back at the sight of it. *Go for it*, the glint in his eye said. *Blow this whole thing wide open.* So she turned back to Sybil. 'What if the Baba Yaga never felt the fog arrive because it's always been here.'

More silence. But this time it was loaded. She could feel the tension rising in the air, thick like tar, as the wolves started to piece everything she was saying together.

'The Baba Yaga said she could sense the remnants of a concealment spell and assumed that was why. But she was wrong. Well, it probably explains why Oren had so much trouble tracking it. We've only witnessed it when it's turned up on its own accord.' Oren let out a little growl of agreement as he realized he'd wasted all that time hunting for nothing. 'But for those seconds you lost a grip on those spells, some of her magic escaped out of the cave. The magic she can't control. And some of that concealment spell just grasped on to the tips of the magic . . . the *fog*, as it floated away.'

The witch with the black hair, who had stood to speak when her mother couldn't, swore under her breath as she pieced it together too.

'Did you know, Sybil?' Oren demanded. 'Did you see it escape?'

She didn't answer.

Which was answer enough.

'Your other witches have seen it, though?' he pushed. 'Even if they didn't realize it was part of Kalinka. How else did they know to repel it down on the riverbank?'

'It has passed through our camp twice,' Sybil admitted. 'Our camp is closer to this cave, so an appearance wasn't unexpected. I feigned ignorance and called on my witches to do what they could. Trial and error brought us to the best repelling enchantments quickly enough.'

'But your missing witch, the one you said went missing recently . . .' Sage said slowly. 'The fog did consume her, right?'

More glances between the witches, but it seemed clear to Sage that whatever they really thought or felt, none of them were willing to openly challenge their witch mother.

'I cannot be certain,' she said honestly. 'She went alone to find some herbs to replenish her potions cabinet and never returned. But . . . after I saw what happened to Chloé's arm, I started to suspect.'

There was no point asking why she hadn't told any of them, the Arcānum or any of her witches, of her suspicions. Because she would've had to admit Kalinka was in that cave, or that she knew what the fog was.

'Do you know what became of Mathilde?' Sage asked.

'She was never seen again. I imagine she fled when she heard Kalinka had been found, and was still alive to tell us her name. The werewolves told us she'd left the mountains to live amongst humans once again.'

Sybil bowed her head, the story told at last.

Sage looked at Oren. She had no idea where to start. On any of it.

Was there a law that Sybil had broken in locking her daughter away like this? Yes. Did the fact she'd done it to protect Kalinka from repercussions for what she'd become, and to protect the rest of her coven from the unpredictability of Kalinka's increasing instability make a difference? Maybe.

Well, it did to her.

'I cannot allow you to keep her imprisoned in that cave, not now I know she's in there,' Oren said. 'You know that, don't you?'

Sybil's head snapped back up. 'And do what instead?'

'It depends.' He shrugged. 'On what state we find her in when you drop the spells imprisoning her, as well as the memory charms on your witches.'

'I will not,' Sybil growled, drawing herself back up, fresh defiance on her face. 'She has not had access to the extent of her power in decades. She cannot control it—'

'Then perhaps you should have tried to retrain her,' Oren shot back. 'Rather than locking her away in a darkened cell. Which no doubt has damaged her even more than you ever intended or realized.'

She heard the undercurrent there that she knew everyone

else had missed. He had told her once that a minotaur had locked him up. Held him prisoner for six years. And though he'd never gone into more detail than that, she knew this imprisonment had been the catalyst for him refusing to serve in the Cariva any longer, opting to demote himself to the Arcānum wherever possible.

'You will do as I say,' he warned her. 'I will grant you tonight to speak with your coven, and tomorrow we will deal with Kalinka.'

'If you put all that power back into her, the magic will kill you, if it doesn't kill her first,' Sybil warned. 'You will not be able to enter that cave.'

Oren's impassive, beautiful face was blank, not a hint of compassion or sympathy on any of his features. All the things she knew he hid away from anyone but her and P.

He nodded at Sage, agreeing with her silent suggestion.

'We know someone who can,' she said quietly.

'Then you sign their death warrant.'

'It doesn't matter.' Sage's chest panged as it always did. 'She's already dead.'

38

SAGE

Oren didn't wait.

He shifted her back across the river, and as her feet touched solid ground she felt the familiar warmth of his magic, a translucent golden blanket of protection settling over her skin.

Then he disappeared again, off to make the long journey back home. To their precious home, and their precious P.

'She will be here by tomorrow morning,' Sage told the witch mother. 'Speak to your witches tonight. Do what you need to do. Tomorrow, we will go up the mountain.'

She was surprised that Sybil didn't argue. The old woman nodded, turned to her few witches still waiting behind her, speaking quietly as they headed for the trees. It would be a long night for them. She wondered if the witch mother would still have control of her coven by morning.

When they were gone, she turned to look at the werewolves.

None of them spoke. All of them turned to head back towards their camp, and a likely debrief with their alpha.

Sage just had to trust that Celeste would keep this contained until the morning.

The truth was that, technically, everything that had befallen them recently *had* been at the hands of the witches. One specific witch. Kalinka.

'Gabriel.' She almost choked his name as he moved to turn away from her too. 'Wait.'

'For what?' He rounded on her. 'For you to tell me how you really hate us?'

It felt like a punch to the gut. 'I never said that.'

'You said you hate the wolf—'

'I do.' She wouldn't be forced to say untruths to save his feelings. '*My* wolf, yes, because I have done terrible things when I'm her, Gabriel, but—'

'But what? What can she have done that was so bad, for you to "hate" her?' He quoted the air with his fingers in disbelief. 'Everything you are. Everything *we* are?' He held his arms out, gesturing to this whole world around them. His eyes flashed and he gave a bitter laugh. 'And let's not even begin to talk about that wolf you killed. I mean, of course you did, you put that – ' he looked around for an insult filled with enough venom to describe Oren – 'that *monster* before wolf loyalty? A monster devoid of any sense of humanity, who you defend to the *hilt*! You put another race before your own?'

She stared at him.

She understood wolf loyalty, but this was the first time

Gabriel reminded her of Roderick. His attitude towards other races, towards her simply for being a werewolf, demeaning and cruel.

'You know, don't you, what he did to the last true werewolf pack he strode into?' he demanded. 'You know what he does to people like us?'

'Amhuinn was turning humans on purpose. To see if he could make magical hybrids,' she whispered defiantly, but hot tears were already spilling down her cheeks. 'Oren had no choice.'

Gabriel stared. He hadn't expected her to know that story. How could she, and still be loyal to Oren? He must've convinced himself that she couldn't know. Or she'd never choose him.

'And the hybrids, they deserved to die too? Was it their fault, what happened to them?'

'He doesn't claim to have always got it right, Gabriel.' Even as she said it, she could hear how it sounded like an excuse. It didn't explain the depths of their conversations, the truths admitted, the never-ending, crushing guilt Oren whispered about when they were on their own.

'He doesn't *care*.' He shook his head, laughing angrily. 'I like you, Sage, I do, but you're young, and I'm sure he can be charming and—'

The crack of her hand across his cheek echoed through the trees around them. And her tears of grief turned to tears of anger.

'Don't you dare,' she hissed, 'patronize me.'

She pulled her jumper and T-shirt over her head and stood there in nothing but her jeans and bra. She wasn't even embarrassed. It wasn't her breasts he was staring at, but the five-centimetre black scar in the centre of her chest, the forks of lightning spearing off it and spreading across her shoulders. As if poison had got into her veins and started to invade her body.

'That was one of Amhuinn's hybrids.' She pointed to the mess. 'At the last moon ball. He stabbed me with a silver dagger. After his father, the alpha of the pack that tried to kill Oren, allowed *five* werewolves to be murdered rather than help us.' It was her turn to laugh angrily. 'So don't you tell me that werewolves are better than warlocks, or any other race, because so far in my experience, they've been some of the biggest bastards of all.'

'That was silver?' He gagged, as if he hadn't heard anything else she'd said after.

His eyes moved to her face at last, and he didn't even ask how she'd survived.

Sometimes, she wondered whether Oren would be able to do it again for another wolf, summon whatever strength he needed without the sheer force of panic and fear and horror they'd all been feeling in the room that night.

'And for what it's worth,' she said, 'he knows my sins too. And he has never once made me feel ashamed. *That's* why you would always be second best.'

He didn't speak. And she didn't know what else to say either. Finally, he nodded and turned to follow the rest of the wolves back to camp.

She waited until she couldn't hear his footsteps any more before she set off to their cabin. She slammed the door and bolted all the locks. She realized it could be the first night in three years, other than a full moon, that she'd spend without either P or Oren somewhere within shouting distance. He wouldn't be able to shift the ghost across the world like he'd done for her, so P would have to travel by human transport and not arrive for some time.

She groaned.

She dragged her duvet from her bed into the little living room, wrapped herself up in a cocoon and collapsed on to the sofa. Then she lay down on her side and let herself cry and cry and cry.

39
SAGE

She drifted in and out of sleep as she wept, until the fading light outside the windows turned black. She didn't even have the energy to get up and turn on a lamp. She had this one night to feel sorry for herself without anyone there to witness it.

She closed her eyes again and listened to the wolf world around her. If she strained hard enough she could hear faint conversations, but they were all in French, so she let her senses tune them back out. She listened to the soft rustle of the highest leaves on the trees all around, moved by a breeze passing over the mountain tops.

'You'd never let me forget it, if you found me self-pitying like this,' Oren's voice said softly into the quiet.

She jumped, eyes snapping open to find him leaning against the kitchen surface opposite where she lay. His arms were folded and he was smiling.

'On the contrary,' her muffled voice came through the duvet cocoon obscuring her mouth. 'I've never once mentioned how P left you crying on our sofa with a bottle of whisky the night of the moon ball, while she sat with me in my bedroom.'

His brow twitched. 'I wondered if she'd told you about that.'

'Where is she?' She sat up, looking around confused.

'Berion and Hozier are bringing her.' He pushed off the kitchen counter and turned on the lamps around the room with a flick of his finger. 'I'll meet them in Poligny, once they make it that far, and bring them up the last bit of the mountains myself.'

'Couldn't you have just brought her?'

'I'm not getting on a plane, Sage,' he tutted as if such travel was beneath him.

She rolled her eyes.

She stood, stretching as the duvet fell to the floor, rubbing at her eyes she knew still looked swollen and red. He watched her, his face hard. And then he sighed. For the second time that day he closed the gap between them and pulled her into his arms.

It was stiff, his back as rigid as ever. It was a gesture he was so, *so* rarely ever willing to offer. But just for tonight, he knew she needed something.

She wrapped her arms around him and clung tightly to the back of his jacket.

'What was it like?' she whispered.

'Like going home.'

'I want to go home.'

'I know,' he said. He pushed her back and looked down at her face, brushing strands of hair behind her ear.

She looked up into his turquoise eyes and wondered what he thought about hers ringed in red – again. Tears cried over another man. She knew it would be foolish to ever wonder if he could feel jealous.

He smiled like he knew what she was thinking. 'Shower. Get changed,' he said, stepping back from her. 'We're not sitting in this cabin tonight, we'll go out for dinner. Somewhere nice.'

She gave him a withering look. 'Stop feeling sorry for me.'

'You're not spending another night eating with those bloody wolves, and neither of us can cook a decent meal between us until P gets here. So come on.' He gestured to her bedroom. 'Get a move on.'

She tutted, but did as she was told.

As she walked into her room she saw there was a bag on the bed. She could hear the smile on Oren's lips. 'P sent you some fancy clothes.'

She walked out of her bedroom an hour later in a dress she hadn't worn since before she'd met Oren. It was sleeveless and black and fitted down to her knees, with the small problem of leaving her scars on display.

Even with her long hair freshly washed and blow-dried, it wasn't enough to cover them. 'Can you mask these?' she asked as she found Oren in a black suit he hadn't been wearing before either.

She refused to look at him for fear of feeling jellied. Sometimes he was just too handsome for her to entirely keep her head.

'Why?' he challenged, coming close enough to gently run a finger over the highest tip of the black scars that just touched her moonstone necklace. 'They're a part of you.'

'It'll freak out the humans.'

'You look beautiful.'

She took the fingers that were tracing her collarbone in her hand.

'Do you have feelings for him?' he asked softly.

'No,' she admitted, a truth she'd settled on in the hours she lay crying, trying to sift through what she felt and why it all hurt so much. Gabriel was handsome, and charming, and he'd been the distraction she'd needed when she'd arrived, and a friend she hadn't realized she'd wanted. But that was all. 'I thought we were friends. But his friendship came with conditions, which isn't real friendship at all. Hurting my feelings isn't the same as having feelings.'

He nodded. She looked back up into his beautiful eyes.

'This isn't over between us, Sage.'

And how she craved the idea of it. Was desperate for that to be true. Grieved the loss of love before it could even blossom. She wanted it so much it made her heart hurt. The fingers of his other hand brushed her cheek, and she had to force herself not to shiver, or lean too much into his touch. With a small wave of that hand she felt the warm touch of his magic, and looked down to see a clear chest free of the blackened scars for the first time in half a year.

He stepped back, observed his work, and nodded. Then pulled open the door to their cabin. 'Let's go.'

'We can't leave from in here?'

'I look just as good as you.' He smirked. 'Let them all see it. But come on, we're going to be late for the reservation.'

She forced herself not to laugh at his endless arrogance and allowed him to lead them out into the street. It was the perfect time. The dinner hall had opened, and wolves were starting to descend. Most in the vicinity looked over. A couple slowed. A few looked her up and down. One even smiled appreciatively. Then she saw Estelle and Gabriel coming out of the next street, side by side, carrying matching bowls covered in foil ready to be eaten. Estelle spotted them first, nudging her brother with her elbow, and Sage was secretly pleased to see a double-take.

'Chin high,' Oren whispered in her ear as his arm snaked around her waist, readying to shift them away. 'Shoulders back.'

Usually, she might've refused this kind of display, but tonight, understanding what she'd sacrificed by admitting what she'd done to save him in front of pack wolves, he was making a point. And he was doing it for her.

'Oren.' She looked up at him. She'd tried to walk away

from these kind of moments between them so many times, but as he held her close, there in front of all those wolves, telling her to lift her chin, to never be embarrassed and never be afraid, how could she go her whole life and not tell him the truth, at least once? 'Oren, I—'

She swallowed. The words caught in the tight lump that'd suddenly risen in her throat.

'I know, Sage,' was all he said. He leant in and planted the smallest kiss on her forehead. 'Don't worry. I already know.'

And they shifted away into Poligny.

Or so she thought.

And all emotions that came with him telling her he already knew that for her it was him, always him, only him, disappeared.

'Oren!' she gasped. He still held her tightly, helping her keep balance with the extra hazard of heeled shoes as the golden beacon of light towered over them. This was not Poligny at all. All around them were couples, families, Parisians and tourists wondering around, smiling, laughing, taking pictures. In the distance was an old carousel, turning gently as music tinkled.

'I didn't specify which city.' He shrugged, but he was grinning in that annoying way as he looked at something over her shoulder, nodding for her to turn and look.

'Table for five at the top of the Eiffel Tower. Fancy.' Berion stood in a deep-blue velvet suit with black lapels,

Hozier and P on either side.

She could've burst into tears again at the sight of them. After the last couple of days, and the growing ache of homesickness in her chest, they were all she wanted.

'Darling.' He swept forward and bent down to kiss both of her cheeks. 'Don't,' he whispered into her ear. 'It'll ruin your make-up.'

She laughed in teary disbelief as Hozier gave her a tight hug, also in a fitted dress, though hers matched Berion's in colour, as she now realized she'd been set up to match Oren.

'I swear, I expected him to take you for dinner in Paris without me,' P laughed when she turned to her at last, unable to throw her arms around the one person she always wanted to touch most.

'He would have, if he thought I'd agree to come without you,' Sage grinned back. 'The nights he complained how bad both our cooking skills are.'

'Oh, I know he would have!' She rolled her eyes in his direction. 'And just hope I didn't find out!'

He held up his hands. 'We're here now together, aren't we?'

P *hmm*ed disapprovingly, but she was trying not to smile.

'You've got a lot to tell us.' Berion's white eyes sparkled. 'We've got a lot to tell you. So come on, at least there will be decent wine.'

As the group of friends set off towards the gates that'd take them up into the tower, fingers twisted in hers to pull her back. She turned to Oren and the lights of the tower flashed, as they did every hour, on the hour, just for a minute. The reflection made his turquoise eyes sparkle.

He smiled as he watched her keep turning, grinning, spinning on the spot as she looked up at the tower glittering over them, and when she was facing him again, so drunk on the happiness suddenly welling in her chest, she didn't even try to stop the hands that came to rest again on her waist, pulling her in close.

'Sage,' he whispered, as her own hands came up to his chest, unable to stop herself leaning into him. She could smell him. She could feel his breath on her lips as his forehead came to rest against hers. How much longer would she be able to resist? 'When we get home, we need to talk.'

'Oren—'

'No, Sage.' He conceded so much to her, she knew that. But the way he said *no* this time was different. 'There are some things we need to discuss. Important things I need to tell you.'

'Like what?' she breathed. His lips were so close to hers. She only needed to lift her chin a fraction and she knew they'd meet.

His other hand came to her face, thumb stroking her cheek. 'Like how I felt like I would've died inside if you'd said you did have feelings for Gabriel,' he whispered. 'Like how I love you too. And I don't *want* to spend the rest of my life pretending otherwise.'

'The rest of *my* life.'

'Sage,' he sighed. 'If I have to ask the gods themselves to let me grow old with you, I will.'

'That's not possible.'

'You've got no idea what could be possible for us,' he told her softly. 'Do you trust me?'

'Always.'

'Then trust me in this. This isn't over. Not yet.'

And just for tonight, as he moved the last few centimetres between them to kiss her, and her lips parted to let him, she decided to believe him.

40

P

'Do we pretend we've not seen that?' Hozier asked.

The three of them stood under the tower, waiting for Sage and Oren.

For all her worry that Oren would struggle to deal with Sage's emotions while they were away, he couldn't have looked more at ease now as he held her close, his forehead pressed against hers, whispering whatever truths he told nobody but her.

'I think so,' P sighed. 'Let them have this moment. God knows it'll only get harder from here, when she finds out the truth.'

'Every romantic's dream.' Berion looked up at the tower glittering above them.

Hozier let out a small, dramatic gasp. 'You owe me a tenner, P.'

A bet they'd made last week as the pair of them had sat up late and watched *The Proposal* and joked that the enemies-to-lovers trope was very Sage and Oren. Hozier had betted that, stuck together up a mountain with no P as their constant buffer, *something* would end up happening. P had thought Sage was too stubborn. Knew she tortured herself too harshly over her mortality to give in.

But for once . . . P was happy to lose a bet.

P was happy to let love win.

She turned her back on them to join the small line of people waiting for the lift, making sure Sage and Oren didn't realize they'd been noticed. She'd be willing to pay a million – which she'd have to borrow from Oren – if it meant her two best friends could find even the smallest chance of happiness together.

And just for tonight, she would ignore the gut feeling in her stomach that warned her this was all just a fool's dream.

41

OREN

'This is so not what I expected.' P gaped at the tiny garden walls and the flower basket windows as they headed through the cabin village that was the Dubois camp. P, Berion and Hozier had arrived an hour before, taking a series of trains across the country to get there from Paris through the night. 'It's . . . it's beautiful?'

'You should see the Monreau camp,' Sage told her. 'It's even better.'

Oren felt a huge, unexpected sense of relief to see them, Sage and P, side by side again as they walked through the trees on their way to the river. Like a missing jigsaw piece had been found and slotted back into place.

When they'd got back to the cabin, after much wine and debate on how to handle what came next, there was a note waiting for them. Gabriel had told Celeste everything. Because of course he had. And she would meet them at the river in the morning.

Oren didn't object. If the alpha stood any chance of controlling the fallout once word about Kalinka finally got round to all the packs, it would be better if she witnessed first-hand whatever was about to happen.

'Ergh,' Berion huffed ten minutes later as they stepped over mud and old leaves. 'This is ridiculous. How on earth do you keep shoes clean . . . well . . . I see . . .'

They'd come out on the bank to a small host of were-wolves, and his eyes had immediately fallen on the battered old hiking boots Benoît was wearing. A far cry from Berion's shining, patent leather brogues.

Oren scoffed a laugh under his breath. He'd been wrapping his own feet in magical shields to protect his shoes all week.

Celeste was surrounded by every wolf that'd been at the riverside to witness Sybil's confession yesterday. He was glad to see she'd learnt her lesson from Patrice at any rate, keeping this lot firmly in her sights.

The only surprise was Sacha, which was somewhat of a boon. Two alphas as witnesses would be better than one. He still looked pale, and there was a darkness to his eyes that Oren recognized as the shadows of grief. But the fresh pink skin he could just see on some of his arm was clean, and the physical injuries seemed to have healed well with his magic.

Every head turned at their arrival.

He felt a flash of anxiety that wasn't his own and sent a waft of the reassuring magic he saved just for Sage down her spine. She threw him a small smile. Something territorial inside him that he hadn't ever let rear its head before purred.

He'd kissed her again last night.

He was *so* over pretending.

The fear in his chest the moment he'd realized where she'd gone yesterday, knowing that the Baba Yaga might well have killed her before he even got there to save her? He wasn't going another day without knowing for certain there was no chance for them.

So he'd told Sage last night they needed to talk. He was going to tell her everything first, and then if she still didn't want him, he'd accept it. He wasn't sure when she found out the truth whether she'd ever want to kiss him again, so he'd made sure he'd savoured the moment. Just in case.

Celeste started to greet them but she faltered, staring at P. All of them, gaping at her hovering a few centimetres above the forest floor, taking in her scars. Wounds that were identical to so many of their own.

'This is P,' he introduced her as Berion and Hozier hung tactfully back, waiting their turn.

'How long have you known each other?' Gabriel asked.

'Since we were very young.' P lifted her chin, understanding the question was about her and Sage, and didn't involve Oren at all. 'We met as small children, at school, when we were both human. This is the longest we've ever been apart since, right?' Sage nodded. 'I died nearly three years ago. We've lived together since then. Oren joined us last year.'

He knew that it took something for Sage to look at Gabriel, because it was obvious that he knew. The eyes that were staring at her now were full of understanding and pity, and maybe even a bit of regret. He hadn't considered that she might hate her own wolf because it'd killed anyone, let alone her best friend.

But everyone seemed to decide they wouldn't acknowledge the obvious elephant in the room as Celeste smiled. 'Welcome, uh, P?'

'My name is Patricia,' P explained. 'But my friends call me P. I suppose it stands for poltergeist too, these days. That's what Oren thought, when we first met.'

Celeste gave a forced-sounding chuckle.

'This is she?' Sacha looked at Sage. 'The chef?'

Sage couldn't hide the relief on her face that Sacha spoke to her at all. Oren knew she was terrified the alpha blamed her for what had happened in his camp yesterday. In reality, it was only ever Sage who blamed herself.

She nodded with a small smile. P beamed at the recognition.

'A poltergeist.' He waved his signature pipe at P like she was a novelty, looking at Celeste. 'Can you believe it? Have you ever seen one, Celeste? I haven't.'

'Oren has forgotten his manners.' Berion cleared his throat, if only to stop P becoming the circus spectacle. He stepped forward, smoothing the front of his forest-green corduroy suit before stretching his bejewelled hand towards Celeste to introduce himself.

Berion smiled politely as she startled, taking in his white eyes properly for the first time. 'They are my grandmother's.' He answered the obvious question. 'She was a witch mother of a coven local to our hometown. She died a long time ago.'

'What a day,' Sacha said under his breath. 'Quarter-witch. I haven't seen one of those either.'

Berion, graceful as ever, ignored Sacha's comment and placed a hand over his chest, bowing his head. 'You must be Sacha Monreau? Sage told me about your wolf. You have my condolences.' And that seemed to stop Sacha in his tracks. He closed his mouth and nodded his thanks.

Then Berion turned an indulgent smile to the wolf loitering just behind Celeste. 'And you must be Gabriel. I've heard all about you too.'

Whatever anyone had told him, Berion left hanging in the air.

Even across the clearing, Oren could see Gabriel's cheeks go red.

He smirked.

'Sorry,' Benoît cut in with his naturally rude tone. 'But why are you here? She' – he gestured to P – 'makes sense. She's going into the cave. Who are you?'

Oren saw P look at Sage, and then at Hozier, and the three girls smother their laughter as Berion's head turned, almost in slow motion. His white eyes looked Benoît up and down, from his battered hiking boots to his balding head.

Then he ignored the advisor entirely.

Somehow, it was even more cutting than Oren nearly breaking his wrist.

'This is my partner, Hozier.' Berion gestured to their tiniest companion, her flaming-red hair shining like molten gold in the morning sunlight.

She came forward to greet the alphas. 'We are colleagues of Oren and Sage, we're also with the Arcānum.' She said it for Benoît's benefit, even as she ignored him too, smiling politely to Celeste, then turned to shake Sacha's hand.

'So, you're going up the mountain?' Gabriel asked P.

P nodded. 'To see what we find, I suppose. See if she's . . . saveable.'

'And if she isn't?' he asked.

'Then I kill her,' Oren said bluntly.

Gabriel opened his mouth as if he was going to retort something that would make Oren summon a dagger to cut out his tongue.

But Berion saw it too and decided to intervene. 'So!' He clapped ring-encrusted fingers together loudly with an air of *getting to business* and headed for the water's edge, looking at Oren. 'Shall I take charge for the next bit?'

Oren raised a brow. *Be my guest.*

'How are you—' Sacha started. But Berion was already waving a purple hand.

The smooth surface of the river started to ripple. One by one, stones summoned from the riverbed began to break the surface, each humming with his magic around the edges.

Well, that was a way of doing it.

Most of the wolves looked horrified at such an open display of magic they weren't used to seeing, ensconced up there in the mountains. They'd watched Oren shift about with horror, but he horrified them regardless of his magic. Only Sacha looked mildly impressed.

'Time to cross, then.' Without waiting, Berion started to stride across the water. 'They will sink once I cross to the other side,' he warned loudly over his shoulder as he reached the middle of the wide river and saw that nobody else had moved. 'I suggest all of you move quickly. Unless you want to shift with Oren.'

P floated forward until her feet were hovering over the water, then turned back with an encouraging smile. 'Celeste? Sacha?'

Oren smiled to himself. Berion's flattering confidence was unrivalled, but P's tact was unmatched too. P knew Celeste didn't really want to be the first one to step on to the stones. But once she did, her wolves would follow. He had to give it to the alpha for putting her own trepidation aside as she stepped on to the first stone.

Sacha followed behind, pipe smoke trailing in his wake.

And then every wolf started to move.

He knew Berion wouldn't actually sink the stones while any werewolves were still crossing, but that twinkle was in those white eyes as he looked back again to check their progress.

Oren took Sage's hand, and she held hers out to Hozier, and he shifted the three of them over. They emerged on the other side just as Berion made landfall, and most of the wolves had cleared two-thirds of the river.

'That's disgusting, you know,' Hozier muttered as she righted herself, clamping a hand over her mouth.

'You get used to it.' Sage smiled, even though he knew she heaved more times than she didn't.

And, of course, it wasn't until the last wolf foot touched the grassy embankment a few moments later that one by one, the stones dropped back to the depths they'd been raised from. Then there was the sound of soft footsteps.

They turned as Sybil Crows-Caw emerged from the trees.

She was still alive then. And unharmed, by the looks of it.

He'd wondered how her confession to the coven would go. Apparently, she'd survived the reckoning. But Sybil only had eyes for Berion. She came up close, tilting her head to the side as she examined his face. 'Were you . . . born with them?'

He nodded. 'Like Kalinka, I believe.'

'And you can control it? The power?'

'Warlock magic is even more powerful,' he reminded her. 'But yes. Not many warlocks know I have witch magic too. They think my eyes are just a quirk. As some warlocks have talons, or cat eyes, or' – he gestured at Oren – 'interesting hair. My parents ensured I had extra training as a child, in secret, to make sure I could control both magics.'

Sybil didn't answer, but her throat bobbed.

Kalinka being born with white eyes had led to many things: her fate, her imprisonment. Perhaps Sybil looked at Berion, tall and confident and unafraid, and saw what her daughter could have become, had events gone differently.

'Where are the rest of your witches, Sybil?' Sage asked.

'They're already at the mountain,' she said. 'They're waiting for you.'

So, they would have an audience, then. And how would they react if the worst came to pass? What if over a hundred witches decided to put themselves between Kalinka and his execution sword?

He had a sneaking suspicion Sybil had placed them there on purpose.

'OK,' Sage said. 'I guess you should lead the way.'

42

OREN

Despite everything he'd allowed to happen to get them to that point, he was annoyed.

He still thought the best course of action, if he was completely honest, was to stride into that cave and kill the witch inside.

Yes, he understood the protests that'd erupted from Sage, P and Hozier last night over dinner when he'd explained the harsh reality of what he'd have to do if they couldn't reach the witch. And even Berion had winced. But at the end of the day, they couldn't contain Kalinka indefinitely. It was cruel and inhumane. She'd been a prisoner for decades already and they were bound to liberate her from that. If she was as unpredictable and dangerous as the witch mother had told them . . . he wasn't sure what else they could do after?

That fog was only a slither that'd escaped that cave, yet it had still consumed a wolf and witch whole, never mind other injuries caused. If that was a precursor for what it was going to be capable of once Sybil Crows-Caw put back the power she'd siphoned, an execution order felt like a mercy.

He loved Sage, and P, but this was one of the rare occasions when their compassion was not a bonus. Look at where compassion had got Kalinka, when her mother had decided to hide her away rather than let the world see what she'd become.

Compassion was only delaying the inevitable.

They stood in a clearing at the base of the mountain. The cave was about seven hundred metres above them at the end of a narrow path carved into the rock. Outside he could just see the remnants of blackened wood, a dead fire giving off its last pathetic hints of smoke. He looked out on the crowd of witches in front of him, all of them sat cross-legged in rows of ten, eyes closed, holding hands and singing quietly.

He was creeped out.

'It reminds me of school assembly,' Sage muttered to P under her breath. Some memory from when they were both human together. 'Remember?'

'That song's not exactly as catchy as "Give Me Oil in My Lamp", though, is it?' P whispered back.

'Give it a fancy name and you could sell this as some kind of meditation exercise at a niche weekend retreat,' Berion said dispassionately. 'Fifty quid a ticket.'

All the girls scoffed.

Oren let them chatter. Sage laughing was one of his favourite sounds. And when it wasn't caused by Gabriel, well, even better. Instead, he watched Celeste at the back of the rows of trance-like witches, lining up her wolves ready to watch whatever was about to happen alongside their adversaries. She was whispering orders. A couple of them readjusted weirded-out expressions into more neutral territory.

Sacha stood puffing on his pipe, looking openly bemused.

'She has told them, hasn't she?' P eyed Sybil standing stony-faced, a little way off to the side as she too watched Celeste arrange more werewolves than had stepped foot on witch territory in centuries. 'Why are they so calm?'

'I told you.' Hozier sounded disdainful. 'They're as bad as pack wolves. If that witch mother has been able to spin her story well enough, they'll accept anything she does.'

Hozier was right, there.

And he was done waiting.

'Sybil.' The witches stopped singing. Everything went silent. All eyes opened and fell on him. Even creepier. 'It's time. Drop your spells of tethering and concealment, and then the memory charms on your witches. They know the truth now, so it doesn't matter.'

'You don't know what you're asking. She's not used to all that power,' Sybil tried one last time. 'It will consume her. It could kill us all.'

Honestly, he hadn't believed much of her defeated act yesterday. Sage had. He'd seen it on her face as she'd watched the witch mother crying over her daughter. But he understood witches too well. It was just as much about pride as about protecting her daughter. Having to admit what Kalinka had become would be a shame on their coven. And having someone like him turn up to execute one of them? A stain on their history. She'd said what she needed to say to get through yesterday, maybe even see if she could somehow convince Sage to let her carry on doing what she'd been doing . . . But this, now, it would infuriate her to have to allow it to pass.

He knew that Sybil Crows-Caw, despite all she had done, would rather have Kalinka die as the force of her power slammed back into her, than let him go in there and execute her. At least then she could spin the story in their favour, make him the ultimate villain, and save their reputation.

He didn't care. He'd been the villain in more stories than he could remember.

'I assure you that I do know what I'm asking,' he said quietly. In his long, awful history, this was nothing. 'Do it, Sybil. Now.'

All the eyes that had fixed on him shifted to the witch mother.

She threw him one last reproachful look, and then she closed her eyes. She held out her hands in front of her. Her lips moved, although no sound came out.

He waited.

He knew what it felt like when these kinds of spells were dropped, and if Sybil was indeed doing what she had been ordered—

There it was. The first thrum of power. Like a breeze that rippled over the clearing. So that was the tethering spell unleashing.

He looked up at the cave mouth: nothing.

He waited.

Then again. Another rush of wind, stronger than before. And when he looked up this time, black fog: thin wisps, small trickles, were swirling about the cave mouth.

Gasps.

Urgent whispers.

Pointing fingers.

The concealment spell was gone. For the first time, the witches were seeing what Sybil Crows-Caw had used magic to hide from them.

His eyes snapped to Celeste. A warning. Keep her wolves calm. He knew they'd heard it yesterday, understood that the fog that'd been terrorizing them had come from this cave, but seeing it like this?

If any of them snapped and reacted with anger, or hurled more accusations of curses at the gathered witches? There would be wolf fatalities before he could intervene.

She nodded, whispering down her line to hold their ground and keep their mouths shut.

Berion threw him a warning glance too. The last spell

left to be broken, the biggest, the strongest, the *darkest*, was about to break. Whatever was just about visible in the mouth of that cave now was nothing. He felt Berion's shield burst from him. The faintest shimmer of purple fitted itself tightly over Sage, Hozier and P. Then he sent his own golden shield to rest over the top.

There was a bang.

So loud he felt his own ears pop.

The blast that hit him now wasn't a gentle breeze. It was like a cannon.

He saw a strange wave of hair, of all different colours, adorned with feathers and beads and ribbons, all moving at once. Blasted back by what felt like the force of an explosion that'd just erupted out of the cave mouth, colliding with them all.

Screams rang out. Wails of pain from the witches as the spell cast over them was ripped from their minds. Hands cradled heads. Noses exploded with blood. He hadn't even realized he'd ducked on instinct until he was twisting round from where he crouched to look back up, Sage, Berion, Hozier and P beside him doing the same.

Darkness roared, the sound in his ears angry and loud, like a fire at the peak of its terror, ripping through whatever was fuelling it. The blackness coming out of the cave wasn't rolling and wisping now. It was surging out in thick angry waves, like black ink dropped into a sea of water, starting to cover the blue sky in darkness.

Some of the witches had already broken ranks, springing to their feet, arms around each other as they cried out in terror, weeping in fear, blood staining the front of their clothes as it poured from their noses. The werewolves across the clearing had thrown themselves on top of both alphas, heads down, arms and bodies covering them.

Oren threw out another shield, stronger this time, a deeper, richer gold as he reinforced his magic, and red and purple from Berion and Hozier joined it too, the colours seeping and twisting into each other as the shield expanded and rose into the air like a giant dome over all that stood below it, stopping the fog descending and devouring them all.

Sybil, he now realized, had fallen to the floor beside him; the effort it'd taken to break the spells she'd kept over her daughter for decades had knocked her out cold. He saw that blood was not only trickling from her nose, but from her ear too. But she was breathing. She was alive.

A couple of witches ran forward, crouching at her side, pushing her hair back off her wrinkled face as they tried to roll her over. He did the old woman the courtesy of summoning some cushions and blankets for them to make her comfortable. Other than that, he ignored her.

His eyes had fallen on P, who had already started to move. Because there, in the cave mouth, between the writhing tendrils of darkness swirling around her, stood a figure. Skeletal and tall, with skin so pale that her white eyes were almost invisible.

The ghost didn't look back. She turned and made her way up the mountain path towards the cave mouth.

43

P

P wasn't afraid.

There wasn't much that could scare her. Not any more.

It was a source of amusement for Sage that one of the only things that'd scared P when she was still alive, truly scared her, was the paranormal. It was her least, *least* favourite type of horror movie, and those late-night ghost hunting shows where guys stood in dark buildings screaming at disembodied knocking sounds? She'd needed an hour of something happy before she went to bed after watching those. Sage had always found it so funny. But she realized now: Sage had seen and talked to ghosts for years Downside without P's knowledge. No wonder they never scared her. No wonder she'd rolled her eyes and assured her there were no ghosts in her house.

As she watched the black fog twisting and rolling behind the magical shield, hammering against it, trying to get through, she knew how terrified she would've been if she were still alive. Convinced the dark mass was some kind of poltergeist activity.

Ha.

Halfway up the path towards the mountain cave, the outline of the figure she'd spotted watching them below had retreated, disappearing entirely back into the darkness.

She glanced down at her watching friends. Oren's arms were folded across his chest. She knew he thought all this was a charade. That he'd be in there as soon as she confirmed Kalinka as lost. For now he was simply humouring them, making it look to the witches like they'd made every effort to save Kalinka first. Sage was pale as she gaped up at the fog that nearly covered all the sky above them, plunging them into a deep gloom, and Hozier looked equally concerned. Berion stood between them, an arm around each shoulder.

He nodded an unspoken agreement. If this all went wrong, he'd make sure Sage and Oren were all right in her place.

'Well,' she said, turning back to the shimmering purple, red and golden veil separating her from that black fog beyond. 'Here we go.'

She lifted her hands, and pushed them through the shield and into the fog.

She'd explained to Oren once that touching another ghost felt like putting her hand through cold, damp mist. And touching a living human felt like sticking her hand in a bag of hot jelly. Stretching out her hand through this black fog felt like thick spider-webs. Like a force that wasn't quite strong enough to hold her back was trying its hardest to slow her down.

It was neither hot nor cold, but there was a sensation like . . . she frowned, and pushed her whole body through the rest of the magical shield and into the fog just to see. And—

She gasped. Thick, dark shadows whirled around the cave like a hurricane, the thundering sound of it roaring in her ears. Her plaits whipped around her head, and the ripped and torn fabric of her jumper flapped about in the wind. She could barely open her eyes against the force of it.

She couldn't quite . . . she didn't understand? Wind shouldn't affect her. In the same way rain didn't get her wet. Yet she could barely turn on the spot, the force of it buffeting against her body, even as she felt it flowing right through her.

For the first time in a very long time, she lowered herself down and allowed her feet to touch the floor. She rarely walked anywhere any more, not over the ease of floating, but as she felt the bottoms of her old, battered trainers against the ground, she felt the grip of their soles hold her steady.

She peered through the darkness. Everything was shrouded in such gloom, but around the edges she thought she could just make out the shadows of furniture, blown back and shoved against the walls. Chairs and a table and some cabinets. A small bed. She took a few more steps, battling the wind. She had no idea how deep this cave was or how far back it went, but the fog ahead was so dense that it looked solid. If Kalinka was anywhere, it was going to be there. She knew it in her bones.

She didn't even think about it. She knew if she did, she would start to feel afraid. So she swallowed, straightened her shoulders, lifted her chin, and headed for the darkness.

The girl was on her knees in the centre of a ball of the thickest fog. The dark shadows so intense that P could only see her for moments at a time between gaps in the whirling fog. It revolved around her like a ball. Locking her in. Another cage – this time one created by herself.

P gazed down on the young woman in a ragged dress of coarse fabric. Long silvery plaits like her own, so long they coiled at her sides on the dusty floor of the cave, tied at the end with small strips of leather. Her face was contorted. Screaming. The sound blending in with the howling wind.

P saw that the fog, the raw magic manifesting itself this way without any tether anchoring it inside the witch's body, was pouring from her eye sockets. It poured out like tears, and her fingers clawed at the sides of her face as if trying to stop it causing terrible pain.

P didn't realize she was crying until she felt her own tears being whipped off the side of her face. She reached out her own silvery hand into the thickest, strongest parts of the fog – a hand that was usually so bright, but even she was muted by the impenetrable darkness. As the black mist rolled through her it made her limbs look solid in parts.

Then she gasped, horrified, and snatched her fingers back, grasping her hand to her chest. She stared at the spot where her own silvery body had started to disintegrate. Specks of silver whirled into the darkness like glitter thrown on to a sheet of velvet. The very tips of her middle and ring finger were gone. Only slightly, but definitely flattened off. As if someone had taken a scrap of sandpaper and dulled them.

A million thoughts raced through her mind. Was that it? Was that part of her gone forever? She'd made peace with the idea that she would exist forever: but the thought of forever *without a hand?*

How else was she going to get Kalinka's attention? She couldn't touch her. She needed to pass through this thickest darkness to get close enough that the witch could hear her voice. But . . . the darkness was so powerful it was disintegrating even her. Nothing should be able to harm her – she was already dead.

If she moved quickly, would it take less of her? Would it need time to destroy her completely? Or would Kalinka react to the shock of finally noticing her so badly that she exploded again, like when the power first went back into the cave, and disintegrate her entirely?

If that happened, she wouldn't even know, so it wasn't worth wasting time thinking on it.

She sighed. She had walked through darkness before. Maybe not darkness like this, maybe not physically, but she'd accompanied Sage through some of the darkest nights, and together they had found the watery light of morning. She'd done it before, and she could do it again.

Whatever happened, happened. If she never walked out of that cave again, Sage would know that she had loved her for the time they'd had together. And Oren.

Taking a deep breath, she braced, and threw herself forward.

44

P

The fog disappeared.

P stumbled, so off-kilter as the wind that was somehow battering her ghostly body stopped, that she had to readjust to right herself before she toppled forward.

The witch, cowering on her knees and screaming in agony as darkness poured from her eye sockets, was gone.

'*Qui êtes-vous?*'

She whirled.

The light of the cave mouth beyond – the sky blue again and peppered with white clouds – made the shape nothing but a black silhouette.

P looked around the cave. Everything was smashed and splintered against the rock, thanks to that initial tremendous outburst of force.

'Hello,' she said, hoping to God that Kalinka understood her.

She realized there was still fog in the cave. But it wasn't seeping out of the witch's eyes now, or billowing in plumes. It curled around her feet and her ankles, where the long white plaits still trailed on the floor about her. Black wisps fluttered like the smoke that rose in thin tendrils from a freshly blown-out candle.

Gentle.

Controlled.

Not volatile and untamed.

Not at all what P had expected to find.

'Was that . . .' She forced her voice to remain light and calm, not giving away any of the rising confusion. She pointed just behind her, where the witch she'd just seen sobbing and screaming was now gone. 'A projection?'

'Who are you?'

'My name is Patricia,' she offered. 'My friends call me P.'

'Why are you here, Patricia?'

P realized there was a lump in her throat. 'To see if I can help you.'

For all Sybil's assertions that Kalinka was insane, she seemed lucid. But did that only make her more dangerous? P floated diagonally a few footsteps, angling herself so that she could see her face a little better.

'I'm here on behalf of the Arcānum. It's been decided that you should leave this cave. I'm here to . . . assess your health first.'

'Does that mean she's dead?' Kalinka asked. 'My mother?'

'What? No.' P held up her hands, seeing that must've been the assumption Kalinka jumped to as the spell on her magic broke. 'God, no, Kalinka, don't worry—'

'I'm not worried.'

P stopped talking.

Something definitely wasn't right.

She looked down at the wisps of black fog flickering around Kalinka's feet again. And, strangely, the first thing she thought of was a cat, a loving pet that was pleased to see their owner after a long day separated, and now wanted to curl around her ankles, welcoming her home.

Then she took in the witch's face. Gaunt. Too thin. Her old, ragged dress hung off her skeletal figure. And those white eyes. Like Sybil's. Like Berion's. Blank.

But not insane.

She tried again. 'Was that a projection I saw, when I first came in here?' She pointed to the spot where the witch had knelt.

Kalinka pulled a face that said yes, and no.

'It was a memory,' she said. 'Of what I was, when I was first locked in this cave.' She paused. 'And for many years after.'

'But not now.'

Kalinka looked down at herself, then looked back at P. 'I guess not.'

'Why did you show it to me?'

'I wanted to see what you'd do,' she said simply. 'I wanted to see if you'd still try to help me, even if you were scared.' A test? Like the Baba Yaga had given Sage, to see if she could trust her? 'And you did.' A small tear seeped from the white eyes, and a bony hand wiped it away quickly. 'I have not known kindness in a very long time.'

'I know.' P nodded. 'What you went through was a terrible thing. The betrayal you must've felt from Mathilde—'

Kalinka's expression flipped, and a fierceness flashed that P hadn't expected such a fragile witch to be able to muster. P had to stop herself from flinching.

'Mathilde did not betray me,' Kalinka said quietly, but with such force P understood it was a warning. P noticed the darkness around her feet start to thicken. All of a sudden, she could see nothing below her knees. 'Mathilde was not *a terrible thing*.'

P held up her hands placatingly, watching the change in the behaviour of the fog, reacting to Kalinka's emotional shifts. 'I'm sorry,' she said calmly, knowing it was not the time to tackle the fact that Kalinka still didn't seem to fully understand what Mathilde had done. 'That was my mistake.'

And it took a moment, but the fog started to retract.

Interesting.

Kalinka looked down at her hands guiltily. 'I apologize.' She gestured to the fog now mellow again at her feet. 'Whatever they did to me . . . broke something,' she whispered. 'And I cannot get it back inside.' She placed a bony hand on her chest, as if to indicate where she wanted to put it all. 'I cannot hide it now. I know the strength scares people, but at least before it was invisible.'

'Your mother already told us that you lost control of your magic,' P told her gently. 'In the direct aftermath of your attack, the magic started to explode in bursts. Hurting the witches around you. We know that your ability to control your magic was altered after the attack, and it was not your intention to hurt those witches.'

Kalinka gave her a quizzical look. 'No, that really was my intention.'

'It . . . What?'

'It was my intention to hurt them,' she repeated. 'I told them not to touch me. I told them to let me go. They told me I was sick, in my mind, and that nothing I was saying made sense. They tried to hold me down. And it made me angry. I just wanted them to let go of me.'

P stared at Kalinka, reassessing everything she'd been told.

Everything she thought she knew.

'Your mother said—'

'My mother—' Kalinka almost shouted, then caught herself. She let out a forced smile, a small apology for raising her voice. 'What they did to me, the pain they caused me, it did change something irrevocably. That's true. When I get angry, or upset, the darkness does . . . become harder to control. But it isn't *uncontrollable*.' Kalinka sounded like she was pleading for P to believe her. 'I am not a lost cause. That was just her excuse. Patricia, I'm not trapped in here because I struggle to control my magic. I'm trapped in here because I tried to escape from my mother. And she will tell you that makes me insane.'

45

OREN

Nearly ten minutes had passed since P had walked through their shield and into the darkness.

'How much longer do we wait?' Hozier voiced his own thoughts.

He didn't know.

Nobody moved. Nobody spoke.

Witch. Wolf. Warlock. All of them stood, watching the dark fog grow and expand until the sky above them was entirely gone. He'd lit a few balls of white light, and he sent them floating into the air above them to illuminate the clearing. But it just made the whole scene look even creepier. Dark shadows cast on pale, bloodied faces.

'Two more minutes,' Oren said.

Then he would go up there. He'd wait until he'd passed into the darkness, surrounded by a bubble of his own magic to shield him, before he summoned an execution sword. If only to stop the witches knowing what was coming before it was too late for protests.

And to stop Sage seeing too.

Despite every promise made between them, despite her knowing everything about his past, despite the fact she'd told Gabriel that he would always be second best, there were still some things he didn't want her to see.

And then . . . light.

He blinked.

The fog disappeared.

Berion's head whipped towards him, eyes wide. Sage was gaping too, and Hozier.

It only took a second or two after that for the gathered witches to react, and the small collection of werewolves. Hands covered eyes, and more gasps escaped lips.

He blinked a couple more times, letting his eyes readjust out of the artificial cold light of his magic back into the real warm sunlight. His heart was pounding and he wasn't sure why, other than feeling sure that something hadn't gone to plan in the way they'd expected.

And where did that leave P?

Sage turned.

She darted for the pathway up to the mountainside, ready to throw herself into that cave and the unknown after her best friend. Berion moved too, and in one quick swoop he had his arm around her middle and practically lifted her off her feet. She writhed in his arms, trying to shove him off her as he held her back. Her demands that he let her go echoed around the otherwise silent clearing.

It was such a funny thing to notice in that moment: that

Berion hadn't used magic to restrain her. Not like *he* had when he'd stopped her killing Flora in that pub. Not like he'd just been about to again, before Berion had snatched her up. Berion simply held her in his arms, held her to his chest with such an ease that was still so alien to him, and let her yell as angry tears rolled down her face.

He realized he'd been so stupid to worry he'd ever lose her to Gabriel, or these mountains. He knew, watching her there now, swearing and hissing at Berion to let her go into that cave, that if there was one person he could ever lose her to, it would be P.

And he realized he was OK with that. That was how it should be.

Berion looked at him over the top of her head. 'I think it's time,' he said, agreeing at last with his proposed execution. 'But, Oren, we go together.'

'No.'

'Yes,' Sage shot back, twisting herself awkwardly still in Berion's arms to look at him. 'If you go in there, I'm coming too. I'm—'

'There's no need,' Hozier cut in, but her voice was heavy with relief.

She wasn't looking at them. She was looking up at the cave.

He heard her name start to ripple across the crowd before he even saw her.

'Kalinka?'

'Kalinka!'

'*C'est Kalinka!*'

And Oren could have doubled over in relief at the sight of P beside her.

Black fog still plumed at her feet, but it didn't float away from her. It hung close, wrapping itself around her ankles.

The crowd of witches moved as one. A wave of bodies surged, all of them, compelled towards the witch they'd believed dead for all those decades. Whose memory they had spoken of reverently. In whose name they had tormented the werewolves across the river for all that time. Hands raised into the air, shouts went up. Of relief, of amazement, of overwhelming emotion. And then chanting started again. A jubilant song of triumph and thanks.

Oren wasn't sure who exactly they were praising. These witches knew the truth now, knew that Kalinka was not the Häxgrotta, was not a goddess or any kind of deity . . . but perhaps at this point it was just habit. Their way of expressing their feelings.

'P!' Sage gaped as the ghost shot back down the mountain path towards them. 'You're still here.' Sage wrung her hands anxiously, her eyes still wild with undisguised panic.

'Only just,' she admitted, holding up her own hand.

Sage looked at it for a moment, not seeing what she was supposed to be noticing. Then she gasped. Berion demanded P show him as she twisted her fingers, the two missing the tips, towards him. But he had no words either.

Neither did Oren. She was dead. Nothing, *nothing* was supposed to be able to hurt her.

'Can you feel it?' Oren frowned.

She shook her head. 'It's just . . . gone.'

'What happened?' Hozier asked. 'What's going on? Is she . . . OK?'

'Well.' P glanced up at the witch, who had stopped and was looking down on the spectacle below. 'It's still up for debate.'

'Is she safe to bring out of that cave, P?' he asked seriously, eyeing the twisting fog.

'I think so. It reacts to her emotions. If we keep her calm, she's OK.'

'And if we don't?' he said pointedly.

'She deserves to tell her story, Oren. Trust me.' Then she looked at Berion. 'Will you escort her down? She . . . struggles with the weight of her hair. And I can't pick it up for her.'

Berion startled at the strange request, but he nodded. 'Now?'

'Just wait a moment. We've got to do this carefully. They're . . .' She looked at the crowd of witches still chanting under the mountain.

'Crazy weird?' Hozier offered.

P huffed a small smile. She shot towards them, rising up just enough that she knew she could be seen by all of them.

'Hello!' she shouted. 'Um, hi!' She waved her arms above

her head. The closest witches turned, looking up at her. 'Hello, up here!'

More of them turned, their singing trailing off as they squinted to see the ghost through the bright sunlight above her.

'That's my cue,' Berion muttered, retreating around the back of them and edging towards the path.

Witches were female-only colonies, only ever encountering men, usually human, to reproduce. The sight of any male, even a warlock with witch-white eyes, being the first to approach their beloved Kalinka would likely not go down well.

'Come on,' Hozier said, beckoning the rest of them to walk into the clearing just behind P, where the witches had originally sat in rows before they'd surged forward, and gesturing at the wolves still standing silently on the other side to meet them in the middle.

A second distraction to keep witch eyes on them.

'Kalinka has been alone for a very long time,' P told the gathered crowd. 'I'm sure you understand that she might feel overwhelmed, and maybe even a little bit confused. Her magic is tethered to her emotions, but she can control it if she's calm. And we need to keep *her* calm in order to keep *you* safe.'

As P talked, the witches listened. She asked if anyone had any questions, and she took them one by one. He watched her in awe, fielding their concerns, cajoling them, until at last she'd managed to convince them to sit back down in their rows in the shadow of the mountain.

He didn't know how she did it.

He was convinced that one day they would learn that she had some strange, unique magic of her own, over and above her superhuman toast-making abilities.

By the time she'd arranged the group, Kalinka had descended and joined them all in the clearing before any of them could really notice Berion stood at her side.

Oren had watched that first meeting too, from the corner of his eye. The witch stretched out a frail hand to touch the side of his face, right beside his matching eyes. They had a brief conversation, and he'd expected Berion to either magic up a bag or gather up the coils of hair in his arms and carry them down behind her. So it was a surprise when silver glinted, and a pair of scissors chopped the plaits off at Kalinka's elbows.

Two snakes of silvery-white hair fell to the floor, discarded.

And Kalinka smiled.

He'd offered her the crook of his arm, and Oren watched, fascinated, as the fog around Kalinka's feet shifted, so that it only manifested on the side of her that was away from Berion.

Her skin was almost translucent in the sunlight that'd been kept from her for so long. Even to his eye, the blue and red veins under the skin on her arms were visible, and the wolves, if they used their wolfish sight, would be able to see a whole lot more.

Celeste muttered something under her breath, and Sacha nodded in agreement, his face pained.

'I think efforts should be made to wake the witch mother,' Celeste said, eyeing the witch still under the blankets. 'It is her daughter, after all.'

'Ergh.' Hozier made a noise. 'Do we have to?'

He wasn't too surprised to notice a few of the werewolves' lips twitching at that. And he was more than happy to let the old witch remain unconscious, if he was honest.

But the look Sage threw him was clear. *She's right. Wake her up.*

'Fine,' he said through gritted teeth.

But it was Kalinka who spoke loudest. 'No,' she said. 'Not yet. Not until I can leave.'

46

OREN

Everyone looked at each other.

Obviously they couldn't let her leave.

Even the witches, who had just heard her request not to wake their witch mother, looked between themselves, confused. Witches did not leave their covens.

One of them stood and started to weave their way through the crowd towards the front. Oren recognized her as the witch with the long dark hair who had spoken in Sybil's place at the riverbank yesterday, the witch who'd explained what Kalinka had been like in the direct aftermath of the attack on her.

She edged forward tentatively, tilting her head to the side, assessing her sister's state. There was dried blood on her face, and the front of her white canvas dress, where her nose had burst open when Sybil had released the memory spell. She looked at Oren, a question in her eyes, seeking permission to approach. He thought about it for a moment, but the look of sadness and concern on her face was genuine.

He nodded.

'Kalinka?' she asked gently. *'C'est moi. Agnes. Tu te souviens de moi?'*

Kalinka squinted, as if her eyes still hadn't fully adjusted to the light of outside, and peered into the witch's face. But then she sparked with recognition.

When Agnes spoke again she kept her eyes fixed on her sister, roving over her skin, taking in her thinness, her jutting bones and her skin as thin as paper, but it was for the benefit of them all. 'Kalinka is my coven sister, but she is my blood sister too. My youngest sister. My name is Agnes Crows-Caw. I am the eldest daughter of the witch mother.'

Every werewolf, warlock and ghost head moved between Agnes and Kalinka, taking in Agnes's long, black, flowing hair and Kalinka's silvery-white plaits. They couldn't be more opposite, except perhaps for height – both of them tall. Oren looked at Berion next to her, and only just then realized that his white hair was a witch trait too. Not a warlock quirk. He couldn't believe no warlock back home, himself included, had ever spotted it.

'Swear it,' Kalinka whispered softly. 'Swear you didn't know I was in there.'

Agnes shook her head. A tear rolled down her cheek and ran tracks through the dried blood on her face. 'We burnt your body on a pyre. Right here.' She gestured to the floor under her feet. 'She admits she faked it all. She says she tricked us.'

Kalinka swallowed, tears rolling down her own cheeks. Her hands jerked, as if maybe she thought about stretching them towards her sister. Then she pulled them back.

Like she'd forgotten how to even offer an embrace. She swallowed and looked down at her feet. 'I want to leave now.'

'Kalinka,' Agnes said gently. '*Maman* knows what she did was wrong, but she was . . . so scared.' Agnes held a hand over her heart, imploring Kalinka to believe her. 'We will protect you, now we know, we will keep you safe together. We—'

Oren didn't want to point out that that wasn't their choice at all, but he would, soon enough.

For now, a more pressing matter was the black fog around Kalinka's feet starting to expand. He threw shields around Sage, Hozier, Berion and P, letting it weld to their bodies, and Agnes as well. Then the werewolves were jerking back. Hands shot out and Gabriel threw himself almost completely over his mother. Some of his guards covered Sacha too.

He tried not to roll his eyes as he threw a blanket shield back over the top of them.

'I want to leave,' Kalinka told her sister. 'I don't want to stay here.'

Agnes glanced at Oren, her eyes pitying.

See, they said. *She's sick. She doesn't know what she wants.*

But he wasn't quite sure that was accurate.

He didn't entirely blame Agnes, it was incomprehensible to most witches that one of their own would ever leave their coven. But every stereotype had an exception to the rule. Maybe Kalinka was that exception here. Now he could see her white eyes, he understood the weight of the pressure the young girl must've been under from a very young age. The assumption she'd succeed her mother's place one day. The expectation for greatness. Had that not been what'd happened to him, hurried into the specialist training school for gold-magic warlocks, a fast track into the Cariva itself, at half the age of all other students?

Maybe Kalinka's desperation to escape was the reason she'd let herself be so easily tricked by Mathilde's apparent kindness, if the young werewolf had offered to show her the way out. If that was the case, all this time she really had been coherent. She had been telling the truth, but these witches had just mistaken it for insanity.

What a mess.

'It's OK,' he said to Kalinka, examining how her fog reacted. 'We won't make you do anything you don't want to do.'

And he was right. Well, P had been right. It was tied to her emotions. The relief on her face was mirrored by the fog's retraction. He dropped the shields he'd just thrown over them all.

Celeste broke ranks from her wolves, gently pushing her son aside.

'*Bonjour*,' she said gently, to get Kalinka's attention without startling her. 'Kalinka?'

Kalinka jumped anyway. Berion leant in and whispered into her ear, to explain who Celeste was. Kalinka looked at him, and he nodded encouragingly. Celeste remained at a respectful distance, her hands clasped together in a way that was obvious the alpha was trying to appear unthreatening. She beckoned for Sacha to join her and introduced him too.

And when Sacha spoke it was in English, because clearly he wanted them to understand it.

Sage gasped. 'Mathilde was a part of your pack?'

Which finally explained why he was really there.

He nodded. 'After Celeste told me everything, and after your conversation with . . . with . . .' He shook his head. 'I looked through old records of my pack, from before I was the alpha. Before any of us even lived here. And I found her. Mathilde came to my pack a long time ago, when she was a little girl. She arrived with an older brother.'

'What?'

But Sacha couldn't say it, genuine hurt flashing across his face. Oren was sure that Sage knew what that meant too, just as well as he did, but it was Kalinka who finished the sentence for them.

'His name,' she said, 'was Eugene Durrand.'

47

OREN

'Eugene?' Sage repeated slowly. She looked back at Sacha in disbelief. '*Eugene* Eugene?'

Sacha nodded, devastation on his face. 'He never . . . in all those years. He never said. I never knew he had any links with Kalinka at all, never mind . . . this.'

'Because he would have had to admit what he did,' Kalinka said softly. 'Mathilde left a letter for their alpha, telling the pack that she was leaving, saying goodbye. Eugene Durrand tracked us down before we could get out of the mountains.'

Sacha looked helpless. 'Our records say that Mathilde left the pack to re-enter the human world. There is record of a letter,' he confirmed. 'The dates correspond. But there was no mention of Kalinka. I . . . I don't think they knew that part.'

Kalinka shook her head. 'Only Eugene knew about me. She told him. He forbade her from ever seeing me again. *Disgusting*, he called her. *Shameful*.' Her face contorted in anger. 'When she left, he knew it was with me. That's why he followed. To punish us for disobeying. He hunted us down. He tied *both* of us up. And . . . And . . .'

But it was happening again as she started to relive the memories. The black fog was starting to billow from her in angry plumes.

Oren threw the shields back up. He didn't know why he'd bothered taking them down.

P rushed in quickly to put herself in front of Kalinka's face, the thin black fog doing nothing but pass through her. He wondered how thick it'd had to be to start disintegrating the tips of her fingers.

'It's OK,' P soothed. 'It's OK.'

'It isn't OK,' Kalinka said, her voice louder now. '*It isn't OK!*'

And apparently it wasn't, because the fog was growing darker and denser. He stared, both horrified and fascinated. All his long years and he'd never encountered anything like it. Surely Kalinka would be a once-in-a-lifetime phenomenon. And then it started to pour out of her eyes like black tears.

What . . . the fuck.

The Elders would love to get a look at her.

Gods. He'd execute her out of mercy before that ever happened.

Sage stumbled back at the sight, grappling for the hand closest to her. Hozier grabbed her hand right back, the pair of them moving away from this new unfolding terror.

Berion's white eyes were wide as he tried to pull Kalinka's hands, now clawing at the side of her face, away from her skin before she broke it with her nails.

Oren shook his head.

This couldn't go on.

He'd given P her chance, but this was too dangerous, and he couldn't allow it.

He let the blade appear, elongating in his hands. The steel glinted, the sun reflecting off its surface. Celeste gasped at the sight of it, an arm on Sacha's as she pulled him back, away towards the safety of their wolves. Agnes started screaming too, some of the witches leaping to their feet, but Oren threw up a barrier of magic to keep them all back. The looks on Sage's, P's and Hozier's faces as they spotted it too almost made him feel guilty. But this was what they'd agreed. Sage would have to witness him do terrible things at his side. And here at last was one of those painful, terrible, awful moments.

He would make it quick.

'Kalinka Crows-Caw,' he said quietly. The start of the official execution order.

'Oren, wait!' Berion pleaded, positioning his body between them as he tried to calm the witch, prising her hands away from her face and grasping it in his own hands. 'Look at me,' he begged her. 'Kalinka, please,' he whispered. 'Look at me.'

He had allowed Berion to come with mild trepidation,

and this was why. Killing Amhuinn had been a difficult choice for Oren, because Amhuinn was not just a werewolf but a warlock as well. The only warlock to ever be bitten by a werewolf. Killing Amhuinn was more than just an execution order. He was killing someone who was partly one of his own.

Oren had known that in letting Berion be a part of this, if the worst had to happen, Berion would be part of a team that killed someone who was partly one of his own too.

And the problem with Berion was that he did have feelings.

He did have a heart and it could feel so much love.

'Kalinka Crows-Caw,' he repeated. He would remove Berion with magic if he had to. 'On this day—'

And then she exploded.

48

OREN

Silence fell.

He was standing in a forest clearing, but not the one they'd just been in outside the cave. Everyone else was gone. He spun slowly on the spot but . . . nowhere to be seen.

He was alone.

Birds sang overhead, and before he could consider his options, or panic that Sage and P were nowhere in sight, in front of him, two young girls materialized.

One, around twelve years old and with dark hair and wearing a long cloak of embroidered, heavy fabric, looked mildly distressed. He frowned as she looked right through him, as if he weren't there at all, never mind holding a long blade.

He watched her turn, peering between the leaves.

She was lost.

Behind a tree, unnoticed by the girl, was another. White hair and white eyes. Watching. Silent. They were like yin and yang. One light. One dark.

What was this?

As he watched the girl with the white hair accost the other, a conversation in rapid and garbled French breaking out, he realized this was a memory.

Kalinka, so lost in her grief and despair, was showing them her story.

The white-haired girl was pointing at a tree, and then along the ground and to another tree in the distance, evidently highlighting some invisible boundary. The dark-haired girl ran back over the invisible line, then looked back at her new adversary with fearful eyes. Oren didn't need to know the language to understand that little Mathilde was apologizing profusely for accidentally crossing on to witch territory.

But little Kalinka only smiled.

Then the world around them melted and blurred, and suddenly he was in the same clearing, watching from a different angle, and the sunlight was different. It was colder. Kalinka still looked the same age – around fifteen years old. But Mathilde looked a little older than in the last memory. The girls were chatting animatedly, sitting on the ground, each of them on either side of the invisible boundary line between the two territories.

They talked in hushed voices, and they were giggling. A friendship being born. A loyalty being forged. It struck him that this was probably what Sage and P looked like, before, when they were both human children. Before one had been changed and one had been killed and their lives were turned irrevocably upside down.

Then everything shifted, and this time he wasn't in a forest clearing. And it wasn't daylight. He was inside a tent and Sybil Crows-Caw looked a lot less wrinkled than she did now, but her hair was still wild. Kalinka looked barely older than Sage. A young woman, but she still cowered in her mother's anger.

Sybil was standing over a discarded cloak, holding up a piece of crumpled paper she'd clearly found in one of the pockets. A drawing, and a signature just discernible in the corner. Her white eyes wide as she hissed at her daughter.

'*Qui est Mathilde? Parce qu'elle n'est pas des nôtres! Elle n'est pas une sorcière!*'

Kalinka shook her head, tears streaming down her face. '*Elle est mon amie.*'

'*Ton amie? Ton AMIE?*' Sybil howled cruel laughter at her daughter, so stupid to believe any werewolf would ever be her friend. Oren waved a hand, and the spell he'd used to translate the bergsmed for Sage attached itself to his ears. He watched mother and daughter scream at each other, arguing as one insisted that witch and werewolf could never care about each other while the other insisted that they could. 'She's not your *friend*, Kalinka! Do you have no shame? Do you not care for the disgrace you bring upon us associating with those *beasts*? You will be a witch mother, you will be—'

'I will not,' Kalinka snapped back, drawing herself up to her full height, as if it was the only thing she had as defence against her mother, tiny in comparison. But it didn't really matter. She still looked afraid. 'I don't want it. I don't care. I will run away before you make me.'

The hand Sybil cracked across her face was hard, the sound echoing around the tent. It seemed to shock them both into silence.

Sybil took a step back. 'You're not going anywhere. I forbid it,' she said simply, ending the conversation as the crumpled drawing in her hand wilted to ash, and floated to the floor in pieces. 'This is over. You do not see that were-wolf again.'

Kalinka stared at the remnants of her note from Mathilde. She breathed in one long, shuddering breath, and then she turned and fled from the tent.

The world melted again and now the girls were walking arm in arm through the forest, all notions of keeping to their own sides of the boundary gone. It was dusk, their tones still quiet but more serious. He followed, keeping up as they hurried through the trees. And when the pair paused, he realized that Kalinka was crying. Mathilde pulled a small cloth handkerchief from the pocket of the simple navy tunic she was wearing and wiped away the witch's tears. And then she leant in, and kissed Kalinka on the lips.

He was Oren Rinallis.

Nothing shocked him any more, not enough to gasp. But this? His breath caught in his throat.

This wasn't just a forbidden friendship.

This was a love story. Forbidden love. This was magic and mortal, forbidden not only by their heritage but by their lifespans as well. Destined to always be parted eventually.

It was him and Sage.

The blade that was still in his hand faded away into gold dust as he listened to the pair come to accept that if they wanted to spend whatever time they had while Mathilde still walked this earth together, they'd have no choice but to leave. Run away from these mountains so steeped in history and rivalry that neither side would ever allow one of their own to be with the other. From Mathilde's responses it was clear that she'd faced much the same reactions from her own family too. From Eugene Durrand.

Kalinka hadn't left because she'd feared the future or resented what was expected of her. It was just that for Kalinka, the power of her magic, or the future as a witch mother one day – none of that was more important than love.

The world changed, and this time it didn't stop. The memories were coming quicker, the world around them shifting and melting and changing with a more frequent rapidity. And some of the memories he could only catch a glance of before they moved on. Every time the girls met in secret, whispering, planning, spreading out maps.

The surroundings changed again and now the girls were hurrying. Running. Bags thrust over each of their shoulders. Then they were in a particularly overgrown part of the mountains, and strange, tiny men stood on each other's shoulders were talking in a weird guttural sound. And then they were running again, panic in Mathilde's eyes as the dark-haired girl looked back over her shoulder.

In the next scene it was raining, although Oren wasn't getting wet. It rained so hard even the thick canopy overhead couldn't stop the downpour. The mountains echoed with screams, and Oren turned to see Mathilde pinned against a tree by two other werewolves, barely into their twenties themselves. In front of Mathilde, the bloodied, beaten body of Kalinka lay in overgrown bracken, her eyes fluttering, barely conscious. Another werewolf covered in blood stood over her, fists dripping as he panted. The young Mathilde fainted and went limp.

Oren felt nothing other than the roaring in his ears as everything faded into total blackness. The sight of the young girl pinned to the tree screaming as the person she loved lay dying at her feet, etched inside his eyelids.

Red flashed.

Sage lay on that floor, Hozier's hands desperately trying to stem the crimson blood that seeped out of Sage's chest between her fingers.

He was glad Kalinka's fog had consumed Eugene Durrand.

Oren was satisfied that once it had been forcefully separated from Kalinka by Sybil's magical barriers, the fog had not been acting on any specific instruction . . . but despite that, something deep inside also knew that the fog had known who it had stumbled upon in the Monreau camp. And it'd taken revenge at last.

It was quite clear to him, based on Sage's descriptions and first-hand accounts he'd gathered from eyewitnesses, that the fog was not on a meaningless chaotic rampage. Multiple people had got the impression it was looking for something. In barns, around trees, through paddocks.

And now he understood.

This piece of Kalinka's magic, independent, yet still so inherently part of her, that understood her heart and soul, hadn't been terrorizing the werewolves at all. It'd just been looking for Mathilde, in any of the places it expected she could be, whether hiding or kept against her will.

With no understanding of time, it hadn't understood that nearly a century had passed, nor that old age would have likely taken her by now anyway, even if she had managed to escape her brother and his cronies and fled to a long and happy life away from the mountains.

Everything else – the dying crops, the sick livestock, the soured milk – he'd wondered why it hadn't consumed or killed the animals like he knew it was capable of. But the fog wasn't out to hurt anyone. All of that was just a by-product, a result of being touched by something so sad, so filled with such pain and grief that nothing good could survive it.

For the first time in a long time, a single tear rolled down his cheek.

The world shifted one last time, and he understood that the darkness he stood in was still part of Kalinka's memories. This was the part where she floated in and out of consciousness, coherent thoughts dulled by both the pain and the tonics administered to heal her wounds.

After a while, he saw flashes between the gloom. A face here, a different face there. He saw a tent being pushed open and the witch mother walk in. Then he saw another witch dab her face with a damp cloth.

He heard snippets of conversations. He heard Kalinka's voice, though it only said one word. One name.

He heard Sybil Crows-Caw muttering to her witches that Kalinka's mind must've been irrevocably broken. Because what she was saying was inconceivable. Of course her daughter had never expressed any interest in leaving their coven. It was incomprehensible that she would choose any other future than the one she had set out for her. Between the flashes of darkness and the snippets of Kalinka's memory as she flitted in and out of consciousness . . . Oren understood.

Sybil Crows-Caw was laying the foundations for what she was about to do to stop her daughter from leaving.

Sybil Crows-Caw had lied about everything.

49

OREN

Then it was over.

He was back outside the cave with everyone gathered. He looked around. Sybil was still unconscious and unaware on the floor behind them, but everyone else . . . The whole clearing was silent. Nobody moved. All of them had seen the truth, even as they'd stood alone in the memories.

And now Kalinka was on her knees, no fog in sight.

He looked down at his hands. They were empty, his blade gone. He looked at Sage. And she was looking at him.

Their worst nightmare had just unfolded before their eyes. The reason she'd been rebelling against the idea of letting him love her, and of loving him back. Because this witch curled on the floor grieving for the love she would never get back, she was him in another eighty years.

Sage stifled a sob, and the explosion of pain in his chest he knew wasn't his but hers. Oren watched her drop to her knees in front of the witch still sprawled on the floor, her head in her hands, and place a gentle hand on her shoulder.

Berion dropped down too, and his own hand went not to

Kalinka, but to Sage. Because he understood too. He'd understood before either of them, hadn't he? He'd seen them falling for each other before they'd even realized it themselves.

Despite his earlier thoughts, he was glad Berion was there. He had the gentleness Oren couldn't ever achieve, and he was glad that P hadn't had to take on the emotional burden of supporting them all on her own too.

'Her magic has run out,' Hozier said quietly.

'What?' He blinked, confused.

'Witch magic depletes,' she reminded him.

The power she'd expended forcing all those memories into so many minds had used up all of her power. Expended it in such a way it almost made her human. How Sybil looked so exhausted when she'd used all her power that first time they'd met her. How she'd literally passed out removing all the spells she'd cast over Kalinka.

'How long do we have, before it comes back?'

'The afternoon, at most.' Berion didn't take his eyes off the witch. 'The more powerful, the quicker it regains strength.'

He looked up at all the gathered witches, and then at the werewolves. Celeste was wiping tears from her eyes and even Sacha looked red-faced.

So now what?

He couldn't let Kalinka go free with this magic she couldn't control the moment she felt any kind of sadness, anger or anxiety. But to pass an execution order now . . . no matter what promises he and Sage had made to each other, he was pretty sure a part of her would hate him forever.

And Sybil Crows-Caw?

Where did he start with her list of sins?

He was about to gather his friends together – he knew he owed them at least the courtesy of an explanation first – when Berion stood and beckoned him to the side.

'Oren, listen. There's another solution – possibly . . .' Berion took a breath. 'I've been working on something in Downside. A spell. It's old magic. Very old. Dark. But it . . . it kills magic.'

'What?'

'It takes it away,' Berion said, almost helplessly. 'It makes you . . . human.'

Berion's white eyes stared at him, and they were full of sadness.

And suddenly Oren understood, his stomach lurching. This spell, Berion had been working on it for him. If Sage didn't settle.

'Does it take away her long life?' he asked carefully, keeping his voice calm even as his heart pounded.

Berion nodded. 'If she takes it now, she will live out a human lifespan. Eighty more years or so. But it's irreversible. Once her power is dead, there's no going back. Not ever. If she agrees and one day changes her mind, there's nothing to be done.'

'Well, that's irrelevant, surely?' Sage asked, the rest of the conversation, its true meaning, going completely over her head. 'She will never be able to control it fully. And she will never be able to hide it, if she wants to go down into the human world to live there.'

'Kalinka's magic is tied to her trauma,' Berion told her gently. 'I hear the humans have excellent helpers, that help to fix that kind of thing.'

'Therapists,' P supplied.

'Those,' Berion said. 'It may be that one day, she could be in a position to regain control of her magic, with the right help. But if she makes this decision now, it's . . . tough.'

'How old is the spell?' Oren asked.

'It's illegal now, for sure,' Berion warned him. 'Amhuinn-illegal. I'd be breaking a lot of laws to carry it out to completion.'

But Berion was offering, willing to do it, for him.

'How long will it take to do it here, for her?'

'The ingredients aren't too obscure, and can be gathered pretty easily,' P said. 'I've already seen it, it's actually more of a potion than a spell.'

Oren's head whipped to her. She stared resolutely back.

And he realized, P knew too.

The way his heart started to thrum anew in his chest as he saw the faintest hints of betrayal – her disappointment that he hadn't told her about Sage being a hybrid – that she'd hidden so well for the time she'd been there with them . . . He knew at once that he shouldn't have decided to wait until this was over. The hurt in her expression wasn't worth it.

But he couldn't do anything about it now.

'Offer. If she says yes, do it. If she doesn't, I will pass the sentence.'

By the time they turned back to the gathering, Kalinka was speaking to more witches that'd approached. And Oren was interested to notice it was Celeste who had stepped in to Berion's vacated position. Kalinka was on her feet again, the alpha holding her up with an arm around her back, keeping the frail woman steady.

The four other witches standing beside Agnes had the same black hair and cheekbones, and Oren could see at once that they were the rest of Agnes's sisters. They were Sybil's other birth daughters. Kalinka's blood sisters. While they hadn't been present at the waterside yesterday, Agnes had clearly seen fit to include them now in their mother's absence.

Berion approached to make his offer, and Sage followed. Oren hung back.

'P,' he said. Hozier hung back with her. He guessed that if Berion had told P, then Hozier knew as well. 'I'm sorry I didn't tell you.'

She gave him a tight smile. 'I will not tell you how disappointed I am, because I know you know.'

'I'm not even certain she is a hybrid yet,' he whispered honestly. 'I can't be completely sure.'

'I'm sure,' she said. 'I went to MacAllister.'

His mouth dropped open. He looked at Hozier, but she nodded confirmation. It was true. They'd made that journey already into the moors while he and Sage had been away. Hozier looked between them, and knew they needed a moment. She turned to join Berion and Sage's conversation instead.

'What if she can't forgive me for not telling her?' He could barely mouth his deepest fear.

The smile she offered was softer. 'But what if she can?'

For the second time that day, he could feel tears welling behind his eyes.

What was wrong with him?

'As soon as we get home?' P asked him. He nodded. So she smiled. 'Then let's save this witch.'

50

OREN

Kalinka had agreed.

She hadn't even wanted to think about it.

She had looked at Berion as if he were offering her a gift from the gods. A second chance at life. Her sisters had tried to step in and object, mutters rippling through the rest of the witches too, and even a few hisses and growls.

But when Berion had warned them that without this, Oren would not simply release her back into their care in this state, they had seemed to get the hint. Kalinka's sisters, apparently acting as the unofficial leaders in their mother's absence – as princesses of the coven, he supposed – looked at each other. When they nodded, the rest of the witches fell into line quickly. When they gave their official blessing, Kalinka burst into tears.

But before anything else happened, she told them that she had one more question, and she wanted to ask it of her mother.

*

When Sybil Crows-Caw woke – when he finally released the magic he had secretly been using to keep her unconscious after Kalinka asked for her to stay that way – the first thing she saw was her daughter, out of the cave and standing in the centre of the clearing. And around her not only the rest of the coven gathered, united, but a werewolf alpha at her side, holding her up, the rest of the werewolves interspersed between her witches. All gathered as one. All of them staring down at her.

And none of them looked friendly.

Oren stood back from where he'd had to lean over her to remove his own magic and then use some of his healing to wake her up.

It took a moment for it all to register on Sybil's face. She blinked, trying and failing to lift herself before falling back.

Then it was like the true realization hit the witch mother all at once, with the force of a train. Her eyes went wide, and the shadow of a monster crossed her face.

She jumped to her feet with a deftness and agility she had not previously displayed, as she took in the sight of her daughter outside her cave for the first time in seventy years. Alive. Undamaged by the force of the magic barrelling back into her.

Oren realized that Kalinka dying was probably what she had expected to happen. Not ideal, since she'd kept her captive for all these years, but better than the truth being outed at last.

Then she burst forward like a bullet from a pistol, again with a speed he hadn't expected. But then again, everything about this witch had been a lie so far, hadn't it? The talons exploding from her nails were longer than she'd ever displayed before, and the sharp teeth that erupted from her mouth were so long that they protruded down on to her chin.

Her meaning was clear. If the magic had not killed Kalinka, if Oren had not yet killed her, she would do it herself. And frame it as what? A mercy?

'Get away from my daughter!' she screeched, her eyes bulging as she took in the wolves, not savage and frothing at the mouth ready to fight her witches, but standing among them, united in one cause.

Kalinka gasped, the sound so tragic for its utter fear.

Oren waved a lazy hand.

He was done.

He wanted to go home.

He wanted to tell Sage everything and see how they could move on with their lives.

He shot out more magic, not a full shield this time that would trap the witch, her talons and her infuriatingly annoying screeching inside – he appreciated that to get this over with, Kalinka needed to be able to ask her questions. Instead he moulded his magic into bars, and he trapped the witch in a cage just in time for her outstretched talons to be out of reach of the crowd she was about to throw herself into.

She howled, screaming and yelling obscenities. At him, for trapping her, at Celeste for daring to touch her daughter, at her own witches for not doing anything to help her other than stand there, staring at her, completely unmoved.

'*Maman*,' Kalinka said. 'I want to ask you something, and you will do the courtesy of telling the truth.'

'Will I?' Sybil's face contorted and she barked out a cold, high laugh. 'You dare command me? You—'

'Who did you burn?' she asked. 'On the pyre. Who was it wrapped in the shroud, that everyone thought was me?'

It was the last question that Oren expected her to ask, but as Sage's eyes met his, as Hozier and P looked at each other, and Berion, Celeste, Sacha and everyone else's eyes went wide, they realized that they already knew the answer.

And the worst part was, so did Kalinka.

She just wanted to hear the truth from her mother's lips.

Oren walked around the witch mother and looked into her face. The gloating pleasure that curled her lips made him want to plunge his favourite dagger into her heart.

'She came for you, you know,' Sybil said. 'Mathilde.' She hissed her name. 'Two nights after you'd come home to us. The little pup, come to see if she could sneak you away.'

He eyed Kalinka for her reaction, and judging by the whites of Celeste's knuckles clamped tightly around her shoulders, the effort she was putting into keeping that witch standing said enough. Thank the gods her magic was temporarily depleted.

But even then, they didn't have long. All of this was taking up precious time before they had to start avoiding flesh-devouring black fog again, until Berion could brew up the potion that'd destroy it forever.

'I caught her,' Sybil said. 'Off the corner of Buttercup Valley. Her face was as bashed in as yours. I guess those dogs don't mind hurting their own, *eh*? But then again, we know they're uncivilized.'

Oren expected an eruption from the gathered werewolves, but it was fascinating to see how an alpha's orders to keep their mouths shut kept them under control, especially in her presence. He should've summoned her to the riverbank every time they'd been down there, and those wolves had worked their damned hardest to find a way round her orders.

'She told me everything. She had escaped her brother that very night they'd found you, and spent a little time resting, letting her wolf blood heal some of her wounds. I guess he thought she'd just left the mountains anyway, as planned. But she waited. She came looking for you. To see if she could get you out one last time. She told me you were in *love*.' Sybil laughed. 'She told me you were running away, because you *loved* her.'

And the scorn in Sybil's voice . . . the disgust. The mocking tone as she ridiculed her daughter for something as pathetic as love? He sent a rush of his magic down Sage's spine, because he saw a flash of yellow eyes and knew that in her fury she was about to partially transform in front of them all.

'Like *love* was more important than your coven?' Sybil tutted. 'Your duty as witch mother was more important than some feral beast, set to die before you even reached middle age.'

'What did you do to her?' Sage demanded, perhaps because she knew Kalinka couldn't.

'I pierced her heart,' Sybil said. 'With my talons. And I let her sink to the floor, and I watched her die. If it's any comfort, dear daughter, your name was the last thing from her lips.'

And with that, Kalinka lunged. She ripped from Celeste's arms and threw herself at her mother. And with the sudden burst of movement there were gasps, and shocked calls of her name, and Sage and Hozier and Agnes all surged forward too, arms outstretched, ready to catch the unsteady, weak witch as she stumbled.

Kalinka was screaming and howling and crying. The sounds closer to those of a dying animal in desperate need of putting out of its misery. Her thin fingers grabbed a handful of her mother's ragged hair, and as she pulled it, Sybil's face smashed into the bars between them. Had Kalinka any more strength, she might've managed to scalp her.

But there wasn't much in her thin, malnourished arms, and understandably, the talons at the end of Sybil's arms were the bigger concern. He threw out more magic, and one by one, the talons dropped out of each finger, falling to the floor in drips of blood.

Sybil screamed in pain. So he muted her voice at last. And then Celeste was there again, gently prying Kalinka's hands from Sybil's hair. 'Come,' she whispered. 'Let go.'

Kalinka crumpled into a ball on the floor again, a heap of howling, crying agony.

They all knew that enough years had passed that even if Mathilde had escaped into the human world to start a new life, she would've died by now. But he guessed Kalinka must've always wondered, sitting there in her dark cave. Wondered what had become of the werewolf she had loved. And some days, no doubt, the thought of her living out her life happy and free would've been what kept her going.

He sighed.

He turned to the gathered witches.

'Sybil Crows-Caw has admitted to the unlawful murder of a werewolf,' he told them.

Formal words, but at least it was more clear-cut now. It was a simple sentence to pass and get this whole thing over with. But Agnes shot him a wide-eyed look.

'The Arcānum has held a long-standing agreement with the packs and the covens in these mountains,' Agnes said. 'That you leave us to deal out punishment, as long as it keeps it contained within these mountains.'

'You would let her live?' He raised a brow, astonished

that this witch might defend her witch mother, even now, to the sounds of her youngest sister wailing.

Agnes looked at her dark-haired sisters.

'I never said that,' Agnes said evenly. The silent witch mother's mouth was wide open, screaming obscenities none of them could hear as she wrenched and rattled at the magic bars of the cage he'd locked her in. Everybody ignored her. 'I'm simply asking you to let us deal with our mother.'

'That rule to let you deal with your own disputes was made to relieve the Arcānum from having to make the difficult journey up here in the first place,' he reminded her. 'What you're suggesting is illegal, since we're already here.'

'Are we?' Hozier asked, sounding confused. She looked at Berion, who was crouched over Kalinka with Celeste. 'Are we not still in Paris?'

P was nodding, rising up to his height, her eyes wide and innocent. 'We just went for dinner, and an afternoon shopping.'

He knew what they were doing.

'That's all very well and good,' he pointed out. 'But Sage and I have been here for days.'

It was Sacha who stepped in next. Oren had no idea how the tip of his pipe was still smoking after everything that'd happened. 'I heard you found the fog off the northern border and killed it. It was a monster of old magic. You got a tip-off from the Baba Yaga. You saved us all.'

Sage looked at him, eyes wide.

'And what about Kalinka?' he asked.

'Kalinka who?' Celeste looked up at him, her expression hard. 'While you were with us, a human woman stumbled into my camp, lost for days, wandered off a hiking trail. No magic, and no idea she was in a commune of werewolves. And why would she? Why would she have any reason to suspect? Humans don't believe in such things, after all. With your permission, we took her in, agreeing to nurse her until she was strong enough to leave.'

He stared at her.

Gabriel, who had been silent for most of this whole ordeal, cleared his throat. But it wasn't Oren he looked at. It was Sage. 'When she is strong enough to leave, I will personally escort her to the human world, to wherever she wants to go.' He glanced at Oren. 'If he will allow it.'

And although he didn't directly say it, it was an offer of peace between them. Some kind of apology, for whatever he'd spat at her about him and the monster he thought Oren was.

She gave him a small smile, and he nodded.

Weirdly, Oren didn't mind.

'And Sybil Crows-Caw?' he asked Agnes. 'Why have your coven turned on her?'

'We haven't.' She glanced at her mother still howling silently behind golden bars, then gave him a confused look. 'She's old and died in her sleep. We will make sure she's given a proper send-off. We will wrap her in white shrouds, so her face is hidden, and place her on a pyre. It is, after all, the least she deserves.'

Brutal.

He looked between them. Witch and werewolf. All of them, all of this history between their packs and coven, spanning decades, centuries, old rivalries, new hurts. All coming together and looking to him to agree to bind them all together in this secret.

Then he looked at Sage, and P. And to Berion and Hozier. Human, wolf, warlock and witch blood between the four of them: who not only lived harmoniously but loved each other fiercely. His own pack, if Celeste had been right. No rivalry. No animosity. Just love and loyalty and friendship. Everything Mathilde and Kalinka had hoped to find in leaving together. Because they certainly weren't allowed to find it here.

'Please, Oren,' Sage said quietly. 'Let them do this.'

Because this was the only way these mountains would find the lasting peace she had hoped to achieve by the time they left.

By letting the witches put it right themselves, by letting them deal out proper justice without him forcing their hand or doing it for them, in the eyes of the werewolves it would be atonement. Recognition for all those years of hurled abuse and misplaced accusations.

And, yes, it had been wolves who'd attacked Kalinka –

although the idea she was lured away and kidnapped was so very wrong – but Celeste's offer to keep Kalinka safe on her land, to heal in her own time and on her own terms, was the werewolves recognizing in turn what Eugene Durrand had done all that time ago.

This was how decades of grudges came to an end. This was how a bridge was built, and trust would be repaired.

'I will make you all swear blood promises,' he said finally. 'What has happened today doesn't leave this clearing. The truth dies here with Kalinka's magic. She never lived.'

Agnes Crows-Caw and her sisters on behalf of the coven, and Sacha Monreau and Celeste Dubois on behalf of the werewolves, all nodded.

51
SAGE

The next forty-eight hours were long.

Celeste had rushed ahead, gathering the rest of her pack in the hall immediately as she instructed Gabriel to lead Berion, who carried an almost unconscious Kalinka in his arms, to an empty cabin. She'd even asked Kalinka's black-haired sisters to join them until she was settled, to see where their sister would be spending her time.

Her fog had already started to return by the time they'd settled her in, tiny black wisps flickering out of the soles of her feet as Berion carried her through the Dubois camp.

Then Berion and Oren set about gathering everything they needed for Berion to brew the potion for Kalinka, Oren shifting them out to God-knows-where to gather strange-smelling ingredients.

She wasn't sure what Celeste had said to her pack, but Gabriel had come by their cabin that evening as she and Hozier were settling down to a meal cooked by P at last, and told them that everyone was relatively calm in the face of the knowledge that a witch was now ensconced on their land.

Once they'd heard what Berion was about to do, opinions had swayed considerably, apparently.

Sage hadn't been there the next evening when Berion had finally prepared the potion and given it to Kalinka. He'd asked them all to leave them while they talked, and she, P, Hozier, Oren and Celeste had backed out of the cabin, leaving the two white-haired, white-eyed, witch-blooded people alone to do this last thing that ended it all together.

On their way into the hall the next morning, she was surprised to hear from Berion that Kalinka's eye colour was now a dark green, although she was too exhausted from a night of sickness brought on by the process of losing her magic to leave her cabin and bid them all farewell.

It was nearly a week after they'd first arrived, but it felt like a lifetime.

In the hall was not only Celeste, but most of her pack too, as well as five black-haired witches who had come back to check in on their youngest sister. One of them, standing beside Agnes, now had white eyes.

So it was done.

The new witch mother had been chosen. Hozier had explained to her and P last night that upon a witch mother's death, the magic passed to whoever it deemed the next most powerful in the coven, strengthening her further and turning her eyes white – as happened to all not initially born with them. It seemed that the magic had chosen another Crows-Caw.

Sage wondered if she'd make a better leader than her mother.

When they approached the throne in the centre of the hall, Celeste stood to greet them one last time. 'Is there anything we can offer you, in thanks for your time?'

'We're not really supposed to accept gifts.' Oren cleared his throat. 'Since it's our job.'

Celeste's gaze slipped to him, and her smile turned to a smirk. 'I was not asking the Arcānum.' She shrugged. 'I'm an alpha speaking to a werewolf. And P is not in your employ at all.'

Sage grinned, and when she glanced at him, Oren was clearly trying not to smile back. He nodded.

She looked at P, and P grinned back.

'We hear the moon ball in the Jura mountains is something to behold,' P said.

Celeste laughed. 'I offer you anything I have available to give, and you ask for an invitation to the moon ball?'

'We have a friend who attended one here about one hundred and twenty years ago.' She glanced at Berion. 'Even now you say it's the greatest party you've ever been too, right?'

Celeste laughed harder, her face lighting up.

Berion bowed his head gracefully. 'It's true.' When he looked back at her he smiled sadly. 'And I suppose we need to make better memories than the last one we attended.'

Sage nodded.

'You're always welcome,' Celeste said. 'We'll send invitations back with you, Berion, closer to the time.'

Because Berion had also agreed to return over the coming months to check in on Kalinka and her recovery, and aid if there was any further sickness as part of her healing process.

'Thank you.' Sage smiled, and she wasn't entirely surprised by the lump in her throat. 'For your hospitality, for . . . everything.'

For proving to her that not all alphas were bad.

She looked at Gabriel at last. He'd been quiet, and there were too many watching for her to offer him anything meaningful without causing embarrassment. 'You'll write?' she asked.

For a moment she was worried he might say no. She knew she'd disappointed him in many ways in the short time they'd known each other.

His eyes flickered to Oren and back to her. Then he smiled. 'Only if you promise to save me your first dance at the moon ball.'

Oren's tut was almost inaudible, but it had her grinning at Gabriel. 'I'll see you on the dance floor.'

Oren took her rucksack from her shoulder and threw it over his own. A clear signal he was ready to leave and never come back. But there would be no shifting today, not until after they got a train into Paris for a little shopping first.

Berion picked up a bag stuffed full of cheese that Sacha Monreau had requested from Matthieu Garnier for P.

Sage looked at P, and Hozier, and Berion, and finally at Oren.

He smiled and put his arm around her shoulder as he turned them for the door out of the hall and towards home. Back to Downside. The safe haven of their own, where they all lived together without rivalry or prejudice forcing them apart – something she'd never appreciated before now.

She thought about Kalinka one last time, and Mathilde, and their love that was lost.

She brushed her fingers against Oren's, and felt the familiar warmth of his magic brush the back of her neck. And, yeah, she supposed . . . maybe she should at least hear him out? When they got home, maybe they could talk.

SAGE AND OREN WILL RETURN IN . . .

ALL
THE
CURSED
CREATURES

-2026-

ACKNOWLEDGEMENTS

Firstly: (again) thank you, Lord, for hearing all prayers.

Secondly: everyone at Chicken House who works for every author under their care. The rest of the world has no idea just how much really goes on in the background to get these books into their hands, and it's down to these people just as much as me.

Thirdly: but specifically my editor, Rachel Leyshon, for continuing to be not-furious with my struggles with word counts (and sometimes deadlines).

Fourthly: and also specifically Ruth, who really doesn't have time for the length of my emails sometimes. But she humours my rambling with a smile, and neither my PR boxes for *All the Hidden Monsters* nor my launch party would have been anywhere near the successes they were without her.

Fifthly: my agent Lydia, for always keeping on top of everything, having my back and expertly executing all the technical stuff I don't understand.

Sixthly: Micaela Alcaino for repeatedly working her cover art magic.

Seventhly: the whole team at Bolinda for making my audio dreams come true. An audiobook was always so important to me as I'm such an avid audio user myself. Listening to *All the Hidden Monsters* for the first time is still one of my favourite moments from this whole journey.

Eighthly: but specifically Kate Dobson, for being the narrator of those dreams. You got Sage just right. It's everything I imagined and everything I wanted for her. Every single reviewer on Goodreads that listened to the first audiobook only had great things to say about your performance, so those stars are on you. I know you'll have to read this out for this audiobook, so from the bottom of my heart, thank you.

Ninthly: Jess Popplewell, who when I went to her with twelve ranting voice notes spoiling this whole book just so I could explain how I didn't know how to fix a plot hole, came back with everything plotted out on a selection of detailed Post-it notes (very P), and with her help we'd figured it out in about three minutes. I can't even remember what life was like before I knew what it was to voice note you nearly every single day. Thank Christ nobody else can hear us.

Tenthly: (again) Becky, who has read every book I've ever written since we were kids first, for ploughing on through a very, very early draft of this book even when it didn't make sense at all.

Eleventhly: technically the 3D printer but also Bea and Dilan for making it work and printing endless little ghosts and badges and all sorts for me. And everything else. I can't say anything more cringe than that but I know Bea gets it.

And finally: Major, the Samwise to my Frodo, the Watson to my Holmes, and without whom I would not be able to do so much. I know to the unsuspecting eye that I don't look all that anxious or overwhelmed at all. But standing in front of crowds or talking publicly about my books makes me want to die inside. There are days all of this still feels so new and overwhelming that I don't even want to step out the front door, but I manage it only because you're willing to walk through with me. Thank you for being the only one in the room to notice I'm holding my breath, and nudging my fingers with your nose when you spot that I can't keep my fidgeting hands still. My beloved best friend, I love you forever.

TRY ANOTHER GREAT BOOK FROM CHICKEN HOUSE

THE DARK WITHIN US by JESS POPPLEWELL

Jenny's felt broken for a long time. Luc has his own issues – you would too if your family ruled Hell. When they meet at a party, sparks fly. She sees a handsome devil. He sees a lost soul. Both sense trouble.

But it will take a journey to the very depths of the underworld to bring a girl and a demon together ...

Witty, original and allusive, this YA take on Dante's Inferno combines gripping quest and unlikely romance.
THE GUARDIAN

Paperback, ISBN 978-1-915947-18-5, £8.99 • ebook, ISBN 978-1-915947-20-8, £8.99

TRY ANOTHER GREAT BOOK FROM CHICKEN HOUSE

THE HIVE by ANNA FEBRUARY

Justice is merciless in the Hive, a monarchy of tomorrow, where young bodyguard Feldspar awaits execution, guilty of being alive when her charge is dead.

The girl has one defender – Niko, a royal maverick. Together they have three days to prove the impossible. Three days to question everything Feldspar knows about the world that raised her and discover who the real murderer is . . .

Paperback, ISBN 978-1-915947-27-7, £8.99 • ebook, ISBN 978-1-917171-05-2, £8.99

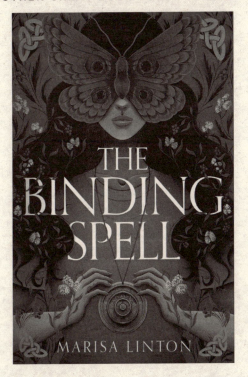

THE BINDING SPELL by MARISA LINTON

What lies beneath must stay hidden . . .

Morgan hopes her nightmares are behind her. Meeting Joe Harper helps. His secrets seem as tangled as hers and their time together is magic.

But Morgan's bad dreams return when her archaeologist father begins work at a local burial site. With every relic he unearths, a creeping horror emerges – a spell that binds them all . . .

Paperback, ISBN 978-1-915947-76-5, £8.99 • ebook, ISBN 978-1-917171-09-0, £8.99